"Tell me, Lucinda, have you ever been tempted to be less than a perfect lady?

"Haven't you ever wanted to strip off propriety and give in to your innermost desires?"

His voice lowered on the last words, vibrating through her with the echo of her unspoken longings. She should be shocked. She should scream or slap him or something, but the image of both of them naked and bared of all inhibitions had taken control of her imagination and would not let it go.

"You are impertinent," she managed to say breathlessly, as her body flooded with the heat of long-denied desire.

"I'm a man," he corrected. He reached out, stroking his fingers down her cheek. "And you, my dear, are very much a woman."

DEBRA MULLINS

A Necessary Husband

AVON BOOKS
An Imprint of HarperCollinsPublishers

This is a work of fiction. Names, characters, places, and incidents are products of the author's imagination or are used fictitiously and are not to be construed as real. Any resemblance to actual events, locales, organizations, or persons, living or dead, is entirely coincidental.

AVON BOOKS
An Imprint of HarperCollins*Publishers*
10 East 53rd Street
New York, New York 10022-5299

Copyright © 2002 by Debra Mullins Manning
ISBN: 0-7394-2569-2

Printed in the U.S.A.

This book is dedicated to
Stephanie Berry and Lisa Presting,
my fellow survivors,
and my mother, Patricia Engel Mullins,
the greatest survivor of all

Prologue

London
May 1805

Eighteen-year-old Lucinda Northcott paused before the doors to the study. Only major transgressions required her presence in her father's private domain, and last night's incident had been her greatest transgression of all.

She took a deep breath and threw open the doors. Behind the massive desk, her father awaited her. General George Northcott was a big man with a broad face and large hands. His massive frame was impeccably dressed in a well-tailored coat of plain blue that emphasized the silver that threaded through his dark hair, as well as the steel gray of his eyes. While normally of an engaging and humorous disposi-

tion, today the general looked every bit the forbidding commander he was known to be.

Lucinda had deliberately worn his favorite of
her dresses, a frock of white muslin with yellow
stripes that emphasized her wide brown eyes,
and she had tamed her curly light brown locks
into a sedate coil at the back of her head to appear dignified. Yet despite her efforts, no hint of
affection shone in her father's eyes. And when
he raised one dark brow and sharply pointed his
finger at a nearby chair, her heart sank.

She had really done it this time.

She sat down, clenched her hands together in
her lap, and waited. She wished her mother were
still alive so she could ask her advice. Ask her
how to erase the disapproval from her father's
face and make him smile at her again.

"It's done."

His words vibrated through the room like
thunder, though he never raised his voice. It was
always thus—when General George Northcott
spoke, his words echoed with power.

Lucinda leaned forward eagerly. "He agreed?"

"In a manner of speaking." The general precisely aligned a piece of paper on his desk with
the edge of the blotter.

"What does that mean?" she burst out impatiently. "Did he agree or not?"

"Don't take that tone with me, Lucinda," her
father warned. "I've spent the morning averting

disaster—no thanks to you and your escapade last evening."

"But—"

"Silence. You are to be married."

The knot of anxiety in her stomach loosened, and she let out a relieved sigh. "When?"

"Three days from now. A special license must be obtained."

"Of course." She tried to suppress her joy—it was going to be all right. Scandal would be avoided, and the famed Northcott honor would remain unblemished. And her father would once more look at her with approval in his eyes. "What did he say when you asked him?"

"The earl was disappointed, which is to be expected. However—"

"Not the earl! Malcolm. What did *he* say?"

Her father cast her a quelling glance. "He said nothing, as he was not there."

She frowned in puzzlement. "Then how could he have agreed to the marriage?"

"He didn't. The earl felt that the daughter of a mere general was not good enough for the heir to his title." His voice tightened. "He offered quite a sum to silence me on the matter, but you will be pleased to know that I would not accept anything less than marriage." The general pushed his chair back from the desk. "You are to wed the earl's younger son, Harry. It was the best I could hope for."

"*Harry?* But I barely know him! It is Malcolm I love—"

"Malcolm is on his way to his father's estate in Scotland. He will return after the wedding."

Scotland? She stared at her father, cold fear in her heart. "I can't marry Harry Devering, Father. I won't."

"You will." His words slammed into her with the full weight of his disapproval behind them. "You have greatly disappointed me and caused nearly irreparable damage to the Northcott name, which has remained unsullied and respected these past two hundred years. You *will* marry Harry Devering, and you will do so willingly and with a smile on your face." He sighed, suddenly looking every day of his fifty-odd years. "I am only glad that your mother was not alive to witness this."

"Father . . ." She came halfway out of her chair, but he stood as well, towering over her and brimming with authority. She sank back down.

"You have shamed both me and all the Northcotts before me, Lucinda. I only hope you can make something of this marriage. Now, leave me." He seated himself back at his desk, pulled some papers in front of him, and began to read.

Slowly she stood and walked toward the door. Her high spirits and country innocence had cost her everything: the man she loved, her father's respect, and her freedom.

She had no choice now. She had to marry Harry Devering.

Chapter 1

Raynewood Abbey, Hampshire
1816

All hope hinged upon tonight's success. As Lucinda Northcott Devering walked through the ballroom of the Duke of Raynewood's ancestral estate, every conversation died as she approached. The silence lasted just long enough for her to pass by before the whispers rose again in her wake. Gossip swept through the room like a gust of wind up from the London docks, rank with the stench of rumor.

"... died in his mistress's bed ..."

"... no one was surprised ..."

"... barren, the poor thing ..."

"... really couldn't blame him, I suppose ..."

Lucinda held her head up high, her impeccable breeding evident in the board straightness of her spine and her dignified poise. The calmest of smiles played about her lips, as if everyone were not talking about Harry Devering's ignominious death in the bed of his mistress, or the fact that his widow was making her first social appearance in over a year.

The skirt of her shimmering gold dinner dress swished in gentle accompaniment to her unhurried pace as she made her way toward the dance floor. It was a small assemblage, only forty people, made up mostly of local gentry. The duke had arranged the intimate dinner party with dancing to follow as the debut for his American granddaughter. An informal affair, it was merely to give the girl a chance to practice the manners she had learned from Lucinda these past several weeks. The real thing, Meg's grand debut in London, would follow.

For Lucinda, it was a test that must be passed at all costs. Her very future depended on it.

For an instant, as she stood watching the couples on the dance floor, she experienced a pang of regret. Once she, too, had danced so gaily without a care in the world. Before she had been so foolish as to believe herself in love. Before she had married and discovered that she had nothing to offer a man, but her sterling breeding. Over the past eleven years she had become known as a paragon of dignified propriety, and never again would she deviate from that course. The cost was much too high.

Still, her heart ached with the longing to dance and flirt with a man. More than that, to be held by a man, kissed by him, made love to by him. But it was not to be. Lucinda Devering was not a woman who drove men to passion.

Shaking off her despondent thoughts, she turned her gaze to the dance floor, where Miss Margaret Stanton-Lynch, the granddaughter of the Duke of Raynewood, danced with the young Earl of Coucherton.

Meg was all that mattered now. With Meg's success would come her own.

On the other side of the dance floor, the elderly duke was watching his granddaughter dance with a fond smile on his sharp-boned face. Despite the fact that Meg had only recently made the acquaintance of her grandfather, there was genuine affection between the two that warmed Lucinda's heart. Meg was as sweet-natured as she was pretty, and both qualities would make her quite sought-after in the marriage mart.

That, and the fact that she was the granddaughter of one of the wealthiest and most prestigious noblemen in England.

The duke looked over and met Lucinda's gaze, then gave her a subtle nod of approval. Lucinda let out a relieved sigh. Meg had made no social blunders; perhaps this madcap plan would work after all. Perhaps Lucinda's future would be assured, despite her dire straits.

Then a crash sounded in the hallway, and the doors to the ballroom slammed open.

"Get your damned hands off me!"

A huge man burst into the room, long dark hair flying about his face and his jaw shadowed with a day's growth of beard. A footman clung to each arm, trying to stop the brute, but he dragged them along with him into the ballroom. Blood trickled from one servant's lip, and the other had lost his powdered wig.

Lucinda placed her hand over her pounding heart. Good heavens, were they to be robbed? Was the ruffian insane, to break into the home of the Duke of Raynewood in such a manner? What sort of lunatic would dare do such a thing?

"Garrett!" Meg gasped, stopping right in the middle of the dance.

Lucinda's mouth dropped open. Garrett? *This* was Meg's brother, the one she could never stop talking about?

She moved toward Meg, keeping her gaze on the windblown wild man. The footmen struggled to hold back the American by the arms, and with a roar of rage he shrugged off his coat, sending the footmen stumbling backward. As the hapless servants crashed into Stephens, the hovering butler, Garrett Lynch faced the crowd in his shirtsleeves with fists clenched, magnificent chest heaving with exertion, blue eyes glittering with the light of battle.

Lucinda's heart pounded. This was the Marquess of Kelton? *This* was the Duke of Raynewood's heir?

Garrett Lynch regarded the glittering assembly of pampered English nobles through a haze of simmering rage and frustration. He had little use for those who disdained good, honest work in favor of living off the efforts of others. Between his own family history and the recent war between England and the United States, Garrett had little love for the so-called superior English.

A deafening silence settled over the room. Even the orchestra had stopped playing. He searched the crowd for the familiar face of his sister, but he was unable to spot her. Damn! One dark-haired girl should stand out easily among so many pale, blond English.

Soft, measured footsteps broke the eerie quiet, and he turned his head to regard the elderly man who made his way to the front of the room. He was tall, and his broad shoulders hinted that he had once been a large, powerfully built man. Age had stolen the brawn from his frame, leaving him bone-thin, but his snow-white hair was still thick and his dark eyes burned in his sharp-boned face. He was dressed in expensive, well-tailored evening clothes of stark black, and he walked with the air of a man in complete control. Garrett took one look at the familiar, bladelike nose and slanted brows—features he himself shared—and knew immediately who approached him.

His grandfather, Erasmus Stanton, the Duke of Raynewood.

"Ah, grandson," the duke said jovially, as if they had not just set eyes on each other for the first time. "I see you were able to arrive in time for the dancing after all."

So the old man was going to play the loving patriarch, was he? Garrett cast a contemptuous look at the duke. He had come all this way for one thing, and one thing only. "My ship is waiting. Where is Meg?"

"I can see you have obviously had a difficult journey," Erasmus continued smoothly. Only the flicker of annoyance in his dark eyes told Garrett that the man was affected by his grandson's rudeness. "Perhaps someone can escort you to your rooms so that you might refresh yourself." The duke glanced at the doorway, where the two footmen and the butler hovered.

Garrett turned and glared at the mincing butler who had refused him entry to his grandfather's house, forcing Garrett to barge past him, and at the ineffectual footmen who had futilely tried to keep him from searching for his sister.

All three looked terrified at the prospect of going near Garrett, which was fine with him.

"I'm not staying a night in your house, old man," Garrett bit off. Impervious to the shocked gasps that echoed through the ballroom, he took grim pleasure in the way Erasmus flinched. "Produce my sister. Now."

The duke's features hardened, and his elderly shoulders stiffened with pride. He narrowed his eyes. "If you want to see your sister, you young whelp," he commanded in a low tone, "then you'll come into the study with me to discuss this like civilized men."

Garrett met his grandfather's furious stare unflinchingly with his own. "The hell I will."

Erasmus continued to hold Garrett's gaze, his entire visage icy. Garrett refused to look away. For a long moment, the two men remained locked in silent combat.

Just as Garrett was certain his grandfather was about to summon his minions and have him thrown out, a new voice broke their visual contest.

"Meg," a woman said loudly. "Come greet your brother."

Garrett whirled at the sound of her voice. Standing behind him was a slender, elegant woman. She was rather tall for a female, but he was a large man, and he appreciated a woman who didn't look as if she might break if he touched her. She regarded him warily with her wide brown eyes, which almost exactly matched the shade of her toffee-colored curls. Her body was slim, her breasts small but plump, and her hips gently curved beneath the shimmering silk of her gold-colored gown.

He wouldn't mind coming home from a long voyage to a woman who looked like this, he thought with a sudden tug of male interest.

Apparently not intimidated by his close study, the beauty gave him a polite smile, then gestured to the dark-haired young woman who stood with her.

Garrett glanced away with effort, then he stared. This was not the Meg he remembered.

She wore a gown of pure white, which set off her dazzling blue eyes, fair skin, and ink-black hair. The gown also clung to her figure in a way designed to make an older brother uncomfortable. Pearls gleamed at her throat and in her upswept curls. Garrett gaped at this familiar stranger in disbelief until she grinned at him, dimples flashing, and suddenly she was his Meg again.

"Meg," he said, and held out a hand.

Before Meg could reach for him, the other woman stepped forward again, placing herself between the siblings. Mere inches separated Garrett's chest from the woman's softly rounded bosom, and the light scent of her perfume soothed his raw nerves in a way only a man who loved women would understand.

"Perhaps you would care to reunite with your sister in private," she said so softly that only he could hear, "rather than embarrass her further in front of her new acquaintances."

Taken aback by her reprimand, Garrett was tempted to roar his outrage, and the crowd be damned. But then he cast a glance from Meg— this new Meg, who looked as primped and polished as the rest of the English beauties—to the well-dressed nobility beyond them.

Damn. He probably had embarrassed his sister with his unconventional entrance. Well, he could act the gentleman for her for one night, much as it galled him to play society's games. Reluctantly, he gave a nod.

Meg's lovely champion glanced at the duke. "If you would lead the way to the study, Your Grace?"

Erasmus jerked his head in a nod. Then he turned to the assembly and smiled with a charm that surprised Garrett. The duke's authoritative voice easily reached the far corners of the silent room as he addressed the crowd.

"As you can see, my grandson is devoted to his sister and is anxious to be reunited with her. His only fault is not sending advance word of his arrival, which has confused my footmen." A ripple of uncertain laughter greeted this announcement. The duke's smile never wavered. "I'm sure you will all excuse us while we repair to the study for a private reunion." Signaling to the orchestra to continue playing, he then held out his arm to Meg.

The girl hesitated, casting a longing look at Garrett, but she allowed her grandfather to escort her from the room.

"Allow me to show you the way, my lord."

Garrett stared after Meg with a scowl on his face, frustrated that his grandfather had absconded so neatly with his sister, but at these words he turned his attention back to the lovely lady with the cautious brown eyes. She watched him coolly, as if he were a barbarian who had been let loose in the palace.

He couldn't blame her, he supposed. It was common knowledge that Garrett Lynch was a terror when in a temper, and he had clearly lived up to his reputation once again.

Even though the pretty peacemaker was part of the English nobility, he was inclined to think kindly of her. Not only was she physically attractive, but she had been the one to bring Meg to him, after all.

Lucinda was completely astonished when Garrett Lynch turned from savage to gentleman in the blink of an eye.

He gave her an irresistible smile that revealed the same dimples his sister possessed, and offered his arm. Startled, she instinctively took his arm. Her fingers curled around warm, hard muscle.

"What's your name?" he asked, leading her from the room.

As the ballroom doors closed behind them, the murmurs of the crowd became a roar. The duke had minimized the damage with his explanation, and his reputation would do the rest. Meg's debut would not suffer, despite the near-scandalous interruption.

The American was staring at her, and she realized she had not responded to his question. "I am Mrs. Lucinda Devering, my lord."

Garrett's dark brows lowered. "*Mrs.* Devering? It figures that a lovely lady like you is already married," he said in a grumble that sounded disappointed.

While he was far too rough around the edges for her taste, a thrill went through Lucinda just the same. To be considered attractive by such a rugged, powerful male made her feel very female in a primitive sort of way—and she was astonished to discover that she liked the feeling.

"You flatter me, my lord," she replied politely, her tone far smoother than her erratic pulse.

"I'm no lord."

"But you are," she replied distractedly. Good heavens, her head barely reached his shoulders! She had never felt more feminine. "You are the Marquess of Kelton, and the Duke of Raynewood's heir."

He stopped in the middle of the hallway and his handsome features hardened once more. "The hell I am."

Startled, Lucinda dropped her hand from his arm. "That is the third time tonight that I have heard you utter a profanity. I will thank you to control your language in polite company, my lord."

"And that is the third time tonight you have referred to me as 'my lord' . . . Lucy," he replied with an insolent smile. The barbarian was back, and her foolish fantasies evaporated instantly.

She drew herself up. "My name is Lucinda," she corrected coolly. "But you may call me Mrs. Devering."

"And my name is *Mr.* Garrett Lynch," he responded. "Or Captain Lynch, if you prefer. *Not* Lord Lynch."

"Actually, the proper address would be Lord Kelton."

"Mrs. Devering, you will find that I am *improper* in many respects."

As he stared at her, color rose in her cheeks. Such boldness! But she would not let him fluster her. "That does not surprise me, my l— er, Captain Lynch."

"See? That was not so very hard, was it?"

"Would you care to see your sister or not?" she asked through gritted teeth.

With an exaggerated sweep of his arm, he silently indicated that she precede him.

Odious man. How could she ever have thought him attractive?

Repressed wench. Garrett stalked along behind Mrs. Devering, watching the way her skirts swayed as she walked. He wondered what connection Mrs. Devering had to his sister. And where, he speculated, was Mr. Devering?

He had been a long time at sea, and he would have worried if he hadn't felt the tug of attraction, especially once he'd looked into her big brown eyes. But then her icy words had reminded him how much he disliked the English.

He had come miles out of his way to collect his sister, and he was in a foul mood. He certainly didn't need some prissy, patronizing *lady* scolding him about his manners. Especially one that he might have tried to talk into his bed, had circumstances been different.

The unwanted attraction worsened his already thunderous mood.

It was bad enough that his mother had died while he was away at sea. Then he had rushed back to Boston, only to find he had missed the funeral by several months. He had reached his breaking point when he'd discovered that Meg had taken off for England, to go visit the grandfather they had never seen.

That had been the old man's choice, he thought darkly as they approached the study.

The Duke of Raynewood had disowned Garrett's father for marrying an Irishwoman against the old man's wishes. And now that the duke's older son had died in a carriage accident, suddenly the old man had come seeking the children of the son he had betrayed. Well, to hell with his precious title.

Garrett strode into the study behind the stiff back of Mrs. Devering, noting that Erasmus had taken the position of power in seating himself behind his desk. Garrett slammed the door behind him, grinning like a pirate as his grandfather and Mrs. Devering both jumped.

Mrs. Devering gave him a disapproving look, and for the first time in weeks, he wanted to laugh out loud. If only she weren't married. If only he had the time—

"Garrett!" Meg launched herself into his arms, and he held her close, all other thoughts forgotten. She was all the family he had left in the world.

Erasmus cleared his throat, and Garrett glared at him over his sister's dark curls. She was all the family he was willing to acknowledge, anyway.

"Perhaps we have gotten off on the wrong foot," the duke said stiffly.

"We got off on the wrong foot the instant you kidnapped my sister," Garrett shot back.

"Kidnapped? Are you mad?" The elderly man's voice shook with proud fury. "If you weren't my grandson, I'd call you out for such an accusation!"

"That wouldn't do your precious title any good now, would it?" Garrett taunted.

"Gentlemen, please compose yourselves," Mrs. Devering said, stepping between them with hands raised in a calming gesture.

"You're not fit to bear the Stanton name," the duke spat, "much less the title."

"Then it's a good thing my father took my mother's name. I bet you hated that, didn't you, old man?" Garrett gave a harsh laugh. "And I don't want your title. It can die with you, for all I care."

Erasmus paled, but then straightened his spine and glared at Garrett with such contempt that he almost felt respect for the old fellow.

"If you despise me so, why are you here?" Erasmus asked stiffly.

"I got what I came for," Garrett said, holding Meg close. "My ship is waiting to set sail for Boston. Tonight."

"No!" both women cried.

Lucinda took a step forward in protest, and Meg shoved out of Garrett's arms. "I'm not leaving, Garrett Lynch, and nothing you say can make me!" the girl vowed.

Garrett stared at his younger sister in shock. "What do you mean, you're not leaving? Of course you're leaving! We're both going back to Boston tonight."

"You go if you want to," Meg returned with a toss of her head, "but I am staying here with Grandfather. I like it here."

"What do you mean, you *like* it here?"

"Grandfather has treated me quite well," Meg informed him. "He's bought me some lovely gowns and is going to take me to London. And Lucinda has taught me all about proper manners and how to dance."

"She has, has she?" Garrett sent a dark glance at Lucinda, who looked at him as if he were an insect. "Meg, your home is in Boston, with me."

"Why should I go back to Boston, just to watch you sail away again?" she snapped. "You left us all alone, Garrett. When Mother died, I had no one to help me make the arrangements for her burial. At least Grandfather isn't going to sail away and leave me, like you did."

Guilt crashed over him like the tide against the shore. But didn't she realize he'd had no choice?

"I did what I had to in order to provide for the both of you," he whispered.

"We didn't need the money as much as we needed you, Garrett," Meg said softly. She laid a hand on his cheek. "I want to stay here in England for a while and get to know Grandfather."

"Don't be foolish, Meg." Desperation made his tone harsh. "Go pack your things. You're coming home to Boston with me tonight."

"No, I'm not." Meg turned and went to stand by the duke. She faced Garrett squarely, and he realized with a shock that his baby sister had somehow grown into a woman. "I'm twenty-two years old, Garrett, and you can't make me do what you want. For once I am going to do what *I* want."

"And you want to stay here."

"Yes."

Garrett looked from Meg's face, so full of determination, to the duke's, silently gloating, and to Lucinda's, quietly compassionate.

When had he lost control of the situation?

Meg was right that he couldn't force her to leave. But he wasn't going to leave her at the mercy of their grandfather, either. The old man had betrayed his own flesh and blood once before, and Garrett intended to be around when Erasmus finally showed his true colors.

"Then I'm staying, too." He glanced coldly at

his grandfather. "I assume there's room for me someplace in this pile of rocks?"

"I'll have Stephens prepare a room," Erasmus said, triumph in his voice.

"Fine." Garrett spun on his heel and left the room, slamming the door behind him.

"Captain!" Lucinda called, hurrying after the American. Her steps were three to his one. Lifting her skirts a bit above her ankles, she ran to catch up to him as he disappeared around a corner of the hallway.

She rounded the same corner at a brisk trot and smacked straight into his broad, muscled chest.

A brief whiff of sea and pure male made her head spin. Strong hands clamped around her upper arms, steadying her and pulling her an inch closer to that powerful, masculine body. Her breasts were pressed against his chest, her legs aligned with his, her eyes even with his throat.

She took a deep breath, and that delicious scent of seafaring male made her body tingle in a way she hadn't felt since she was a girl.

"Is there something I can do for you, Mrs. Devering?"

For some reason, that innocent question asked in such a low, masculine voice sparked the naughtiest of ideas in her head. She opened her mouth to blurt out what she was thinking, but the smug gleam in those bluer-than-blue eyes stopped her.

Good Lord, what was she doing?

She jerked from his hold so quickly she stumbled again. He steadied her with a hand on her arm—a hand she shook off the instant she regained her balance.

Stealing a moment to gain control, she tucked a stray curl back into place, then smoothed her skirts, *not* looking at him. What was the matter with her? She had been reacting like a bedazzled schoolgirl ever since she had set eyes on the man!

"Your grandfather sent me after you," she told him, her voice calm despite her tumultuous emotions.

"I'm certain he did. However, you can assure the duke that I have no intention of stealing the silver."

Her mouth fell open. "His Grace would *never* think such a thing!"

He gave a snort of derision and traced a gentle finger along her jaw, and she shut her mouth with a snap. "I'm sure you believe that, too."

She stepped back, calling upon all her training to calm her skipping pulse and maintain an unruffled demeanor. "Actually, he wanted me to make sure you have everything you need for the night."

"Did he?" He glanced over her from head to

toe with frank male approval. "Well, there might be a thing or two . . ."

Speechless, breathless, she felt her heart pound with shock at such brazenness. She couldn't possibly feel excitement. Summoning all her control, she replied coldly, "Captain, I believe you have misunderstood me."

He gave a harsh bark of laughter. "No, Mrs. Devering, I understand you all too well. More's the pity."

With that, the arrogant beast set off down the hall, leaving Lucinda staring after him.

Chapter 2

Garrett slept soundly in his grandfather's house, a fact that irritated him mightily. But after so many months of sea travel, he supposed it was natural for a man to sleep like a babe in such a huge, soft bed, especially one that wasn't moving.

As he descended the staircase at half-past eight the next morning, he thought about the lovely Mrs. Devering, who had looked so scandalized when he'd flirted with her. Had he passed the night wrapped in those soft white arms, he could have forgiven himself the indulgence of sleeping late that morning—but since he'd slept alone in that big bed, he was only annoyed.

Too bad she was married. He would have liked to thaw her prissy English ways with some hot-blooded American loving. Perhaps this evening he'd have better luck, and find a pretty lass to tangle the sheets with him.

But for now, he had business. He followed a servant to the Green Salon, where Tim O'Brien awaited him.

Tim was the son of a seaman and the grandson of a seaman. First mate of the *Trinity*, he aspired no further and had made it clear that he was content to remain with Captain Lynch for as long as he was able-bodied enough to sail. Garrett rewarded skill, and he rewarded loyalty. Tim O'Brien was a master of both.

Tim now stood in the middle of the opulent room, mouth agape as he stared at the fine furnishings. Pale green silk lined the walls, and his feet sank into plush, verdant carpet. Against the backdrop of such wealth, Tim should have looked ridiculous with his simple clothing, day's growth of beard, and mouse-brown hair sticking out beneath his dark blue cap. But to Garrett, he looked like all that was familiar and dependable in his world.

"Good morning to you, Tim," he said as he entered the room. "And thanks for coming so quickly, and for bringing my sea chest. I was desperately in need of a change of clothing."

"I'm thinking you should have brought your evening clothes," Tim answered, his lined face creasing in a grin.

"We need to discuss the change in plans." Garrett paced, wishing he had a wooden deck under his feet. "As I said in my message, there has been a delay."

"Not too much of one, I hope," Tim replied, his eyes serious. "You're aware we have to be in Calais at the end of the month to fetch that shipment of silk. If we're not there, that snake Edmond Fouliere will sell the lot of it to someone else and leave us to pay the forfeit fee."

"I have every intention of being in Calais by month's end. I just need a day or so to talk some sense into my sister."

Tim grinned. "Captain, I have three sisters myself, and such a thing cannot be done that fast."

"I will make Meg see reason," Garrett vowed. "However, should she prove stubborn about the matter—"

"A sister of yours, stubborn?" Tim rolled his eyes. "Perish the thought."

"*Should* she prove stubborn," Garrett repeated with a glare, "we shall need an alternate plan. If she does not see reason within two days, I want you to take the *Trinity* to Calais and seal the bargain with Fouliere. Once you return, my sister will be ready to leave, if I have to tie her up and carry her."

Tim chuckled. "You'd best start practicing your knots, then."

"Why do I keep you on?" Garrett growled

with fond exasperation. He strode to the door and swept it open. "Be off with you then, and watch over my ship and my men." Garrett signaled to a nearby servant in the hall. "Please see Mr. O'Brien to the door," he instructed.

"What, you'll not escort me yourself?" Tim placed a hand over his heart. " 'Tis crushed I am, Captain."

"I don't know where the blasted door *is*," Garrett muttered.

Tim laughed. "I'll bid you farewell then, Captain. And I'll see you and your sister in two days' time." The mate followed the footman down the hall, like a breath of fresh air departing the stilted atmosphere of Raynewood.

Garrett's stomach growled, and he realized he was half starved. He glanced around for a footman—there was generally one underfoot at every moment—when his attention was snared by a movement on the stairs. He looked up into the cool visage of his grandfather.

The duke was not one to be cowed, especially by his own grandson. He ignored Garrett's glare and continued to descend the stairs at an unhurried pace, as if the air between the two men did not suddenly thrum with tension.

Even though it was daytime, the duke wore somber colors. Today's coat was a shade of claret so dark it bordered on brown. His neck cloth was tied in precise folds, and every snowy hair was in place. Garrett's stomach grumbled, sounding like a roar in the silence, and making him feel about as socially polished as a beggar.

The duke's lips twitched. "Good morning, grandson. I expect you are hungry this morning?"

Garrett eyed the man suspiciously. "I could eat."

"The breakfast room is down that hall and to the right," Erasmus said, pointing. "Are you in need of an escort?"

"I can navigate a ship to any place in the world," Garrett replied. "I'm certain I can find a room in a house, even one as oversized as this one is."

"Then if you will excuse me, I have estate business to attend to. I shall be in my study if you need me."

"I won't," Garrett said curtly.

Erasmus raised his brows in an expression Garrett had seen many times in his own mirror— condescending amusement. "Should you require anything, simply ask a servant. I'd like you to feel at home here." The old man gave him a small smile before he turned down the opposite hallway to his study.

Garrett headed down the hallway toward the breakfast room. "Feel at home?" he muttered. "The hell I will."

*   *   *

Lucinda sat alone in the breakfast room, moving her eggs around her plate in a pretense of eating.

Aside from the unexpected arrival of Meg's brother, last evening had gone splendidly. Meg was so bright and beautiful that she was bound to make an excellent match before the season was out. And once Meg was betrothed, Lucinda's future was assured as well.

When the duke had first proposed his plan, Lucinda had thought it impossible. Make a proper English lady of an American hoyden in time for the season? See the girl well married to a titled peer? Yet Meg had proven an able student. Lucinda was well pleased with the girl's progress, as was the duke.

The only one *not* pleased was Garrett Lynch.

Lucinda frowned. She knew the duke was secretly thrilled that his grandson had come to England, but she feared Meg's brother was going to be an immense obstacle.

He seemed to honestly care for his sister, so she couldn't understand his selfish desire to return the girl to the wilds of America. Had he no idea of the advantages Meg would claim simply by being the granddaughter of the Duke of Raynewood? Had he no comprehension of the life of luxury she would lead married to an English nobleman?

Not every woman was handed the opportunity to be a guaranteed social success, and Meg had it by virtue of her birth. By escorting Meg in Society, Lucinda would also find the one thing she most needed to survive in the polite world—a husband.

She didn't really want another husband. One had been more than enough; look where that disaster had landed her! But since she was not an heiress, she had no other options.

The duke had put it about that Lucinda was simply a good friend of the family, somewhat close to his granddaughter's age, who had graciously agreed to take the young lady under her wing. No one knew the truth: that Lucinda was all but destitute and homeless, thanks to her philandering husband. Marriage would allow her to keep body and soul together and her family honor and dignity intact. If her despicable brother-in-law had not managed to destroy her chances with his unfounded rumors.

"Well, now, a bit early for a visit, wouldn't you say, Mrs. Devering?"

The deep voice jerked her from her musings. Garrett stood in the doorway of the breakfast room.

"And good morning to you, Captain," she answered tartly.

He grinned at her, flashing those ridiculously appealing dimples as he walked over to the sideboard where breakfast was laid out. She couldn't help but notice again what a large man he was, especially since the savage appeared before her in merely his trousers and shirtsleeves. The white shirt fit him well, emphasizing his broad shoulders and the ripple of his muscles as he walked. But really, had they no modesty in America? Where was his coat, his cravat?

He turned to face her, his plate piled high with eggs and sausage, and he raised his eyebrows as he caught her looking at him.

"Did you need something, Mrs. Devering?"

She refused to be embarrassed. "I was simply wondering where the madman from last evening had disappeared to."

He laughed and those dimples flashed again, drat the man. His teeth were white and even, and now that he had shaved and cleaned himself up, he was just as handsome as Meg was lovely.

He had combed his dark hair, and while the length was most unfashionable, the way he had it tied back gave him the look of a pirate. Since he was more presentable, she could see a resemblance to the duke in the sharp blade of a nose and the dark, slanted brows. If only his manners matched his looks, she thought as he sat down and dug into his breakfast like a man who had been fasting for a week.

He paused in his single-minded devouring of his food. "You never answered my question, you know."

"I don't recall your asking a question."

"I asked what you are doing here at this hour, Mrs. Devering. It seems a bit early to be paying a visit to Meg after her late evening last night."

"Surely you are not lecturing *me* on the social proprieties! You, who walk around half dressed and attack your food like a starving wolf?"

He frowned down at his clothes, then turned the frown on her. "There's nothing wrong with the way I'm dressed. And if you did not come calling at such an early hour, perhaps your delicate sensibilities would not be offended."

"I have not come calling," she replied impatiently. "I am a guest of the duke's."

"Really." He sat back in his chair and raised his brows. "And what does *Mr.* Devering think of that?"

Lucinda flushed, taking his meaning immediately.

"Mr. Devering passed away just over a year ago, Captain," she replied sharply. "I am a widow."

His face softened in sympathy. "I'm sorry," he said softly. "I didn't know."

"You don't know a great many things, Captain," she shot back coolly. "Since you inquire, I will inform you that your grandfather asked me to help Meg in assuming her rightful position in society. As he and my late father were friends, I naturally agreed to assist him, and accepted his gracious invitation to stay here at Raynewood so that I might be closer to your sister. Now, have you any more questions, *my lord*?"

"Yes. Where do you live ordinarily?"

She gave a thought to the lovely country house she had been forced to sell to pay the first of her husband's debts. "I don't see how that is your concern. You are very rude, my lord."

His expression darkened at the title. "I'm not the one who has to worry about a reputation," he said pointedly. "Isn't there some English rule that says an unmarried woman can't live alone with a man not her husband?"

"Your grandfather is nearly eighty-five years old!" she exclaimed. "But to put your nasty mind to rest, let me assure you that we are well chaperoned."

"And who is this chaperone? Meg?" He laughed.

"No, you scapegrace," came a new voice. "I am."

Garrett was obviously startled by the aged female voice that had interrupted their conversation. And when he got a good look at the lady, the comical expression of disbelief on his face had Lucinda suppressing a giggle.

Tiny enough that she would barely come up to Garrett's chest, the white-haired lady was fashionably dressed in a dress that matched the dark purple turban on her head. Ropes of snowy pearls all but obscured the delicate embroidery of the gown, and large diamonds sparkled at her ears. She glared at him, and Lucinda was struck by the resemblance between them, right down to the Stanton nose.

"Have you no manners in America?" the old woman demanded. "Do you not even rise when a lady enters the room?"

Garrett got to his feet, a flush spreading across his cheekbones. "I apologize, madam," he said with hastily gathered charm. "You took me by surprise."

"Who is this strapping lad?" the old lady demanded of Lucinda.

"This is your great-nephew, Garrett Lynch from America," Lucinda replied, biting the inside of her cheek to keep from laughing. "Captain, this is your great-aunt, Lady Agatha Strathwaite, your grandfather's sister."

"Nephew, is it?" Lady Agatha demanded.

"He's William's son, my lady."

"Ah, you would be Kelton, then," Lady Agatha said with a decisive nod. She peered closely at him, her dark eyes searing. "You like females, don't you?"

"Ah . . . yes." Clearly puzzled, Garrett looked at Lucinda, who refused to meet his gaze. It was all she could do to maintain decorum, torn between shock at Lady Agatha's bold question and outright laughter at Garrett's discomfort.

"You'll do," Lady Agatha declared.

"Thank you, ma'am," he responded, his tone doubtful.

She clucked her tongue at him. "You may address me as Lady Agatha—everyone does, even dear Lucinda—or even Aunt Agatha, as we are family. And perhaps the next time we meet, you will be properly attired, as well."

Again he glanced down at his clothes. Lady Agatha saw his puzzlement and sighed. "You'll have your hands full with this one," she said to Lucinda. "He's got looks, I'll grant you that, but he definitely needs polish."

Lucinda allowed herself a smile. "Luckily, he is not my problem, my lady."

Lady Agatha let out a cackling laugh. "Isn't he?"

With that cryptic remark, she left the breakfast room.

Garrett slowly sat down again. "Why did she ask if I like females?"

"Perhaps you should ask your grandfather."

"No, Mrs. Devering. I'm asking *you*." Something about the way he said the last word made her want to blush. It sounded so . . . intimate.

"It's a rather indelicate matter," she stalled.

He leaned back in his chair and folded his arms, grinning from ear to ear. "That's even better."

The man was a scoundrel, to sit there and fix

those stunning blue eyes on her while demanding that she speak of things no lady was supposed to know about! "It's something of a family secret," she admitted, heat creeping into her cheeks. "I really do think you should ask your grandfather to explain."

"I don't agree," he said softly. "You're blushing, Mrs. Devering."

"Of course, I'm blushing!" she snapped. "You are making me quite uncomfortable."

"Good," he said, dimples flashing. "Now what was this deep, dark secret you were about to reveal?"

"Captain, please. I really cannot."

"I like the way you say that," he murmured. " 'Captain, please.' I'd like to please you, Lucinda."

His warm, low voice stirred longings she hadn't felt in years. She squelched the rebellious emotions. "My name is Mrs. Devering," she corrected, but her tone wasn't as chiding as she would have liked. "And I will thank you not to seduce me at the breakfast table."

"My apologies," he replied. "Where would you like me to seduce you, then?"

"Your uncle did not like females," she blurted out. "Obviously, we do not have that concern with you!"

Garrett burst out laughing as understanding lit his features. "Old Erasmus really did it, didn't he? He disowned the one son who could provide him with an heir!"

"You *are* his heir," she snapped. "And you have quite ruined my breakfast."

She stood to leave, but he held up a hand, still chuckling. "Sit, Mrs. Devering. I apologize."

She hesitated.

"Sit," he told her again, his face creasing in amusement. "I promise to behave."

Slowly she sat down again, watching him closely. "I shall hold you to that, Captain."

"Let's change the subject," he suggested. "I had heard that the English do not rise before noon, yet everyone seems to be up already."

"We keep country hours at Raynewood," she informed him, taking a bite of her now cold eggs. "Only Meg is still abed, but as the dance master arrives this afternoon, she will be rising soon as well."

"I see." Garrett attacked his breakfast again. Then he looked up and pointed his fork at her. "If Lady Agatha is the chaperone, why does Meg need you?"

Alarm streaked through her at the question, and her heart skipped a beat. Then she took a deep, calming breath. No one knew her true circumstances. Well, almost no one.

"The duke felt Meg needed someone younger, to be a companion," she replied evenly, managing somehow to keep placidly eating her eggs.

"Lady Agatha is a lady of some years, and His Grace felt that a high-spirited young girl might be too much for her."

"So he hired you."

She clenched her teeth in annoyance. Was the man never satisfied? "I assure you, Captain, that I am *not* His Grace's employee. I am simply a friend of the family who is doing him a favor."

"And for that favor, you get to stay here in this huge house and live off my grandfather?"

Color rose again in her cheeks. She jerked to her feet and threw her napkin down on the table, her entire body quivering with fury and fear. The irritating man was skating uncomfortably close to the truth.

Fascinated, Garrett put down his fork. Her flushed cheeks and anger-bright eyes contrasted with the pale green of her dress, bringing her loveliness to life.

"You, sir, do not know what you are talking about," she said in a low, clipped tone. But her fingers crushed the napkin where it rested on the table.

"Maybe I don't," he agreed, watching her with interest. "But something sure has you all worked up."

"Good day, Captain," she said tightly, and swept from the room as if she couldn't stand his presence another moment.

Garrett looked at her empty chair and the

crumpled napkin. So the lovely Mrs. Devering was a widow. That changed everything, as he was now free to seduce her with a clear conscience. She looked like a woman who could use a good romp between the sheets, and he was just the man for the job. Which brought him to his grandfather.

Was there something illicit going on between the duke and Mrs. Devering? She had acted very strangely when he had suggested it. Did she see the duke as a meal ticket? Was she his mistress?

If something was going on between the two of them that he didn't like, there was no way Meg was staying another day. He dug into his breakfast. He would have his answers soon, one way or another.

The man was a complete barbarian, Lucinda thought, storming down the hallway. And his remarks had been far too close for comfort.

She paused in her flight, pressing her palms to her flaming cheeks.

The American was too bold and spoke too easily of things that should be left unsaid. He would never understand her reasons for accepting the duke's bargain. How desperate she had been. How trapped.

She closed her eyes to will away the memories, but they came anyway. The tradesmen pounding on her door the day after her husband's death. The salacious lord who had approached her at Harry's funeral to collect a gaming debt—any way she cared to pay it. The lovely country house, the only place she had been happy during the ten years of her marriage, sold to cover Harry's vowels. Yet it still wasn't enough.

And then there was Malcolm.

Just his name made her drop her hands from her face and straighten her spine. Malcolm would *not* defeat her.

She would survive, even if she had to go around Garrett Lynch to accomplish her objectives. He had no concept of correct social behavior, and worse, she wouldn't put it past him to deliberately sabotage Meg's chances to make a good match—especially once they moved to London for the Season.

And the way he looked at her! She had heard tell of lusty sailors, but last night . . . No one had *ever* looked at her that way. It was . . . indecent! Yes, that was the word. *Not* exciting. That was not what she had meant at all.

With any luck, Garrett would soon return to America and leave her—leave all of them—in peace.

"Mrs. Devering, a word if you please," the duke said from the doorway of his study. "*Now*, if you please," he repeated, then disappeared into the room.

With a feeling of dread shadowing every step, she walked into the study.

"Kindly close the door," the duke said, seating himself behind his desk. He hadn't raised his voice. He didn't have to. The Duke of Raynewood had spent eighty-five years learning how to command people with the sheer power of his presence.

And it was effective, Lucinda thought, taking the chair the duke indicated with a sweep of his hand. No one could intimidate better than the Duke of Raynewood.

"Have you just come from breakfast?" he asked, glancing through some papers.

"Yes, Your Grace."

"Then I take it you must have seen my grandson."

She folded her hands tightly in her lap. "Yes, I did, Your Grace."

"He's grown into a handsome lad." He looked at her expectantly.

"Indeed, sir."

The duke leaned back in his chair. "He does credit to the Stanton name—though he would deny the connection if he could."

Unsure where the conversation was going, Lucinda could only murmur, "Yes, Your Grace."

"But he's my grandson and my heir, Mrs. Devering, whether he wills it or no. I would like time to convince him to stay in England and take on his responsibilities."

Though she fervently hoped otherwise, Lucinda pointed out, "He has said he will not leave until Meg does. She intends to stay the full season, if not permanently, which should give you plenty of time to get to know each other."

The elderly man tapped his fingers on the desk. "I do not think Garrett will wait that long. I saw him this morning, speaking with one of the men from his ship. It wouldn't surprise me if he means to take Margaret away with him by force."

"What!" Lucinda rose to her feet. "Your Grace, are you certain?"

"No, I am not certain, but the possibility does exist." He raised his brows at her, and she slowly sat as he continued, "I am very fond of my granddaughter, Mrs. Devering, and being a selfish man, I would like to keep her with me as long as possible. It is my greatest hope that she will marry well and settle here in England. Should Garrett succeed in spiriting her away, I doubt he would allow her to return until long after I was in my grave, if then."

"Surely he would not be so cruel?"

"I'm certain he would not see it that way. But he is very angry with me, and he sees me as a threat to Margaret."

Lucinda nodded. "I believe you are correct. He is very protective of his sister."

"As am I, Mrs. Devering. I want what is best for my granddaughter, but that is where my grandson and I have differing opinions." He gave a small, sardonic smile. "Among other things."

"Perhaps, over time—" she began.

"Over time, I shall be in my grave, with my estates abandoned and my granddaughter an ocean away!" The duke took a deep, calming breath. "To make certain none of these things comes to pass, I am charging you with keeping an eye on my granddaughter, Mrs. Devering."

Lucinda nodded. "Of course."

"And my grandson."

"What?" Once more, Lucinda surged out of her chair. "Your Grace, it is one thing to have charge of a young girl, but quite another to attempt to keep track of a grown man!"

"Be seated, Mrs. Devering."

"You can not ask such a thing of me," she continued, her voice rising. "It is impossible!"

"*Be seated!*" he thundered.

Lucinda sat.

"Perhaps you misunderstood me," the duke said in a low, dangerous voice. "We have an agreement, Mrs. Devering."

"Garrett Lynch was not part of the agreement."

"I have changed it." Calmly, the elderly man folded his hands before him on his desk.

"You cannot do that!"

He raised his brows. "I have just done so. Mrs. Devering, you have always maintained an impeccable reputation for good breeding and elegance. You have done your family name proud, and I am certain your father would have been pleased."

Lucinda nodded stiffly.

"However . . ." He paused. "Before his death, your husband acquired a shocking amount of gaming debts. And for some reason, his brother, Lord Arndale, has not paid these debts of honor."

Lucinda set her jaw at the mention of Malcolm Devering, her brother-in-law. She knew exactly why Malcolm had not paid Harry's debts, and it had nothing at all to do with honor. "That is correct, Your Grace."

The duke continued, "You are in a difficult situation, madam. Without my help, you do not have the means to repay the amount."

"I have my mother's pearl necklace," she whispered, desperate to gain some control over the situation.

The duke shook his head. "You and I both know that the necklace would make but a small dent in such a sum."

Feeling trapped, she said, "It is all I have, Your Grace."

"Not at all, madam." He steepled his fingers. "You have a respectable family pedigree and excellent social standing. You have entrée into the salon of every society hostess, and your demeanor is that of a lady in every way. Your reputation is quite unassailable, despite the current gossip."

Her cheeks heated. "You mean the tale of how my husband died."

"Indeed. While the gossips have continued to chew on this particular tidbit, I have noticed that your husband's actions have not injured your own consequence. It's quite remarkable."

"I'm glad you approve, Your Grace," she said with a tight smile.

He looked uncomfortable for a brief moment. "Yes, well, it is an uncommon tale, and you have weathered the storm quite exceptionally."

Uncommon tale indeed! *My husband died in his mistress's bed. He broke his neck during one of their shocking games with whips and ropes.*

"A woman of your fortitude should have no trouble handling my grandson," the duke continued, "so I want you to keep him in your sights as much as possible. I have plans for him, as well. I intend to arrange a match for him with Lady Penelope Albright."

"He will never agree," she blurted out.

"I am aware of this, Mrs. Devering." She flushed. "You will assist me in making sure Garrett and Lady Penelope spend time together while we are in London. Once he marries the daughter of an English peer, he will be more inclined to stay here in England and tend to his responsibilities."

"It is not my place—"

"Your place is where I say it is, Mrs. Devering! I will arrange the introduction to Lady Penelope, while you turn my grandson into a proper Englishman."

"Impossible," she whispered.

"You must make it possible." He stood. The sunlight streamed in through the window behind him and shadowed his face, making him seem all-powerful. "For if you fail in this, if my grandson returns to America, then our bargain is forfeit."

"But, Your Grace—"

"Forfeit, Mrs. Devering." He stepped forward and held her trapped with his cool, dark gaze. "Without me, you will never be able to fund your own season, and your reputation will be ruined once word of your financial difficulties gets out. Which it must, at some juncture. You will never be able to make the match you so desperately require. We need each other, madam."

"But—"

"Good day, Mrs. Devering."

The words were a dismissal. Rising, she left the study, remembering how less than an hour ago she had been hoping to rid herself of Garrett Lynch.

Now she was totally bound to the man. Turn Garrett Lynch into an English gentleman? Impossible! He would resist every step of the way. Yet if Garrett succeeded in convincing Meg to leave with him before the end of the season, he would take Lucinda's future with him.

She had no choice. She had to make him comply with the duke's wishes—by whatever means possible.

Chapter 3

Garrett descended from his room shortly after two o'clock. He had been waiting all day to speak to Meg, but first she'd been sleeping, and then she was dressing.

He was not used to being idle.

Pursuing Mrs. Devering would have been an amusing pastime, but the lady had not reappeared after her dramatic exit from the breakfast room. No matter. Their paths would cross again, and he would have another opportunity to charm the lovely widow into his bed.

He had been over a year at sea, and he didn't dally with innocents or other men's wives. But a widow . . . He grinned wickedly.

Since Mrs. Devering had gone to ground, he sought other means of passing the time. He had already been down to the stables to take a look at

Raynewood's admittedly excellent horseflesh, then he had perused some titles in the library. He had walked the grounds. Twice. He had viewed the gardens. Finally he had attended to some correspondence that had been neglected while he chased all over the world after his errant sibling. Letters in his hand, he stopped one of the maids as she passed through the foyer.

"Excuse me, miss. Do you know if my sister has come downstairs yet?"

The young girl bobbed a quick curtsy. "Not yet, Your Lordship. She's dressing."

"Still? She's been dressing for the past hour!" He scowled. How long did it take the girl to put on a dress and brush her hair?

As if that did not make him impatient enough, the servants insisted on addressing him by the blasted title, no matter how many times he had tried to convince them otherwise. He had finally given up.

Catching the nervous look in the maid's eyes, he deliberately softened his expression. "What's your name?"

"Alice, Your Lordship."

"Alice, would you please let my sister know that I need to speak to her? I'll be in the gardens."

"That won't be necessary, Alice. I'm right here."

Garrett looked up and saw Meg coming down the stairs. Once again, he was struck by how much she had changed. She wore a fashionable dress of pale pink, and her dark hair was carefully arranged in cascading curls. And she walked down the stairs. Slowly. Elegantly. He remembered, on the rare occasions he had come home, how she used to run down the stairs of their house in Boston to throw herself breathlessly into his arms.

Were the English stifling every bit of spirit she possessed? Where was the feisty girl he loved so much? The sooner he got her home, the better.

"I've been waiting for you," Garrett said as Meg reached them. "You never used to stay in bed until noon or take over an hour to get dressed."

"I never used to stay up late at a soirée thrown in my honor, either," Meg replied coolly. "Do you need to post those letters?"

Soirée? Frowning, he looked down at the letters in his hand. "Actually, I wanted to send them over to Tim O'Brien so they could go out with the *Trinity*."

"We'll have a footman take them." Before he could respond, Meg plucked the letters from his hand and turned to the maid. "Alice, would you please have Stephens send one of the footmen to deliver these to my brother's ship?"

"Certainly." Dipping a curtsy, Alice took the letters and hurried off.

Garrett peered at his sister skeptically. She

seemed so poised. Where was the little minx who had once tried to stow away on one of his ships? Where was the laughing, vivacious young woman he had left in Boston over a year ago?

"What did you want to talk to me about?" Meg asked politely.

She spoke to him as if he were some vague acquaintance and not the brother who had practically raised her! He didn't like this one bit. She reminded him of some unfeeling Englishwoman, afraid to put a hair out of place. How was he supposed to talk this cool stranger into coming home to Boston with him?

"Well?" she asked, lifting her brows in that condescending manner that seemed to run in the family.

"Let's go out to the garden," he replied. "I'd like some privacy."

"As you wish." Head held high, Meg led the way.

Garrett felt a small sense of accomplishment as they arrived in the garden, once he realized that he could have gotten there without Meg's guidance. It seemed his navigational skills were still intact.

Meg led the way down the path to a stone bench surrounded by young cherry trees bursting with pale pink blossoms. She turned and faced him, her expression still unreadable.

"What did you want to speak to me about, Garrett?" she asked. "My dance master arrives in less than an hour."

"You already know how to dance," he pointed out.

"Hardly." With a haughty toss of her head, she drawled, "I know the colonial dances. Today Monsieur Collineau is going to teach me the waltz."

"Colonial? Have you forgotten that you *are* a so-called colonial?"

"Not here, I'm not. Here I am Miss Margaret Stanton-Lynch, granddaughter of the Duke of Raynewood."

"Stanton-Lynch? What the hell is that all about?"

"Garrett, really! Your language!" She gave a sniff of disapproval that made him want to throttle her. "Our father's name was Stanton, after all. He only changed it to annoy Grandfather."

"It was always good enough for you before," Garrett ground out. "Meggie, what are you doing? Why don't you quit all this foolishness and come home where you belong?"

He finally caught a glimpse of the old Meg as her blue eyes sparked with temper. "Home to Boston, you mean? What is there for me now? Mother is gone, and you'll go sailing off again as soon as we arrive."

"Meg—"

"At least Grandfather won't abandon me."

"You don't know that!" Garrett roared. "He abandoned our father, didn't he? He's only playing at this because he needs us. He needs *me*. *I'm* his precious heir!"

"Grandfather loves me!" she shouted back. "This is not about you, Garrett William Lynch!"

Garrett's heart lightened. *Here* was the Meggie he knew.

"Don't fool yourself, Meg. Once his older son died, the old man had no one left to take on his precious title. That's all he's ever cared about. That's why he disowned our father."

"That was over thirty years ago," she snapped. "People change."

"Not that old coot. If I ever saw anyone set in his ways, it's him."

"There's no talking to you," Meg declared, throwing her hands in the air. "As long as I can remember, you've given the orders, and I was supposed to obey them. Did you ever once consider that I might want some say in my future?"

"You were just a child."

"Garrett, I'm twenty-two years old. I haven't been a child for a long time," she said quietly.

Had she screamed the statement at him, he might have been able to ignore it. But her sad solemnity made him pause. *Had* he been too overbearing recently? Meg was eight years younger than he was, and he was used to taking care of her. But she wasn't a little girl anymore.

"You're right."

She had actually parted her lips to argue before she realized what he'd said. Closing her mouth, she looked at him curiously.

"You're right," he said again. "It's just that I've been in charge of the family for so long, I never noticed when you grew up."

"You weren't home enough," she said, but the words had no heat.

"I was trying to support a family, Meg. I know you can't understand that, but it was important to me to give you the best I could."

"No, I do understand it." She began to stroll as she spoke, reaching up to gently touch one soft, pink cherry blossom. "But what you don't understand is that I don't remember our father, Garrett. I was only three years old when he died at sea. You're the closest thing to a father I have ever had. And I needed you."

"I've always been here for you."

"No, you haven't." Plucking the bloom from the tree, she met his gaze. Her eyes were sad. "I didn't need the money you sent as much as I needed you, Garrett."

He sighed. "We've been over this, Meg. I can't change the past."

"Neither of us can. But things are different now. Mother is gone and now we've found

Grandfather. You don't need to work so hard. You've done well, Garrett, but it's time to make changes."

"I don't want anything to do with that old man," Garrett grumbled. "He can keep his stiff-rumped English ways and his precious fortune and his blasted title."

Meg let out a sigh of exasperation. "Has it occurred to you, Garrett Lynch, that maybe Grandfather is sorry for what he did?"

Garrett laughed harshly. "*Him*? Hardly."

"You are so stubborn! Why can't you stop being so angry at him and see that he regrets what he did?"

"Because of what he did, our parents are dead," Garrett ground out. "Da would never have had to go to sea if he'd been here in England, living the life he was raised for. And Ma got so sick after I was born that they almost didn't have any more children. If the duke had accepted her as our father's wife, she would have had better medical care. She was never really strong again after you were born, and that's probably what killed her."

"And I feel guilty every day because of that," Meg said, her voice catching on the words.

"It's not your fault, Meggie." Hurting for her, Garrett searched for words of comfort. "You know how much she wanted children. If you want to blame someone, blame that selfish old bastard for denying her a life she should have had, a life where she might not have gotten so sick. Where neither of them would have died."

"And don't you think *we're* entitled to that life?" Meg's voice was thick with unshed tears. "Don't you think he owes us? Even if you can't believe that he's sorry, Garrett, can't you find some way to accept what he's offering?"

"I'm sorry, Meg, but I don't want anything from him. And I don't want you near him, either. I can't stand to see you hurt."

"*You're* the one who's hurting me, Garrett!" She threw the flower at him. "For once, I want something for myself. Did you know Grandfather is going to present me at court? That he's going to take me to London and buy me beautiful clothes and introduce me to earls and princes and grand ladies? I want that! I've never wanted anything so much in my life."

"Damn it, Meggie, *why*? I've tried to give you everything. What can I do to make it better?"

"You can let me do this, Garrett." She gave him a steady look full of so much maturity that he was shocked. "I know you, and you probably thought you would take a couple of days to talk me into going home with you. And then once you got me home to Boston, I bet you'd never allow me near England again."

"I . . ." Garrett shut his mouth. She had him there.

She narrowed her eyes at his guilty expression. "I bet you even sent Tim off to handle business while you bided your time to talk some sense into me. Well, I have news for you, Garrett. I am *not* leaving England until I get what I want."

Garrett rubbed a hand over his face. "What *do* you want?" he asked wearily.

"I want to go to London. I want to be presented at court. And I want you to be there with me."

"Me, in London?" He snorted. "With those primping idiots and those empty-headed women? Are you crazy?"

"Yes, you in London," Meg said with a steel in her voice that he had to admire. "We'll get you some clothes, and you can come with me to all the parties."

"Clothes again?" he grumbled. "What's wrong with the way I'm dressed?"

"It's not correct dress for an English peer. Which you are, whether you like it or not." She put her hands on her hips. "I want to spend some time with you, Garrett, and I want a taste of what Grandfather is offering. Then I'll discuss going home with you."

Garrett remained silent for a long moment. She really wasn't asking so much. And once she saw what fools the English nobles could be, she'd be eager to return to sensible Boston society. Once she was back in Boston, maybe he would see about being home more often and throwing a party or two for her. Young girls liked that sort of thing.

"All right," he said finally. "I'll come to London, but I can't stay there forever. I still have a business to run."

"Oh, Garrett, thank you!" She ran and threw herself into his arms. He held her tightly, relishing this glimpse of the old Meggie.

"Just don't marry some damned Englishman," he murmured into her hair.

She just hugged him more tightly. For now, that was enough.

The dance master's name was Monsieur Collineau, and he looked, Garrett thought, like a stork dressed in expensive clothing. The tall, thin fellow had a beak of a nose and spindly legs, and his shirt points rose so high that Garrett was amazed he didn't put an eye out every time he turned his head.

And if "Monsieur Collineau" had been born anywhere near France, Garrett would eat Tim O'Brien's hat.

No one had spotted Garrett yet. He stood in the door of the music room and watched as Lady Agatha played the pianoforte for Meg, who danced with Lucinda. The lovely widow had changed her gown to one of soft brown, which molded her slender figure and emphasized the whiteness of her skin. Her tawny curls bounced as she waltzed with Meg, yet a small frown creased the delicate skin between her brows.

"No, no, no!" Monsieur Collineau cried, clapping his hands together. Lady Agatha stopped playing. "This is wrong, all wrong."

Lucinda sighed and brushed a stray curl back into place as the tall, thin dance master paced the floor of the music room.

"You should be graceful," Monsieur declared, "not clomping about like a dairy maid through a muddy field! Let us try again."

"This is not going to work," Meg said, folding her arms obstinately.

"It *must* work, my lady," Monsieur Collineau said sternly. "You must learn to waltz if you are going to be a success this season! Come, Madame Devering, take your places again."

Lucinda hesitated. "Monsieur, perhaps Miss Stanton-Lynch is correct. I am not used to playing the man's part in the waltz, and I am finding it difficult to remember where to put my feet."

"Nonsense! You will begin again!" He signaled to Lady Agatha, then dropped his hand, an uncertain expression on his face. "Uh, my lady?"

Lucinda glanced over at Lady Agatha, whose head bobbed forward on her chest even as a soft snore echoed through the music room. "Oh, dear, not again," Lucinda sighed.

Again? Garrett thought. Their conversation in the breakfast room came back to him, and everything rapidly fell into place. No wonder the duke had arranged for Lucinda to help with Meg: Lady Agatha apparently had a tendency to drift off to sleep at any moment!

Lucinda hurried forward and gently nudged Lady Agatha, who came awake with a loud, "Who's there?"

"Monsieur would like to try the waltz again, my lady," Lucinda said respectfully, remaining close until the elderly woman gathered herself.

"Well, why didn't he say so?" Lady Agatha demanded.

Lucinda went back to her place with Meg. Lady Agatha launched into a robust waltz, and Monsieur Collineau quickly took up the count again. "Now then . . . one, two, three, and one, two, three—smile, Miss Stanton-Lynch—and one, two, three . . ."

Garrett chuckled as Lucinda spun haltingly around the room with Meg. He knew the exact instant that Lucinda caught sight of him standing in the doorway. Her eyes widened, and she stumbled.

"Ouch!" Meg stopped dancing to hobble on one foot. "Lucinda, you stepped on my toes."

"I'm so sorry, Meg." Lucinda turned her back on Garrett and helped the limping girl to a nearby chair.

"I say, who is this?" Monsieur Collineau demanded, catching sight of Garrett. The dance master regarded Garrett's simple attire through his quizzing glass. "Sir, this is a private lesson!"

"I won't interrupt." With a bland smile, Garrett went over and seated himself in a chair beside the pianoforte, long legs sprawled before him. He nodded at Lady Agatha, then folded his hands over his stomach and prepared to watch the lesson.

"See here!" the dance master burst out, puffing up with outrage.

"I see no reason why my nephew cannot watch his sister's dancing lesson, do you, Mrs. Devering?" Lady Agatha asked, her words stopping the dance master's protests mid-breath.

"Of course not, my lady," Lucinda replied, looking as if she longed to say the opposite. She gave Garrett a furious look, then turned back to Meg.

The dance master paled. "Your . . . er, nephew, Lady Agatha?"

"Yes, my great-nephew, the Marquess of Kelton. He is Miss Stanton-Lynch's brother. I trust you have no objections, Monsieur Collineau?"

Garrett raised his brows in the most arrogant way he could.

"Objections? Of course not!" The dance master cleared his throat. "Welcome, my lord. Please, stay as long as you like."

Garrett bared his teeth in a grin. "Thanks, I believe I will."

"Now, where were we?" Monsieur Collineau asked, looking back to Meg and Lucinda.

"My foot hurts, and I'm tired," Meg complained.

Monsieur hurried over to his student. As both the dance master and Lucinda fussed over Meg, Garrett noticed Lucinda kept her back to him the whole time. Of course, this meant that he had a very nice view of her lovely backside. Despite the layers of petticoats and whatnot that ladies wore beneath their clothes, he could clearly make out the womanly curves of her buttocks and thighs.

What would she do if she caught him staring? He thought of the glare she had given him, and couldn't help the grin that tugged at his lips. She was still mad at him. And when she turned all that passionate anger in his direction, it made him hotter than a summer day in Savannah. Watching her bend over like that gave him a few ideas that would scorch her petticoats, if she only knew.

Lady Agatha leaned forward and whispered, "What did you say to Mrs. Devering, you young scoundrel?"

Startled from his lusty fantasy, Garrett tore his attention from Lucinda's lovely bottom. "What?"

"Come, now. What did you say to her? She's furious with you," the old lady confided in a low voice. "She's a pretty thing. I know you like her."

"I—why wouldn't I like her?"

"Have you made untoward advances?" she asked, her dark eyes gleaming with something that looked like anticipation.

"Of course not!" At least, not yet.

"You didn't?" His aunt seemed disappointed. "Too bad. I had such high hopes for you."

Before he could answer, Meg's voice rose to a pitch he knew signaled trouble. "I told you, I'm tired and my foot hurts! Are you deaf? Shall I say it in French?"

Monsieur Collineau's face had turned red, and his pale eyes bulged in his thin face. He whirled on Lucinda. "Madame Devering," he implored in a voice taut with frustration, "you know we do not have much time. I am expected at the Grendales' residence promptly at five o'clock, and I cannot return to further instruct Miss Stanton-Lynch until the day before you leave for London. We have but a half an hour left of our lesson. Will you *please reason with the girl*?"

Lucinda raised cool brows at Monsieur's irate tone, but she turned to Meg anyway. "Meg, perhaps—"

"No, Lucinda," Meg interrupted. She turned her attention to the dance master. "*The girl* is sitting right here and speaks English, Monsieur Collineau. *The girl* is tired and has sore feet! *The girl* cannot dance again for at least fifteen minutes!"

"*Mon Dieu!*" Monsieur cried, spinning away in dramatic horror. "Fifteen minutes! We are undone!"

Even Lucinda looked worried. "Meg, you know you need to master the waltz. And Monsieur Collineau cannot return until next week."

"I don't care." Meg folded her arms, blue eyes welling with tears. "Can't I just watch for a few minutes?"

Lucinda sighed. "Meg, the waltz takes two people."

"Perhaps I can assist." As all heads swung toward him, Garrett looked at the dance master. "Monsieur, I can help by demonstrating the dance with Mrs. Devering while my sister observes."

"*Merveilleux!*" Monsieur cried. "We are saved!"

"I don't think—" Lucinda's words faded away as Garrett came to stand before her. "Can you even dance the waltz?" she demanded.

"I'm certain I can follow Monsieur's instructions." Grinning, Garrett held out his arms, hungry to touch her even in this innocent way. "Mrs. Devering, I await your pleasure."

Chapter 4

Lucinda stared at the arrogant devil tempting her to step into his arms. His blue eyes gleamed with warm appreciation, and dimples creased his cheeks.

"Go on, Lucinda," Meg said from behind her. "If I see how it is supposed to be done, it will help me learn."

"Come, Mrs. Devering," Garrett urged. "We are well chaperoned. You have nothing to fear."

"I hardly fear *you*, my lord." Chin held high, Lucinda stepped forward into his arms.

He quirked his brows at the use of his title, and sent her a private look bold enough to make her breath catch.

"Excellent form, my lord!" the dance master exclaimed, fluttering around them. "Now, your hand rests here, at her waist—very good—and you take her other hand in yours . . . yes, yes, perfect!"

The casual weight of his hand settling at her waist made her flesh tingle. Good heavens, how long had it been since a man had touched her? Years, certainly; Harry had stopped sharing her bed long before he had died. As she breathed in the scents of soap and man, an unexpected thrill went through her.

She met Garrett's eyes as Monsieur adjusted the American's fingers where they closed over hers. Garrett's hands were big and a little rough, yet he cradled her hand with a gentle warmth that echoed the heat of masculine interest in his eyes.

"My lord, you are familiar with the waltz, are you not?" Monsieur asked.

"I'll muddle along," Garrett murmured.

"Very well. Lady Agatha, if you please . . ."

The music began, and with a knowing smile, Garrett swept Lucinda into the dance.

The first turn left her spinning. She had expected to have to step carefully, lest she tread on his inexperienced feet, but instead she found herself in the arms of a man who could waltz with a grace that stole her breath.

His steps were sure, his arms strong, as he swept her around the room. His thighs brushed hers now and again as he whirled her around and around, making her flush with unexpected delight.

Her heart seemed to burst open with forgotten feelings, emotions she had carefully locked away. It felt glorious to be held again, magnificent to be able to let go of her control and trust a man to guide her for this fleeting moment in time. She began to hum with the music, eyes sliding closed, lips curving in a smile.

For this brief instant, she wasn't Harry Devering's long-neglected widow or Meg's companion or the daughter of General George Northcott. She was simply a woman—a woman who had gone too long without being touched by a man. Oh, the sensations were exquisite, and she never wanted this waltz to end.

Garrett relished the feel of her in his arms. It had been nearly a year since he'd held a woman who was not his sister, and he was enjoying the experience immensely. Her head just reached his shoulder, making them a perfect fit from chest to thighs. He watched her face as she relaxed in his arms, saw the pleasure spread across her delicate features as her eyes closed, and she began to hum with the music. A small smile curved her lips.

Desire flared hotter. Her expression resembled that of a woman who had just been thoroughly made love to, and suddenly he could imagine her lying on the bed amid tangled sheets, those toffee-colored curls spread across the pillows, that very smile of satisfaction on her lips.

Oh, yes, and he could imagine every touch, every kiss, that would bring that smile to her face. He slid his hand more firmly around her waist, longing to pull her closer.

Eventually they would be alone. And then . . . Going to London no longer seemed so intolerable with the prospect of enticing her into his bed.

Lucinda's eyes drifted open, and she gave him a sincere smile of pure enjoyment. He couldn't help but smile back and whirled her in a turn that made her laugh out loud. Her eyes glowed, and she tightened her fingers on his shoulder as he swept her into another turn.

Dear God, he had to have her.

She must have seen something in his face, because her smile faded. She held his gaze as the tension rose between them.

He slowed, making every movement a seduction, every step a caress. He squeezed her waist, watching the awareness slip into her eyes. Her lips parted, and he swept her into another turn, pressing his body against hers for the merest instant before allowing the proper distance between them again.

Lucinda felt as if he were making love to her through the waltz.

His intent expression, his blue eyes focused so

fiercely on her face, as if willing her to fall under his spell . . . The brief brush of his body against hers, so carefully orchestrated that no one but she was aware of it, all bespoke his feelings.

He wanted her.

The knowledge made her heart pound and her head spin. Men had shown interest in her before, but this was the first time she had wanted one back.

She had to get control of herself. Had to rein in her emotions. This could not happen!

But how could she resist those blue eyes, the color of a cloudless sky, looking at her as if he could see her soul? How could she ignore the alluring power of his body, the ease with which he guided her through the dance? How could she not notice those broad shoulders that seemed capable of taking on innumerable burdens with ridiculous ease? His hands, strong enough to crush her bones but gentle enough to hold a newborn kitten? The clean scent of man that tempted her to taste his sun-kissed skin?

How was a woman supposed to resist a man who loved his sister so fiercely that he would sail halfway around the world to be with her?

She couldn't stop the emotions that flooded her, the longing and the wanting and the sheer pleasure-pain of *feeling* again. He had brought her back to life. Somehow, with one dance, this

American with the work-roughened hands and the summer-blue eyes had resurrected the spirit of the woman she had once been.

She wanted, fiercely. She desired, hungrily. And had she been any other woman in any other circumstance, she would have taken the handsome American to her bed—knowing he would leave her, but also knowing that somehow he would unlock the prison where her spirit had resided these past ten years.

But she was Lucinda Devering, pawn of the Duke of Raynewood, and this man was a danger to her future.

Somehow she had to resist him. Somehow she must dredge up the will to deny herself the joy of finally living again. To find the power to turn away from something she wanted more than she wanted her next breath, and concentrate on what had to be.

The music came to an end. With a flourish, Garrett swept her into one more turn and then bowed, pressing his lips to her hand in a courtly gesture she hadn't expected. The feel of his warm mouth on her flesh surprised a gasp from her, and he met her eyes with unabashed desire.

She shivered at his power over her. Thank God she would be rid of him once they went to London. If she could manage to resist him for one more week, then she and Meg would be gone from Raynewood and Garrett would go back to America.

Somewhere she would find the strength to deny her innermost longings. If she gave in to Garrett's advances, not only would she be risking her only chance at a decent future, but he would no doubt become disappointed with her, just as Harry had.

It was much better to quietly glory in the fact that he was attracted to her than to torment herself worrying about what could not be.

A burst of applause brought her back to reality with a jolt.

"That was wonderful!" Meg cried, clapping. "Garrett, you must dance with me next!"

"Splendid, my lord!" Monsieur Collineau trilled. "Quite splendid!"

Lucinda slowly stepped away, slipping her hand from Garrett's. His other hand dropped from her waist. She had to swallow hard before she could speak. "You are an excellent dancer, my lord."

"We do dance in America," he replied easily.

Trying to pull her scrambling emotions together, she gave him a polite smile. "I simply didn't expect a man like you to be so big . . . I mean," she hurried on, cheeks flaming, "I mean, I did not expect a big man like yourself to be so good at this. Dancing, that is. You are quite graceful."

"Why, thank you." The twitch of his lips indicated that he knew her thoughts had drifted onto the path of impropriety. His voice held seductive nuances that only she seemed to hear, as he said, "I look forward to dancing with you again, Mrs. Devering."

"Yes, how regrettable that we shall not have the opportunity," she said coolly.

"Oh, but you will!" Meg cried. "When we go to London you'll have plenty of chances to dance together, since Garrett is going with us."

Lucinda's heart stopped. "Wh-what?"

"Meg has asked me to accompany you to London," he said. "I've agreed to go."

"How splendid!" Lady Agatha chimed in from the pianoforte.

"Yes. Splendid," Lucinda echoed hollowly. "If you'll excuse me, Captain, the dance has left me a bit breathless."

"Are you certain it was the dance?" Garrett murmured.

Ignoring his comment, she walked stiffly to the chair beside the pianoforte as Garrett took his position again with Meg as a partner.

"Simply keep the count and follow his lordship's lead," Monsieur said to Meg. "Lady Strathwaite, if you please."

Lady Agatha started playing again, and Garrett swept his sister into the waltz to the accompaniment of Monsieur's counting. Meg's giggle of pleasure echoed over the well-tuned notes of the pianoforte.

Lucinda found herself captured by the sensual grace of Garrett's movements. His lack of coat allowed the flexing of his back and arm muscles beneath his white shirt to be easily seen. Against her will, her eyes were drawn to his well-shaped thighs and tight buttocks, moving in rhythm with the music. An image drifted through her mind, of Garrett sans clothing, his muscles rippling as he tumbled her onto the bed . . .

"He's a handsome devil, isn't he?" Lady Agatha murmured, still playing.

Lucinda took a moment to calm her pounding heart. "My lady?"

"My great-nephew. He's a handsome devil." Lady Agatha glanced over, her dark eyes twinkling. "A woman would be lucky indeed to attract his attention."

Lucinda straightened her spine. "I'm not interested in his attentions," she said firmly. "Meg is my concern." *And the duke has plans for him*, she reminded herself.

"Meg may be your concern," the old lady said with a chuckle, "but you've just become my nephew's. If you don't welcome his attentions, I suggest you lock your bedroom door at night."

"My lady!" she exclaimed, shocked, even as a ripple of heat went through her at the thought.

"I may be old," Lady Agatha said with a snort,

"but some things haven't changed, and this is one of them. As far as I'm concerned, you could use a man like him, even for a little while. And if you're any bit the woman I think you are, you'll know exactly how to handle my nephew."

"This discussion is quite improper," Lucinda whispered, breathless at the mere idea of *handling* Garrett Lynch.

"When you get to be my age, Mrs. Devering, propriety falls by the wayside. I hope you'll give that young devil a chance."

The idea of Garrett Lynch as a potential lover continued to haunt Lucinda as she watched Garrett sweep Meg into a waltz.

He had to have her.

As he danced with Meg, Garrett cast a quick glance now and then at Lucinda. It didn't matter to him if she *was* interested in his grandfather—something he was not at all certain of anymore. He was certain that his youth and virility would be more enticing than the duke's fortune. And if the lady required hard, cold proof of his devotion, he was a wealthy man in his own right.

But given the heat he had just seen in her eyes, he now knew the key to winning her. Beneath that proper veneer beat the heart of a passionate woman. Unrelenting seduction was called for in this situation, and he was eager to begin.

The more he thought about it, the more he

came to believe that Lucinda had not lied when she claimed to have no interest in the duke. From her reactions, he deduced that she was a woman who had not been touched in a long time.

He would remedy that.

He swept Meg into one last turn and caught Lucinda's eye. She pointedly looked away, and he grinned. Soon he would turn Lucinda's protests into purrs of pleasure.

Very soon.

Chapter 5

Lucinda made her way to her room, having deftly avoided Garrett's attempts to speak to her privately after the dance lesson. She was well aware of the lusty gleam in his eye, and her own emotions were so churned up that she dared not be alone with him. Needs she had not felt in years had awakened with a vengeance, demanding immediate attention.

She was not some green girl to be bowled over by a handsome man, she chastised herself. She had been married for ten years and knew what the world was like. Even if her marriage had been mostly a sham, she had learned much about the ways of men and women during that time, and there was no need to become moony-eyed over broad shoulders.

No matter how much she had longed to stroke her hands over them.

Stop it! She was a grown woman, well able to take care of herself. *Then why did you deliberately use Meg to avoid being alone with him?* She had stayed with the young girl until he'd finally given up trying to get her attention, and gone upstairs to dress for dinner. Lucinda had just left Meg to do the same.

Coward.

"Practical," she argued aloud. "You know what would happen. Better that you stay away from him."

But she wouldn't be able to evade him forever; she couldn't avoid him at dinner or when Meg desired his company. All she could do in those situations was maintain a disapproving exterior when he looked at her with those blue eyes that hinted at such sinful delights.

Even if her woman's heart melted beneath her icy veneer, making her yearn to lose herself in the pleasure promised by his single-minded pursuit.

A vigorous man like him would soon get bored with a battle he could not win, and take himself off to the village for female companionship. And if not—well, London was full of demi-reps who might entertain the American. All Lucinda had to do was maintain her position of chastity.

Easier said than done.

She arrived at her chamber and reached for the doorknob.

"Mrs. Devering."

She jumped, letting out a little shriek as she whirled around. Garrett leaned against the wall opposite her room, his arms folded across his impressive chest. His dark coat blended in with the shadows, as did his ink-black hair. He grinned, his teeth a flash of white in the semi-darkness, and he moved away from the wall.

"Calm yourself, Mrs. Devering," he said as he walked toward her. "Or may I call you Lucinda?"

When had the hallway gotten so small? She wet her dry lips. "You may call me Mrs. Devering," she said weakly. "What are you doing here, Captain?"

"Surely you know the answer to that." He stopped only inches away and reached for her hand, then raised it to his lips, his eyes fathomless in the dimly lit hallway.

She should snatch her hand away. She should give him the sharp edge of her tongue. Instead she only whispered, "No."

"No?" He cocked his head to the side, his long hair sweeping his shoulders with a soft swish. "No, you do not know the answer? Or are you saying no to something else?"

"Give me my hand." She tugged, but he did not release her. "You should not be here."

"You knew I would come." He took a step closer, releasing her hand only to crowd her back against the door of her room.

"My lord," she said, "please go. What if someone should see us?"

"Always the proper English lady," he teased, and leaned closer. "Tell me, Lucinda, have you ever been tempted to be less than a perfect lady? Haven't you ever wanted to strip off propriety and give in to your innermost desires?"

His voice lowered on the last words, vibrating through her with the echo of her unspoken longings. She should be shocked. She should scream or slap him or *something*, but the image of both of them naked and bared of all inhibitions had taken control of her imagination and would not let it go.

"You are impertinent," she managed to say breathlessly, as her body flooded with the heat of long-denied desire.

"I'm a man," he corrected. He reached out, stroking his fingers down her cheek. "And you, my dear, are very much a woman."

Her knees turned to pudding, and she struggled against the urge to press her lips to the delicious masculine mouth that hovered so close to hers. "How clever of you to notice," she breathed. "Now that the biology lesson is over, I must change for dinner."

"Perhaps you would allow me to assist you."

Those strong fingers trailed down her neck, paused at the pulse that pounded in her throat, then continued down to trace teasingly over her bare shoulder, along the edge of her gown.

Lucinda clenched her hands into fists at her sides and leaned heavily against the door as her body melted beneath his touch. "Please, I cannot," she whispered, no longer able to maintain even the slightest façade of resistance. "My lord, I beg you."

"Garrett," he corrected. He leaned in and inhaled the scent of her hair, his mouth hovering above her ear. "I want you, Lucinda."

She squeezed her eyes closed as his warm breath swept her ear. "No. Impossible," she said weakly.

"Not impossible," He cupped the back of her head in his big hand and tilted her face back so that she looked at him. "We are adults, you and I. You're a widow, and I am a man alone in a strange country. Perhaps we can make this trip to London more interesting for both of us. I want to be your lover, Lucinda."

The blunt words devastated any arguments she might have summoned. He lowered his head, hesitating for the briefest instant before taking her lips in a sweet kiss laced with unmistakable hunger.

He kissed the way he did everything else, powerfully and without apology. He pressed her back against the door with the weight of his body, his hand still cupping her head as he devastated her defenses with his mouth. His other hand rested along the curve of her hip, and she brought her own hands up around his waist to find balance in her tilting world. His lips were appealingly soft for such a large, strong man, and she willingly opened her mouth to him, surrendering to the desire between them.

Their kiss went on and on, and with every stroke of his tongue, every nibble of his teeth, her passion overrode her common sense. Finally, he broke the kiss and rested his forehead against hers, his breath coming in fast pants. Sandwiched between him and the door, she could easily feel his arousal through their layers of clothing. For one wild instant, she was tempted to open the door behind her and take Garrett into the intimacy of her chamber.

A footstep down the hall and the voice of one of the maids jerked her back to reality with a violent jolt. What had she been thinking? She had been about to jeopardize her entire future for a few moments of passion!

She attempted to push Garrett away, but he was heavy and not inclined to move. "Someone's coming," she hissed.

He took a reluctant step back, his fingers lingering to stroke her cheek. "I will come to you tonight."

"*No.*" She shoved at him, and his surprise at her answer made him fall back a step.

"What do you mean, no?" he demanded. "What about—"

"No," she said again, shoving open the door to her room. She darted behind it, peering at him from behind the sturdy wooden shield. "I want no lover, Captain Lynch. What I need is a husband."

"Husband!"

"Yes, a husband. Now please take yourself off before someone sees you and starts gossip."

He slapped his hand on the door, holding it open. "You may want a husband, Mrs. Devering," he growled, "but what you *need* is a lover. And I am just the man to accommodate you."

"I am not some tavern maid for you to tumble at your whim," Lucinda snapped. "I am a woman of good family, and here in England, a man marries such a woman if he wants her."

"I have no intention of getting married."

"And I have no intention of being your lover," she shot back.

He gave her a scorching look that was a combination of lust and anger. "We'll see about that."

"Indeed we will."

She slammed the door in his face, then leaned against it, her heart pounding and body singing with unbridled passion, until she heard him storm down the hall.

She had won this battle, but he would be back. And she needed a husband to survive, no matter how tempting a lover might be to her now. In the end, a lover would probably be disappointed in her anyway. Besides, the duke planned to see Garrett wed to Lady Penelope. She shuddered to think what His Grace might do if she interfered with those plans.

Everything depended on her keeping a level head. She *must* resist Garrett's seduction. No matter what.

A husband!

He should have known, Garrett thought darkly, as he made his way to the drawing room where everyone gathered before dinner. Was there not one woman on earth who could honestly enjoy a man's attentions without attempting to trap him?

He had presented Lucinda with a simple proposition. She had been a widow for over a year now, and he had been at sea for almost as long. It seemed a neat and enjoyable solution to him.

Leave it to her to complicate the situation by mentioning marriage!

Garrett strode into the drawing room and stopped just inside the doorway when he saw that the only occupant was his grandfather. Blast it all! The last thing he needed now was a battle with the duke. Garrett's black coat and trousers, which he reserved for business dinners, were not as formal as British evening wear, but it was all he had with him.

The duke also wore plain black, but there the similarity ended. The stark color, relieved only by his snowy shirt and cravat, emphasized the harshness of his features and his white hair. The old man stared somberly at the portrait of his younger self, which hung on the wall above the mantel.

Garrett moved to step out of the room unnoticed, but suddenly his grandfather looked up.

For an instant Garrett thought he glimpsed anguish in the old fellow's eyes, but then the proud aristocrat was back, his gaze coolly polite, his smile bland and practiced with only a hint of arrogance.

"Good evening, grandson."

Garrett gave a curt nod, but said nothing. He uncurled his hands, which had somehow formed into fists, and relaxed his stance, realizing that he had automatically shifted to the balls of his feet as if preparing for a fight.

A smile of genuine amusement tugged at his grandfather's lips for a brief instant. "So," Erasmus said with polite interest, "I am told you have decided to accompany us to London."

"Yes."

"Excellent! Will you stay with us at Stanton House, or would you prefer your own rooms?"

"I'll be wherever Meg is." The words were a warning, and the duke's raised eyebrows indicated he had received it.

"Margaret will naturally be staying at Stanton House," the old man replied. "As will my sister, though she has her own home in London. And Mrs. Devering, of course."

A new thought occurred to Garrett. Good Lord, what if Lucinda's aim was *marriage* to the duke, and not a simple affair as he had surmised? "Mrs. Devering is a beautiful woman," he commented casually.

"So she is."

"A beautiful widow, who lives in your house, even though she is not a member of your family." His tone rose at the end of the statement, making it more of a question.

The duke let out a startled laugh. "Devil take you, boy, are you implying that she's my mistress?"

"Is she?" If Lucinda was involved with his grandfather it would explain her reluctance to enter into a perfectly harmless affair with *him*, especially if her goal was marriage.

The duke shook his head, unable to disguise his amusement. "I thank you for the compliment, my boy, but Mrs. Devering is too young for an old man like me. She is merely the daughter of an old friend and is teaching your sister to get on in society. That is all."

So, even if she did plot to wed the old man, her plans would come to nothing. Good. "I like to know who the players are," he said with a careless shrug.

"A wise precaution."

"After all," Garrett continued, frowning, "just because you aren't a young man, don't assume that a woman wouldn't be interested in your company. Many women go after wealth and position rather than physical appearance."

"Ah, yes." Erasmus gave him a considering look. "No doubt you have encountered such females yourself. I understand that you have done quite well in America. You have your own business and a fine house in Boston. No doubt there were women who found a young man of such means to be irresistible."

"They found my coffers irresistible," Garrett scoffed. "It was one of the reasons I went to sea. There are no women there."

"I daresay it's not much better in London," the duke warned. "You will encounter the same type of female, who hungers for riches and longs to increase her social standing. Especially now that you are the Marquess of Kelton."

"I'm not interested in the blasted title," Garrett ground out. "I'm going there for Meg, and that's all."

The duke drew himself up and looked down his blade of a nose at Garrett. "The 'blasted title,' as you put it, has been in the Stanton family for six generations. And my own title goes back to the Conqueror himself, some eight hundred years. While you are in London, you shall not disgrace either. Do I make myself clear?"

"I have no intention of disgracing your precious title," Garrett retorted. "I just don't want it. Meg is the only reason I have remained beneath your roof."

"You have made no secret of that. Just remember, no matter what your feelings for me, your behavior directly affects your sister's reputation."

"I am aware of that."

"We shall have to get you some clothes and a proper valet, and I shall see that you have membership to all the clubs. I'm certain Mrs. Devering will be more than happy to teach you what you need to know."

"I know how to eat with a fork and dance without stepping on anyone's toes," Garrett said tightly. "Mrs. Devering doesn't need to teach me anything."

"And I think you will find it convenient to answer to 'Kelton' while in London," the older man continued. "The Stanton name has more power in London society than you realize."

"The only power I want is the command of my ship."

Before Erasmus could answer, Meg swept into the room, Lucinda behind her. "Good evening, everyone. Are we late?"

"Of course not, my dear," the duke replied, his expression softening. He sent a nod to Lucinda. "Good evening, Mrs. Devering."

"Your Grace," she said with a curtsy. She glanced at Garrett. "Good evening, Captain."

"Mrs. Devering." This evening she wore a Nile blue gown cut low across her bosom, baring her shoulders in a creamy display that rivaled the pearls at her throat in its beauty. Her curling brown hair was swept up and threaded through with a matching ribbon, and her brown eyes widened with awareness as he openly appreciated the picture she made.

The memory of their kiss heated his blood, and he knew from the rosy flush that swept her cheeks that she remembered, too.

"We have only to wait for my sister, and then we can go in to dinner," Erasmus said.

"I'm here," Lady Agatha announced, stepping through the doors. She was dressed in layers of tulle that made her resemble a puffy, pink wedding cake. A diamond the size of a baby's fist glittered at her throat. "Don't just stand there," she commanded. "I'm hungry!"

"Then arrive on time," Erasmus grumbled. He offered Meg his arm and escorted her from the room, leaving Garrett to escort the remaining ladies to the dining room.

From the moment they arrived in the dining room, Lucinda knew she was in trouble.

Meg sat at the duke's right, Lady Agatha on her other side. With a sweep of his hand, the duke indicated that Garrett sit at his left.

Which left Lucinda to sit next to Garrett. The wicked man had the nerve to wink at her as she seated herself, but she ignored him, resolved to treat him with an icy politeness that would make it clear she was absolutely *not* interested in his attentions.

She might even convince herself.

Under the table, his foot brushed hers. She snapped her head around, prepared to deliver a scathing setdown, and met his startled, blue-eyed stare.

"My apologies," he murmured in a low voice, then spread his napkin in his lap.

Lucinda hesitated, unsure if it had been deliberate or not. When he turned his attention to the footman who entered the room with the tureen of soup, she relaxed. Perhaps it had been innocent, after all.

And perhaps pigs would sprout wings and fly them all to London.

But as the meal progressed and he engaged in polite conversation with Meg and Lady Agatha, Lucinda began to think she was indeed mistaken. Maybe he really had accepted her refusal to start an affair with him. Maybe the talk of marriage had changed his mind.

He had no doubt bedded women in every port of call in the world, and she didn't need an itinerant lover who would leave for Boston as soon as he could do so.

But at least she had the memory of that kiss.

Over a plate of roasted chicken, his hand brushed her arm as he reached for his wine glass. She darted a glance at him, but he seemed completely engrossed in the anecdote being told by Lady Agatha.

Close quarters, Lucinda reasoned. Determined to ignore the tingle brought on by the memory of his body pressing hers into the door of her room, Lucinda reached for her own glass of wine.

Everyone burst into laughter as Lady Agatha finished her tale. Lucinda smiled and sipped her wine, having not heard a word.

"Garrett will be joining us at Stanton House," the duke announced. "I trust you will assist him with whatever he desires, Mrs. Devering."

Lucinda choked on her wine. *Whatever he de-*

sires? Garrett's rakish grin indicated he knew where her thoughts had taken her. The duke was talking about London, not about ... "As you wish, Your Grace."

He looked at Garrett. "Mrs. Devering can ease your way into society, my boy. I hope you will stop being so stubborn and use her expertise wisely."

"I'm certain Mrs. Devering is more than capable of easing me in," Garrett remarked, his expression bland despite the devilment gleaming in his eyes. "But I hesitate to ask her to bear my weight when she already does so much for Meg."

Lucinda gulped down another swallow of wine. The images his words brought to mind were not the ones a lady usually entertained at dinner. They weren't ones a *lady* entertained at all!

But a woman who had tasted passion—ah, that was another story.

Garrett's knee bumped hers beneath the table, and this time she knew it was deliberate.

Damn his dimples, he knew *exactly* what he was about. Garrett Lynch was toying with her— and enjoying her discomfort immensely.

Two could play at that game, she thought recklessly.

"Your Grace," she said, watching Garrett from the corner of her eye, "I am more than happy to lend my expertise in this matter." As she spoke, she stroked her fingers up the stem of her wine-glass. Then down again. Slowly. Caressingly. Again. And again. Garrett's gaze locked on her teasing fingers. With a secretive smile, she continued, "I have considerable experience in such things."

Lucinda trailed her fingertips languorously around the rim of her glass, then stroked them down over the goblet and along the stem. "So I will be delighted to give your grandson any instruction he should require."

Garrett choked.

"Are you quite all right, my lord?" she asked solicitously. "You must have a care when swallowing. It is best to sip slowly, so as not to catch something in your throat."

"Fine," Garrett croaked.

"Do let me know when you require my services," Lucinda said with a smile. Then she picked up her fork, stabbed an asparagus spear, and bit the tip off.

Garrett flinched. "I will."

"Ugh," Meg said from across the table. "I hate asparagus. Here, Garrett." She lifted her plate and held it out across the table.

Lucinda, Lady Agatha, and the duke all put down their silverware with a clank as Garrett scraped her vegetables onto his own dish. He started to dig into the asparagus, then noticed the stark silence. He looked from Lady Agatha to the duke to Lucinda. "Is there a problem?"

"Something must be done," Lady Agatha said, turning beseeching eyes to the duke.

"Indeed." The duke's dark brows slashed down in a frown. "Mrs. Devering, you will see to it."

"Someone mind telling me what's going on?" Garrett inquired, his scowl mirroring his grandfather's.

Meg bit her lip. "I've done something wrong, haven't I? I'm so sorry, Grandfather."

"Don't worry about it, my dear," the duke said, patting her hand.

"I shouldn't have passed the plate, should I? And now Garrett's in trouble, too."

"It's all right," the elderly man said. "Mrs. Devering will take your brother in hand, won't you, Mrs. Devering?"

The wicked gleam in Garrett's blue eyes made her breath hitch.

"Of course, Your Grace," she agreed. "For it seems to me that he is in desperate need of instruction."

Garrett's eyes widened in surprise, and he choked on a mouthful of food.

Lucinda smiled serenely, the picture of English femininity as she hid her satisfaction in a swallow of wine.

As conversation picked up again, Garrett reached for his wine and leaned closer to murmur in her ear, "First point to you, Mrs. Devering."

Pleased with herself, she raised her goblet a bit in a mock toast. "To you, Captain."

One corner of his mouth lifted in a wicked grin that she found incredibly appealing. "Enjoy your victory, Lucinda. The game is not yet over."

He turned to speak to Meg, and Lucinda shrugged off his words. She would win this battle of wits, no matter what Garrett thought. She was a survivor, and she would resist him without fail until Captain Lynch had sailed his ship back to Boston.

Chapter 6

He didn't come.

As the clock in the hallway chimed two, Lucinda stared at her closed bedroom door. She had stayed dressed, fully expecting Garrett Lynch to come to her room that night, and equally determined that he'd never make it past the threshold.

She had been prepared for an all-out seduction, given their wordplay at dinner. And that kiss in the hallway! Enough said.

Yet as the hours passed, no knock came at the door. Obviously, moving the dresser in front of the door would have proven unnecessary, even if she hadn't discarded the notion for fear of servants' gossip. She should be relieved. After all, had Garrett come to her bedchamber as he had implied he would, the outcome could have been disastrous.

Completely disastrous, she repeated to herself firmly.

She let out a deep sigh and leaned back in her chair. Her shoulders were stiff with tension; the anticipation—no, anxiety!—had robbed her of all composure. Sleep would surely elude her this night, unless she did something to calm her tattered nerves.

The thought slipped into her mind as innocently as a rose petal fluttering to the ground. Her mother had always sworn that a drop of sherry could calm the most rattled composure, though such a measure should be saved for drastic circumstances.

Lucinda rose to her feet and opened the door. A bit of sherry was just what she needed. She would slip down to the drawing room for a moment, while the household was still asleep. After all, it wouldn't do for the servants to be gossiping about how Mrs. Devering imbibed spirits in the wee hours of the morning!

Garrett grinned around the unlit cigar clenched between his teeth as he mounted the stairs from the servants' quarters, counting the money he had won from the footmen. They'd been hesitant about playing cards with the crazy American, but the bottles of fine whiskey that Garrett had produced changed their minds rather quickly. He imagined that footmen generally did not have access to such high-quality spirits. The whiskey had also smoothed over any hard feelings about Garrett walking away with the lion's share of the winnings.

He hummed a tune as he tucked the money into the pocket of his coat, draped over his arm. Then he straightened his waistcoat and finger-combed his hair. After all, he didn't want Lucinda to reject him for looking slovenly when he presented himself at her bedchamber.

Despite her claim that she desired a husband, he was sure she was only playing coy. Why else would she have engaged in such flirtation with him at dinner? When he thought of how her delicate fingers had caressed the wineglass, he couldn't help but become aroused.

Some women enjoyed being pursued, and Lucinda Devering was apparently one of them. That was fine with him; he didn't mind seducing her, if that was the game she wanted to play. As long as he ended up in her bed.

No doubt she had fretted the night away, waiting for him to break down her door. He chuckled as he continued up the stairs to the main level of the house. If she had fallen asleep, he doubted she would mind being awakened. He just hoped she wasn't too angry with him for taking so long to come to her.

He tucked his cigar into the pocket of his coat and whistled softly as he passed through the grand foyer and headed toward the staircase. He imagined the things he wanted to do and the positions he wanted to do them in, arousing himself further. Pausing before the staircase, he adjusted the demanding flesh straining at the front of his trousers. It wouldn't do to arrive in the lady's boudoir as hard and horny as a bull. He had no intention of rushing anything, and he meant to make sure both of them enjoyed this night thoroughly.

A sound, like glasses clinking together in toast, drew his attention. He moved away from the stairs and looked down the darkened hallway. A sliver of light peeped from beneath the door of the drawing room. Then a woman's voice softly uttered, "Blast it!"

The voice was not Meg's and sounded too youthful to be Lady Agatha's. Unless one of the maids had taken to nipping the duke's spirits in the middle of the night, that left one possibility.

Lucinda.

Lucinda stared at the small stain spreading across the skirt of her favorite dinner dress. Between her earlier anxiety and her fear of being discovered, her hands were shaking so much that she'd spilled the sherry. She had no idea how she would explain it to her maid. Perhaps she could say it was wine spilled at dinner. Yes, that would work.

She closed her eyes and took a deep breath. Was she really worrying about something so trivial as explaining a stain to her maid? Sweet heaven, she had to get control of herself! Her entire life was falling apart. She was backed into a corner, and only fulfilling her agreement with the duke would get her out of it. That meant teaching Garrett how to win Lady Penelope Albright. She opened her eyes and lifted the sherry to her lips.

"Well, well, Mrs. Devering. I would never have taken you for the type to drown your troubles in drink."

Her hand jerked at the sound of his voice, and she spilled more sherry on her gown. Clenching her fingers tightly around the heavy crystal glass, she slowly turned her head to look at him.

Garrett lounged in the doorway, his cravat dangling around his neck and his shirt unbuttoned at the throat, revealing a hint of black chest hair. He still wore his waistcoat, his coat was folded over his arm, and his well-fitted dark trousers emphasized his lean hips and long legs. His hair hung loose and wild to his shoulders. He grinned at her, a pirate's grin, his blue eyes sparkling with mirth.

Her knees felt as if they had turned to pudding. Why did the man persist in going about half naked? She wondered that he even dressed at all!

"What are you doing here?" Her voice might have sounded strident, but it was difficult to tell, as her heart was thundering in her ears. Why, why, *why* did her body always turn wanton whenever she saw him? The infamous Northcott dignity crumbled in his presence.

"Investigating a mysterious sound in the middle of the night." He shrugged away from the doorjamb and sauntered into the room. "I thought to find a thief, but instead I found you."

"Keep your distance, Captain," she demanded, holding out her free hand as if to stop him.

He halted, still grinning, the rogue. His appreciative gaze swept her from head to toe and left her tingling. "Whatever the lady wants." He casually seated himself on the arm of a sofa, tossing his coat over the back of it.

She watched him warily, as she would a wolf about to spring, and took a slow, steadying sip of sherry. "What are you doing up at this hour, Captain?"

"I was just going upstairs." His gaze dropped to her lips as she licked a drop of sherry from them.

She set down the glass, then realized she didn't know what to do with her hands and picked it up again. "It's very late. I shouldn't want to keep you from your bed."

"You won't, as it wasn't my bed I was going to."

She bobbled the glass, just barely keeping the last of the sherry from spilling on the carpet. "Excuse me?"

He rose to his feet. "I was coming to *your* bed."

The breath whooshed from her lungs, and her heart stopped.

"Surely you knew that." He stopped in front of her and gently stroked her cheek, his smile not fading as she stepped away from his touch. "I told you I would be back."

"I told you no," she squeaked, finding her voice at last. "I thought you understood *that*."

"I understand you just fine." He shrugged. "Many women like to make a man chase them. I don't mind."

He stroked her cheek again, and this time, she caught a whiff of whiskey. "You're foxed!" she pronounced with a combination of horror and relief.

"Not exactly. Just very, very . . . warm."

She slapped his hand away. "I don't care how warm you are, *I* shall not be the one to offer you relief!"

"You're trembling," he said.

"Did you hear what I said? I have no intention of having an affair with you, Captain."

"Are you cold?" His hand slid down her shoulder and stroked across her nipple. It immediately peaked, and triumph lit his eyes. "Seems that you are."

"Captain!" she gasped.

"Let me warm you." He slipped his arm around her waist and scooped her against him, his palm still cupping her breast, and kissed her.

Desire roared forth like a beast released from a cage, and drowned the small voice of reason that was trying to make itself heard over the clamorous demands of her body.

She should protest. She *would* protest. In a minute.

His mouth seduced hers with a gentleness that was just as powerful as the passion of their first kiss. He nibbled at her lips, tasted her, took his time savoring the delicious tangle of their tongues.

She sighed and relaxed in his arms, just for a moment. His hand kneaded her breast with a firm pressure that contrasted with the soft play of his lips, and the swell of pleasure made her want to stay in his arms forever. The tugs of desire made her feel like a real woman, attractive, wanted. And for the first time since Malcolm, she honestly and truly wanted a man.

The thought terrified her.

With a forceful push, she broke off the kiss, straining backward when he would have rejoined their mouths. The last time she had been attracted to a man, it had ruined her life. She'd vowed never again to let her heart rule her head.

And even if she wanted Garrett Lynch, she couldn't have him.

"Stop," she whispered. "We can't."

"We can." He pressed his erection against her stomach. "In fact, I bet I 'can' more than once."

Her face flushed with heat as desire streaked through her belly. Good Lord, the man had no shame at all! Someone had to set an example for him, and the duke had declared that she should be the one.

"Let go of me, Garrett." Once more, she strained backward in an effort to free herself. Heaven help them if any of the staff heard them and came to investigate! She pushed at his shoulder with her free hand, uncomfortably aware that he still fondled her breast in a distracting and arousing way that almost made her forget the duke and Lady Penelope and her own name.

He leaned down and pressed an open-mouthed kiss to her throat, since he couldn't reach her mouth.

Her knees almost collapsed out from under her. She was going to explode from the overflowing passion that had been restrained for the last ten years, and that would only lead to disaster.

He tugged at the bodice of her dress, stringing kisses down her throat to her—

"Stop!" Desperately she threw the last of the sherry in his face, then shoved hard, pushing him away from her. She stumbled backward and hit the sideboard. The sherry decanter wobbled precariously, but she caught it before it fell to the floor.

"Argh! Woman, are you mad?" Garrett pulled his wrinkled neck cloth from around his neck and dabbed at his eyes.

"You aren't listening to me, Captain. I have no *intention* of sharing your bed. None. At. All."

He blinked at her through the sherry dripping from his hair. "You're serious."

"Of course I'm serious!" She gave a sweeping gesture with her free hand. "I've been trying to tell you that all evening!"

"Then what was going on at dinner? Did I imagine that you were flirting with me, Mrs. Devering?"

She colored. "I don't know what possessed me to do such a thing. You were just making me so angry with your persistence."

"So you *were* flirting with me."

She lifted her chin. "Only in self-defense."

"And what about this?" He gestured at her breasts, her nipples embarrassingly prominent beneath her gown. "How do you explain those?"

Feeling as if her face were on fire, she crossed her arms across her chest. "It's cold in here."

He gave a derisive snort and swept his wet hair back from his face. "You are the damnedest woman."

"I told you in the hallway that I am looking for a husband, Captain, not a lover."

He slid her a glance that made her pulse skip into double time. "I could change your mind."

She stiffened her spine. "I very much doubt that."

"Is that a challenge?" He moved swiftly, crowding her backward toward the sideboard. "We Americans love a challenge."

She slapped a hand against his chest to halt his advance. His heart thundered beneath her palm. "I see you are too foxed to be reasonable this evening, Captain. Do you intend to force me?"

His smile was pure male confidence. "I don't have to force women, Mrs. Devering. They come to me *very* willingly."

"Not this woman." She held his gaze firmly, though her insides quaked. "Now please step back."

He did so with obvious reluctance, and she could see the puzzlement in his eyes.

"Thank you, Captain," she said softly.

"This has been . . . the damnedest day." He turned away and stood with his back to her, shoulders stiff and fists clenched. He sounded like a man who had reached his limit.

"I'm sorry if I misled you—"

He silenced her with an impatient slash of his hand. "It's not just you. Nothing has gone right since the day I heard that my mother died."

Silence settled over the room as she searched for a suitable reply.

"I'm sorry for your loss," she said finally. "Meg has told me that your mother was a wonderful woman."

"She was," he said softly.

Again, silence.

Lucinda bit her lip as she stared at his back. "Meg also told me that it took several months for the news to reach you."

"Aye," he replied. "That blasted letter followed me around for six months before it caught up with me. As I was in Amsterdam at the time, it took another four months for me to get home. By then, Meg was gone."

"And you immediately came after her." She paused as a thought occurred to her. "You haven't had a chance to grieve, have you?"

He turned, and she caught a glimpse of torment in his eyes. "I had plenty of time aboard ship."

"I don't think so," she said slowly, her heart going out to him. "I bet you distracted yourself with captaining your ship. And then you came home to find Meg gone to England, and you were able to distract yourself again with your anger at your grandfather."

"You think after a day's acquaintance, you know me so well, Mrs. Devering?" he sneered.

Knowing he was lashing out from pain, she kept her voice calm. "No, but Meg has talked of you constantly since her arrival here."

The ferocity faded from his expression. "What did she say?"

Lucinda smiled. "According to her, you are the bravest sea captain in the world, and the handsomest. You have women the world over in love with you, and you are the shrewdest businessman in the world."

His lips twitched into a smile.

"She loves you very much."

He sighed, his tense shoulders relaxing. "She's all I have left."

"That's not necessarily true. You have your grandfather and Lady Agatha and her grandson, the Earl of Knightsbridge."

"Meg is my family. And once she has gone to this court presentation thing and maybe a ball or two, I am taking her home to America."

"She may not want to go with you."

"She will. She knows I will not have her stay here in England."

Lucinda arched her brows. "Well, Captain, one does not always get what one wants."

"That's right. And my grandfather had best remember that."

Lucinda threw up her hands. "The both of you are too much alike, always issuing orders and expecting everyone else to fall in line with them!"

"Meg is young and impressionable," Garrett argued, clearly ignoring her comment. "Her head is easily turned by pretty clothes and fancy titles, but she'll come to her senses."

Lucinda frowned. "Meg strikes me as a very intelligent and independent young woman. Here in England, many of our young ladies are wives and mothers by her age."

"And no doubt you see the same future for Meg," Garrett snapped. "My dear Mrs. Devering, do not assume that just because you are desperate for a husband that my sister wants the same thing."

"And don't you assume, Captain, that she does not! The duke can offer her a wonderful opportunity to marry quite well so that she can live in comfort the rest of her days."

"I'll see her married to a beggar before I allow her to marry an Englishman!"

"Most young ladies would kill for such a chance, yet you would deny it to your sister!"

"With my last breath," he vowed.

"And I would see her marry well—with *my* last breath," she retorted. "You let your own anger blind you to what is right for her."

"What makes you think you know what's right for Meg?" he demanded. "I am her brother. I'm the one who knows what's best for her!"

Lucinda took a step forward. "Meg says differently. She *wants* to be here, Captain. She *wants* to have her debut in London."

"She doesn't know what she wants," he said with a dismissive wave. "When she's had her fill of your prissy English ways, I will see her home to Boston where she belongs."

Lucinda took a deep breath. "This is getting us nowhere. You are determined to see that she goes back to Boston, and I am equally determined to see that she weds an English peer. We are at an impasse."

"The hell we are. I'm her brother. Who the hell are you to make such a decision for her?"

The cutting edge of his words wounded, but outwardly, Lucinda did not even flinch. "I am only seeing to your grandfather's wishes."

"My grandfather doesn't give a damn about Meg," Garrett snarled. "He lured her here so he could get me here, the wily bastard."

"Captain, kindly watch your language."

Garret gave a sharp bark of laughter. "I'm a man, Mrs. Devering, not one of those prissy Englishmen of yours. I talk like a man, and I have a man's needs."

"Are we back to that again?" she retorted. "Why is it, Captain, that whenever we begin to discuss your feelings for your grandfather, you try to distract me with innuendoes? What are you afraid of?"

"You're a fine one to be talking about being afraid. There is more to life than the careful rules and regulations of your precious society, Lucinda."

"An easy thing to say for a man who seems to heed no one's rules but his own! And I did not give you leave to use my Christian name, sir," she added, her spine stiff.

"It's difficult to seduce a woman and not call her by her given name."

"We have already established that I am not interested in your attentions, Captain."

"I think you're interested, all right," he shot back. "It's just that your precious breeding won't let you admit it."

How had she lost control of the conversation? "My answer will stay the same, my lord, no matter how ardent your pursuit."

A cocky smile curved his lips. "You only call me 'my lord' when you are trying to push me away. I've caught on to your game."

"You're the one who is playing games, Captain—games that do not interest me."

"Shall we put your resolve to the test?" He reached for her, and she jumped back, bumping into the sideboard. The decanter wobbled, then smashed to the floor, sounding like a pistol shot in the silence.

Lucinda stared at the broken decanter with horror. A servant would come to investigate at any moment. If she was caught alone in the drawing room with Garrett, everything would be ruined!

She fled, Garrett's mocking laughter chasing after her.

Chapter 7

"**M**y servants tell me," the duke said to Garrett the next morning, "that you have taken to drinking in the wee hours."

At the sideboard, Garrett placed another fat sausage on his plate. It was bad enough that his head was throbbing from the whiskey he had consumed last night. After stupidly drowning his grief over his mother afterward, did he also have to be scolded as if he were still a lad?

When Garrett didn't answer, Erasmus continued. "While I understand a man's need for spirits, I do trust you will be more discreet once we arrive in London. One generally goes to a gentlemen's club to indulge in such behavior."

Garrett placed a third sausage on his plate. "I'll remember that."

"The decanter can be easily replaced," Erasmus said, "but a reputation cannot. See that you heed my words."

Garrett turned toward the table and caught a flash of color outside the doorway of the breakfast room. If he wasn't mistaken, the lovely Lucinda was lurking outside the room in a crisp yellow gown, trying not to be seen. A smile quirked his lips.

"It seems that reputation is everything to the English," Garrett remarked, raising his voice slightly. "What about a man's character? Doesn't that count for anything?"

"Society is unforgiving of breaches in etiquette," the duke said. "Once an error in judgment is made, the stigma lasts forever." He paused, then said quietly, "I was trying to save your father from that stigma all those years ago."

Garrett jerked his attention away from Lucinda. "Is that what you call tossing a man from his home for marrying the wrong woman?"

"She was an Irishwoman," the duke replied evenly. "English society tends to regard the Irish as little more than peasant upstarts. I was trying to save William pain."

"Instead you lost him," Garrett retorted. "I bet you didn't expect that."

Erasmus sighed and sipped his tea. "No, I didn't. But I should have. William had more than his fair share of the Stanton pride." He met Garrett's gaze over the edge of the teacup. "As do you."

Garrett ignored the statement. "What will your precious society say about the fact that your grandchildren are half Irish? Won't that get Meg ejected from the palace or something?"

"I don't see any need to belabor the fact," the duke replied. "And I have settled enough of a fortune on her that she will be well sought-after."

"*I* can provide my sister's dowry—she doesn't need your money. Not that she's going to marry some damned Englishman, in any case."

The duke's lips curled in a small, humorless smile. "What you do not seem to understand, Garrett, is that it doesn't matter if she needs it or not. I choose to give it to her because I care for her."

"You care about your title and your family name," Garrett said. "What's your plan, to get Meg married and have her child be your heir?"

"Hardly," Erasmus drawled, "as that would not be possible given the law of primogeniture. The title can only pass through the male line."

Garrett leaned back in his chair. "Which leaves you with me or nothing."

"So it would seem."

"Too bad, huh?" Garrett stabbed his sausage and bit into it with relish.

The duke's hands clenched into fists, then

slowly uncurled. "You may not want anything to do with your family, Garrett, but at least your sister understands what I can give her."

Garrett shrugged. "She's young, and you're turning her head with all the fancy clothes and snobby titles. She doesn't know any better."

"You obviously do not know your sister very well."

"The hell you say," Garrett snarled, slamming down his silverware. "I practically raised her!"

"From aboard ship?" When Garrett only glared in response, the duke smiled and steepled his fingers. "I am here for her, Garrett. You are not."

"The hell I'm not. I'm right here in blasted England eating at your blasted table. If that's not love, I don't know what is."

"Good morning!" Meg sang as she entered the room, Lucinda following after her. Meg wore a white morning dress with blue stripes, and her hair was artfully arranged in tumbling curls. She bent to kiss Garrett on the cheek, then did the same to Erasmus.

"Good morning, my dear." The duke patted Meg's hand, his expression softening. "And good morning to you, Mrs. Devering."

"Good morning, Your Grace," Lucinda replied. She glanced at Garrett. "Captain."

"Good morning, Mrs. Devering." Garrett

grinned. "My, don't you ladies look lovely this morning."

Ignoring him, Lucinda turned to the steaming platters of food.

"We're going into the village," Meg chattered as she perused the delicacies spread along the sideboard. "I'm going to get some new dresses for Town."

"Don't you already have lots of new dresses?" Garrett asked with a frown.

"Oh, these are fine for the country, but I need much grander clothing for London. We are only going to get one or two things from the village seamstress, as I will be visiting Madame Toulon in London."

"Who's Madame Toulon?" Garrett asked.

Meg brought her loaded plate to the table and sat down at the duke's right. "She's the best modiste in London. She will make all my ball gowns."

Garrett only shook his head and applied himself to his breakfast.

Silence settled over the table. Lucinda picked at her eggs and tried not to look at Garrett. His behavior this morning confused her even more. She had overheard the duke's words about the decanter and had fully expected Garrett to implicate her in the crime. But instead he had taken the blame upon himself.

The man constantly surprised her. First there was his devoted love for his sister. Then his unexpected vulnerability last night when they spoke of his mother's death. Now he'd preserved her reputation by acting the gentleman.

Many men had handsome faces and ugly characters, and their advances she could easily repel. But a man who looked like him and showed glimpses of a gentler side . . . That made him dangerously attractive.

She clenched her fingers tightly around her fork. It didn't matter that she was attracted to him. She knew firsthand how chaos ensued when one was ruled by one's emotions, and she had no intention of doing *that* again.

When she wed again, she would select a man who was kind and amiable and able to support a wife, but love would not enter into it. Everything was much easier that way.

"Are you going to attend the dance lesson again, Garrett?" Meg asked excitedly, breaking Lucinda's train of thought. "Monsieur Collineau comes again in a few days."

Lucinda jerked her gaze to Garrett's as heated memories of their waltz together flooded her mind. He met her gaze, blue eyes hot, and smiled slowly. Lucinda's heart began to pound.

"I would love to, puss," he finally drawled, "provided it does not interfere with something equally important, such as an appointment with the tailor. I've been told that I will embarrass you if I arrive in London wearing my own clothes, so I hope you appreciate the sacrifice."

Meg made a face at her brother. "Garrett, you are such a ninny. He will look fine in English clothing, won't he, Lucinda?"

Lucinda licked her dry lips. "Of course he will, Meg."

Ignoring Garrett's knowing smile, she concentrated on her breakfast.

"I've also engaged a valet for you," the duke announced. "His name is Stobbins, and he will be coming with us to London. He arrives in a few days."

"Yet another sacrifice for you, dear sister." Garrett wiped his mouth with the napkin and rose from his chair. "If you will all excuse me, I have an appointment with a stallion."

"Tea is at four o'clock," the duke reminded him.

"Fine!" Garrett's voice was ripe with annoyance as he left the breakfast room.

Meg bit her lip as she watched her brother's retreat. "Oh, dear, he's in a temper now."

Lucinda snorted. "I have never seen your brother when he is *not* in a temper!"

"Oh, he's just not happy to be here," Meg replied, dimples flashing. "Garrett likes to have his own way in everything."

"So I surmised," Lucinda said dryly.

"I do want him to have a good time while he is here," Meg continued, a wrinkle of worry forming between her brows. "I certainly hope he behaves himself for the tailor."

"He will or answer to me," the duke declared.

"Oh, Grandpapa," Meg giggled. "No one can make Garrett do anything he does not want to do. He reminds me a great deal of you."

The duke grunted, but then smiled at Meg. "Let's hope you are right, my dear."

"Come, Meg," Lucinda said, rising. "The seamstress awaits."

Garrett rode off most of his headache on Mercury, the swiftest stallion in the duke's stable. He rode for hours, taken in by the beauty of the Raynewood lands despite himself.

Someday this might all be his . . .

No. He jerked his thoughts from that dangerous path. He would not be caught in such a trap. So his grandfather was older and frailer than he had expected. That was no reason to forget all that had happened and forgive the wily old bastard for the unforgivable.

He reined Mercury to a stop atop a hill and slid from the horse's back to look out over the endless green hills of Raynewood. No amount of money, no fertile lands, no blasted title would ever balance the scales of his parents' deaths.

He had lost his father while still a child, and

when he had signed on as a cabin boy at the age of eleven, his shipmates had taken over the task of turning a boy into a man. And when he had come home from his voyages, his mother had smoothed out the rough manners he had learned aboard ship.

"Eating with your fingers is not permitted at my table, little man!" she would say in her Irish lilt, swatting his fingers with a wooden spoon for good measure.

"And since when is a son of mine too good to go to the Lord's house on a Sunday morning?" she would demand when he dawdled about going to church.

And the thing he heard the most often, the words he had taken to heart: "You're the man of the house now, Garrett, and you must always take care of your sister."

Good Lord, he could hear her voice as clearly as if she stood beside him. Of course, that was impossible. He would never again hear her scold him, the thickness of her accent indicating exactly how angry she was with him. She hadn't been a tall woman, but what a huge heart she had packed into that tiny body. She had loved with the fierceness of a warrior, and he couldn't believe that she was gone.

He swiped at a tear that trickled down his cheek as grief welled up, the fresh wound threatening to choke him.

The horse shifted, seeming to sense his emotional turmoil, and Garrett patted the stallion's neck to soothe him, trying to distract himself. Trying to control the flood of pain that threatened to overwhelm him. He willed back the feelings, but still they surged forth, unrelenting. A hoarse sob escaped his lips.

The floodgates opened, and, shuddering, he gave in to the inevitable and sobbed like a babe, openly mourning the loss of his mother for the very first time.

She was gone, and his life would never be the same again.

Lucinda settled herself on the stone bench amid the rosebushes with a sigh of relief, stealing a few quiet moments to watch the sunset. Going to the dressmaker was always hectic, and never more so than when a young girl was involved. The dressmaker already had Meg's measurements, so most of the afternoon had been spent looking over styles and selecting materials.

In accordance with their agreement, the duke had also arranged for Lucinda to have some new gowns. Much fewer than Meg, but it was enough. She would wear the dresses proudly to London, and perhaps she would attract a suitor or two.

Unfortunately, she would probably attract Malcolm as well.

The thought of her brother-in-law threatened to steal her enjoyment of the beautiful sunset, and she fought not to let that happen. But the memories came anyway.

Malcolm was a handsome man, and as a young girl, Lucinda had been taken in by his blond good looks and impressive pedigree. Innocent of how predatory men could be, she had been lured by him into the conservatory one evening, where he had attempted to seduce her. He would no doubt have taken her innocence as well, had her father not come upon them. To avoid scandal, marriage had been proposed. However, it had not been Malcolm that Lucinda married.

And she thanked God for that every day.

Ah, how young she had been, and how naïve. In the early days of her marriage to Harry, Malcolm's brother, she had fancied that she and Malcolm were tormented, star-crossed lovers. Malcolm seemed to feed her fantasies with the smoldering looks he would send her way whenever no one was looking. At first she had thought his love was as unrequited as hers, and that his father's high standards were to blame for their unfortunate circumstances. But she soon learned the truth.

Dutifully, she had tried to make her marriage work, but after the first few months it became painfully clear that she and her new husband were not well suited. By mutual agreement, they decided to live their own lives. While Harry went off with his mistresses, Lucinda quietly tended the gardens at their country home in Surrey and filled her time with local social events, haunted by the knowledge that she did not possess whatever quality it was that made men desire women. Then Malcolm started to come to visit her whenever Harry was away, and for a brief time she had believed that he still loved her.

Silly, naïve girl. Malcolm soon made it clear that he only wanted to bed her, and not even because he particularly desired her. It was only because he had been thwarted in his seduction that fateful night that he wanted to complete what he had started.

He had never loved her. He had never intended to wed her.

Disillusioned, Lucinda had refused him, and continued to refuse him all through her lonely marriage to Harry. And then Harry had died . . . Dear Lord, she could see the scene as if it were yesterday.

She'd been sitting in her parlor, dressed in her widow's weeds, reeling from the knowledge that Harry had run up extensive gaming debts. One lord had even dared approach her at her husband's funeral to slyly suggest an alternate method of payment, should she not have the funds Harry owed him.

Numb with shock, humiliated by the gossip associated with her husband's death, she hadn't even begun to contemplate how she would pay off the notes. And there were so many of them! Dozens of gaming debts for staggering amounts. Bills from the tailor and the jeweler. And the rent was overdue on his mistress's townhouse.

Then Malcolm had arrived, looking exceedingly handsome in mourning black.

"Dear sister-in-law," he had crooned, seating himself without invitation on the settee, "I have recently received the sad news that my brother was quite under the hatches when he died. Allow me to help you in this time of need."

She had stared at him warily, even though, traditionally, an honorable man would step in and pay his brother's debts. "He gambled away my widow's pension," she said dully. "I have nothing but this house and my mother's pearls."

"Scandalous," Malcolm agreed, shaking his head solemnly. "I sympathize with your predicament. And I will pay all of it—every last coin," he said, leaning close to place a hand on her knee. "All you need to do is become my mistress."

"What! Are you mad?" She leaped to her feet, dislodging his hand. "Your brother is barely in the ground, and here you are trying to seduce his widow!"

"Not true," Malcolm said, standing as well. "I have been trying to seduce you for years." He caressed her shoulder, smirking when she jerked away. "It's a simple business arrangement. You become my mistress, and I will see all Harry's debts paid. If not, well then . . ." He shrugged. "You will have to find some other means to pay the notes."

"I *will* pay them," she vowed.

"How? His obvious amusement only fired her anger. "Will you take a position somewhere and eke out a few pounds a month? At that rate, you will end up in the Fleet before the year is out."

"A man of honor would pay his brother's debts," she said pointedly.

"You are much too preoccupied with honor, my dear. This is the real world, and this is how things are done in the real world."

"My honor is all I have left! And I will keep it no matter what happens."

"Dear Lucinda," Malcolm said, mirth heavy in his voice, "by accepting my proposition, Harry's debts will be taken care of and you will live in the lap of luxury until our association ends."

"I will live in complete dishonor," she corrected. "No, thank you, Malcolm. I'll find some other way to meet my obligations."

"Oh, really?" He folded his arms across his chest and looked at her as if she were an entertaining child. "I will ask again: what do you intend to do?"

"I could marry again," she said proudly.

"Really? And who would have you?"

She fisted her hand at her sides. "I still have my reputation, my family name."

"I can see this is going to be quite amusing," he said with a chuckle. "Very well, Lucinda. Try it your way. But when you fail, remember that my offer still stands."

"Get out of my house!" She pointed at the door.

"I'll be back," he said. "And I guarantee, you will be happy to see me."

He had gone, leaving Lucinda alone with her resolve to survive.

Hard to believe that was only a year ago, she mused now, watching the sky take on a pink glow. Since then, Malcolm had done his best to sabotage her efforts and force her into a corner where she would have no choice but to become his mistress. He had started rumors that she was barren in order to discourage potential suitors. The only thing he hadn't advertised was her financial circumstances, probably because the situation reflected badly on *him*. But she had managed to thwart him time and again, first by selling her house to pay some of the debts, then by accepting the duke's offer.

She still had no idea how the duke had known of her circumstances, but she did not question her luck. She merely accepted the offer and thanked God that staying at Raynewood got her out of Malcolm's reach for a short time.

And God willing, a marriage would get her out of his reach forever.

The sound of the garden gate broke her train of thought, and Garrett slipped quietly into the garden. There was a slump to his shoulders that she had never seen before, a weariness to his step that tugged at her heart.

He looked as if he didn't have a friend in the world.

Where was the charming scoundrel she had come to expect over the past couple of days? What trouble had befallen him that he looked like the loneliest man in the world?

Good breeding dictated that she remain quietly hidden in the rosebushes, since he clearly had no desire to be seen. She should just let him pass and leave him to his privacy.

But as he came closer, she saw the look on his face—bleak and lost. Her heart went out to him, and she stepped into his path before she could stop herself.

"Good evening, Captain."

His head jerked up, and for a moment she could have sworn that his eyes looked red, as if he had been crying.

Ridiculous. It must be a trick of the fading light.

"What are you doing here?" he asked, an edge

to his voice. "I thought you and Meg had gone to the dressmaker's."

"That was hours ago." She came closer to him. "Captain, are you feeling quite the thing?"

He stiffened. "I'm fine."

"I don't think you are." She laid a hand on his arm. "Is there some way I can help?"

He looked down at her hand, then raised his gaze to hers and gave her a mocking smile. "I do believe that's the first time you've ever touched me voluntarily."

She snatched her hand back. "There's no need to be nasty. I will be more than happy to leave you to your misery!"

She spun away, the peace of the garden shattered, but he caught her by the crook of her elbow.

"Wait," he said quietly. "I'm sorry, Lucinda. I'm not fit to be around people at the moment."

His sincerity soothed her ruffled feathers, and she couldn't walk away from the sorrow in his blue eyes. She relaxed, not protesting when he left his hand on her arm. "I'm just trying to help."

"I know. I'm just . . . having trouble dealing with things at the moment. But I appreciate the gesture."

He sounded so desolate, and now she could see that it wasn't the light—the redness of his eyes clearly indicated he had been crying.

"Sometimes emotions are more crippling than physical wounds," she said quietly.

He stared at her for so long that she began to regret her words. But then he gave her a crooked smile. "I'd much prefer a bayonet to the belly."

"I'm sure you would."

"I'm no good with feelings," he said. "Unless it's lust."

She laughed, and he grinned along with her. The moment caught the both of them. Her laughter faded. His smile slipped away.

He held her gaze as he leaned forward, giving her every chance to back away. But she didn't. Something rose between them, some sort of kindred connection, and she stood captured by its spell as his lips sought hers.

Their lips met softly and clung, and he gently caressed her face. The sweetness of it destroyed her defenses as hot passion never could. Aching to be closer to him, she lifted her hand to cover his against her cheek.

He pulled back and looked into her eyes for a long moment. Then he took her hand in his and brought it to his lips in a simple, affectionate gesture. "Thank you," he whispered, squeezing her hand. "I'll be all right in a little while."

"If you need to talk—" she began, wanting him to linger.

"I'm fine."

Then he was gone, striding rapidly up to the house and leaving her alone in the garden with the sunset and the memory of his tender kiss.

Chapter 8

That evening Garrett spent a lot of time watching Lucinda, first at dinner and then as everyone relaxed in the drawing room after the meal.

He had regained control of his emotions, though he was still unsettled by that moment he had shared with her in the garden. Why had he been talking to her about his *feelings*? What kind of a man did she think he was, to have practically cried on her shoulder in such a manner?

He caught her looking at him now and then with concern in her gaze, and it made him damned uncomfortable. Did she now think that he was one of these frail and fainting Englishmen? He would have to get things back the way *he* wanted them; that is, pursuing his goal to get Lucinda naked in his bed.

And she played right into his hands by sending Meg up to bed with Lady Agatha after the duke had retired. She deliberately lingered in the drawing room after the others had left, though for propriety's sake, she left the door open.

"Are you all right?" she asked quietly, coming to stand beside his chair. "I've been worried about you."

"I appreciate your concern," he said, though he winced inwardly at the compassion in her voice. Damn, she did think him some sort of blubbering fool, didn't she?

"I imagine the events of the past few days have been somewhat taxing for a man who's used to being in charge all the time," she continued.

"Quite so." He rose to his feet, unable to sit placidly. He was no babe in swaddling to be so coddled! "Come to think of it, I have been feeling somewhat . . . lonely."

She backed up a step, wariness slipping across her features. "May I remind you that you are surrounded by family, Captain?"

"That's not the kind of loneliness I've been feeling." He gave her a charming smile, advancing on her even as she retreated. "A man such as myself misses the comfort to be found in a woman's arms more than anything else." She bumped up against the sofa, and he took another step, bringing their bodies within inches of each other.

"Captain, we have discussed this," she said primly, but he saw the way she swallowed hard. The very proper Mrs. Devering was more rattled than she was willing to admit. "And the door is open," she added.

"Shall I close it?"

"Certainly not!"

"Then let's get back to the subject at hand. You said you were worried about me," he said, caressing the rim of her ear.

"Only that the pressures of your situation may have become overwhelming." She met his gaze squarely, clearly ignoring his flirting. "You don't want to be here, you dislike your grandfather, and you have just lost your mother. I imagine anyone would feel overburdened in such circumstances."

"So you think you know all about me, Lucinda?" He took one last step, trapping her fully between his body and the sofa. Her scent teased his senses, soothing his raw emotions. This was what he needed: the softness of a woman to ease his aching heart.

"This won't stop the pain, you know," she said quietly as he bent down to nuzzle her neck.

He stopped and leaned back to look at her, brows raised. "So wise, Lucinda?"

"I've lost more than you know," she said. "Physical pleasure won't ease what bothers you."

"Have you tried it?" He gave her a rakish grin.

She sighed in exasperation. "I have already told you that I do not indulge in casual affairs, Captain."

"And is this where I am supposed to ask you to marry me?"

She raised her chin. "No, Garrett. Even if you were to ask me to marry you, I would not do so."

"Is that so?" He brushed his chest across her breasts, smiling as she gave a little shiver. At last he was starting to feel in control again.

"Why should I marry a man who hates my country, hates my way of life, and is gone most of the year?" Lucinda demanded. "If I want to be alone, Garrett, I might as well stay a widow."

"I don't hate your country," he corrected, leaning forward again to place soft kisses along her throat. "In fact, I am becoming quite fond of England."

"You could have fooled me." She pushed at his chest, but didn't succeed in moving him an inch.

He laughed outright at the annoyance on her face. "Why are you fighting this?" he asked, teasingly flicking one fingertip over her nipple. Her flesh responded, hardening visibly beneath her dress. "You can see how good we can be together. This kind of attraction is rare and should be treasured."

"As you no doubt have more experience than I do, Captain, I shall have to trust your word on that." She pushed against his chest once more. "Do let me go before the servants see us!"

"Come to my bed tonight," he murmured, nuzzling his face into her hair. Emotion welled up, desire tangled with a dozen others he could not name. Somehow he knew that making love to Lucinda would ease the darkness shrouding his soul.

"I can't," she whispered, her voice uneven. "Even if I wanted to, I can't."

He pulled back, cupping her face in his hands and staring into her eyes. "But *do* you want to? Tell me the truth, Lucinda."

She tried to turn her head away, but he held her gaze steadily. Her eyes were amazing, revealing everything she was thinking and feeling, even as her facial expression remained neutral. He could see the confusion, see the indecision. And he could see the desire.

"Tell me, Lucinda," he commanded.

"Yes." The word escaped her lips as a strangled sob. "Yes, I am tempted. But I can't. Don't you understand? *I can't.* Is that what you wanted to hear?"

He hungered for her nearly to obsession, and he had been determined to reestablish control of their relationship. But now he had forced this admission from her, and the suffering in her voice robbed him of any pleasure he might have taken in it.

"Actually, I wanted to hear that you would come to my bed tonight." He tried to grin, tried to inject humor into the situation, but the distress in her eyes did not fade.

"I can't."

His grin vanished. "I know."

She pushed at his chest again, and this time he stepped back. She darted away from the sofa and turned to face him. "Garrett, my . . . promise . . . to your grandfather is important to me. I need to concentrate on getting Meg ready to face London, and frankly, having to avoid your attentions is distracting me from that goal. Do you want your sister to make a fool of herself? To be ostracized as the uncivilized American?"

"Of course not."

"Then leave me be," she beseeched him. "If not for my sake, then for Meg's. She needs me right now."

Her words made him feel like a cad. "When do we leave for London?" he asked.

"In five days' time."

"All right, then. You have my word that I shall not pursue you."

Her shoulders sagged with relief. "Thank you for being reasonable, Captain."

". . . until we get to London."

"What!"

"At that time," he continued, "all bets are off. I still intend to make love to you before I leave England, Lucinda. You'd best get used to the idea."

"You'd best get used to a lonely bed." Turning on her heel, she sailed from the room.

Garrett grinned as a weight seemed to lift from his shoulders. Things were getting back to normal.

Four days later, as she climbed into the coach to return from the village, Lucinda pondered the amazing fact that Garrett had kept his word.

Monsieur Collineau had returned only that morning for Meg's last dance lesson, and the girl seemed to have picked up the rudiments of the waltz at last. Garrett had made an appearance at the lesson, partnered Meg while she mastered the steps, and then left again, all without one improper remark.

Astonishing.

Lucinda had gone on to spend the afternoon in the village with Meg, getting last-minute adjustments done at the dressmaker's and shopping for shoes and hats and other accessories. Garrett's only response to their plans had been "Enjoy yourselves," before he had gone riding.

No innuendoes, no disparaging comments about the English, nothing.

His new behavior had been noticed by Lady Agatha and the duke, as well. Lady Agatha didn't seem surprised, but the duke credited the change to Lucinda's influence.

He was right, Lucinda thought wryly, but not in quite the way he thought.

Garrett had spent most of his free time these past few days either riding or at the tailor's, and he even managed to keep his disagreements with the duke to a minimum. If only it could last, Lucinda thought as she listened to Meg's idle chatter on the way back to Raynewood. But the household left for London on the morrow, and like Cinderella's pumpkin, the spell would be broken. Once they were in London, Garrett would once more be in pursuit of her, and it was getting harder and harder to resist him.

He still sent sizzling looks toward her whenever no one was watching. Sometimes he would find little ways to touch her, grazing her hand or taking her arm to escort her in to dinner, nothing more forward than any English gentleman would dare. Yet it was that one remembered glimpse of his vulnerability that fascinated her.

So while she smiled and nodded at Meg's conversation as the coach rolled up the drive, her mind lingered on Garrett, and the kiss in the garden that haunted her still.

* * *

Having returned from a long, sweaty ride, Garrett tried to make his way up to his room, but it was slow going. He encountered so many servants darting about, packing for the move to London, that it was like trying to navigate the main streets of Boston just to get down the hall!

One more day, he thought. One more day and he would be able to actively pursue Lucinda again. The subtle flirting they had been doing had only fueled his desire for her.

He finally made it to his bedroom and pushed open the door, only to see a young man rummaging in his sea chest.

"What do you think you're doing?" Garrett demanded.

Startled by Garrett's shout, the young man straightened abruptly, but Garrett was already moving. He grabbed the fellow by the shoulder and slammed him up against the wall in one swift movement. A threatening hand around the young man's throat brought fear to the lad's eyes.

"What the devil were you doing in my sea chest?" Garrett demanded again.

"I . . . I . . ." the fellow stuttered. He was pale now, his brown eyes wide with alarm. He couldn't have been more than five and twenty, though his sparse light brown hair and round, moonlike face made him look older. Garrett towered about a foot over his head, and the fellow's sturdy body seemed more the result of good English cooking than physical activity.

"I didn't catch that," he said, tightening his fingers around the fellow's throat a fraction.

"St-St-Stobbins," the intruder finally gasped. "I-I'm Stobbins, m-my lord."

Oh, Lord, the valet. Garrett jerked his hand away from the servant's throat. "Sorry about that, Stobbins," he apologized, taking a step back. "I thought you were a thief." Now that he was thinking clearly, Garrett noticed that Stobbins wore decently cut, clean clothing, which should have given him pause before attacking the fellow.

Stobbins felt his throat and cast Garrett a wary glance. "Of course you did, my lord."

"First rule," Garrett said, "is to stop with the 'my lord' stuff. I don't like it. If you cannot address me by my given name, then you may call me Captain Lynch."

"I would never presume to address Your Lordship by your given name!" Stobbins gasped in shock.

"Then let's settle on 'captain,' shall we?" Garrett said, slapping the fellow on the back. "So tell me, Stobbins, what does a valet do?"

"Sir?" The manservant's eyes bugged out, as if he could not comprehend that anyone should *not* know what a valet did.

"Calm yourself, Stobbins. I'm an American. Surely they told you that?"

The valet seemed to relax. "Of course, my . . . er, Captain. I should have realized. A valet takes care of a gentleman's clothing, helps a gentleman dress, and assists in a gentleman's toilette."

"So basically you take care of my clothes and help me get dressed every day?"

"Indeed, sir." Stobbins bobbed his head. "My father is also a gentleman's gentleman, to Lord Knightsbridge. And my grandfather served the duke for many years before his death."

Garrett bit back a smile. "I'm certain I don't deserve you, Stobbins, but I shall count myself lucky to have a man of your experience to help me while we are in London."

Stobbins beamed. "Indeed, sir."

"So tell me, what were you doing in my sea chest?"

"Starting to pack your clothing from the wardrobe, Captain, to go to London. By the way, your new garments have arrived from the tailor."

"Good. I'll try them on as soon as I change my clothes. I smell like a horse."

"As you wish, Captain."

Stobbins reached out to remove Garrett's coat, and Garrett jerked away from him. "What the devil are you doing?"

Stobbins swallowed hard. "I was assisting you in removing your coat, sir."

Garrett sighed and rubbed his eyes with one hand. "There is no need to undress me as if I were a babe, Stobbins. I am quite competent in that area."

Stobbins wrung his hands. "Then what shall I do, sir?"

Garrett thought for a moment. "You can take away the dirty clothing." Stobbins reached out again, and Garrett stepped away, clarifying, "*After* I have taken it off myself!"

"Of course, sir." The valet all but pouted.

What was with the people in this crazy country? They all seemed to live for waiting on others hand and foot! Exasperated, Garrett stripped off his coat and handed it to Stobbins. "Here you are. This should cheer you up."

The valet's face brightened as he took the garment. "Thank you, sir!"

Garrett tugged at his neck cloth. "You know, I could probably use a bath. Does arranging that fall under the duties of a valet?"

"Quite so, Captain. I shall order one up immediately." With a skip in his step, Stobbins hurried away.

Garrett began shedding his clothing in haste, lest the man return to try and strip him again.

The only one he wanted to do that was Lucinda.

The thought cheered him, and he began to whistle as he prepared for his bath.

*　*　*

"I am so tired!" Meg declared as they entered Raynewood's foyer. "I can't believe we bought so much!"

"Only the barest necessities," Lucinda replied airily, the girl's enthusiasm infecting her as well.

An army of footmen trooped into the house behind them, bearing boxes of all descriptions. And some of those boxes were for *her*, Lucinda thought with a thrill. At last she had some clothing suitable for attending London functions.

Of course, Malcolm would also be there, as he was still the darling of the *ton*, but she refused to let him spoil her excitement. Her plan *had* to work. She *would* find another husband, and once the duke discharged Harry's debts, she would no longer be threatened by destitution.

She only had to find some way to keep Garrett at bay.

As the stream of footmen showed no sign of letting up, she said to Meg, "Let's go into the Green Salon and have Cook send us something delicious to have with our tea."

"I could certainly use it," Meg agreed.

"Stephens," Lucinda said, drawing the butler's attention. "Meg and I would like some tea in the Green Salon, please. Would you see to it?"

"Very well, Mrs. Devering," Stephens replied.

"I love the way you do that," Meg said as they

shed their bonnets and gloves and went down the hall. "You always sound so gracious, even when you are giving orders to the servants."

"A lady never raises her voice," Lucinda replied, sitting down on a sage-green settee. Her aching feet rejoiced.

"I do," Meg said with a sigh. "I yell at Garrett all the time."

Lucinda smiled. "Well, your brother has a very hard head and probably needs to be yelled at. Being a sea captain, he seems unable to resist issuing orders."

"I wish he wasn't gone so often," Meg said wistfully. "He certainly doesn't need to travel so much anymore."

"He's the captain of a ship, Meg. That usually involves going to sea," Lucinda reminded gently. "I know you miss him when he's gone."

"But he owns the whole shipping business, all six ships. Why can't he stay in Boston and run the company from there?" Meg complained.

"Your brother owns the whole shipping company?" Lucinda repeated, startled. "I thought he just captained one ship."

"Oh, no!" Meg laughed. "He did that when I was little, but now he's built a whole company."

"I had no idea." So Garrett Lynch was an aggressive businessman. Not exactly the most fitting occupation for the duke's heir, but she knew from personal experience that desperate circumstances made a body do things he or she would never do otherwise.

A sound outside the door drew her attention. "Oh, good. The tea is here."

The door opened, but instead of a servant with a covered tray, there stood Garrett.

Lucinda gaped.

After a moment of shocked silence, Meg squealed, "Garrett, you look wonderful!"

Lucinda was amazed. He wore an impeccably fitted coat of hunter-green superfine that emphasized his broad shoulders and large frame. His dark hair was pulled back neatly in a queue. His waistcoat had a subtle pattern of gold and green stripes, and a snowy cravat precisely tied in a Mathematical completed the picture. The sight of his muscular thighs clearly outlined by the clinging material of his buff-colored pantaloons made the breath hitch in her throat. His black Hessians gleamed, emphasizing his long legs.

He looked every inch the fashionable English gentleman.

"Well?" he said. "What do you think? Everyone keeps telling me I need a decent set of clothes to wear to London."

"You look perfect!" Meg exclaimed. "Doesn't he, Lucinda?"

Lucinda forced herself to speak. "My word, Captain, you look quite dashing."

"Stobbins had a time of it getting me into this rig." He met Lucinda's gaze in challenge. "Would you say I would embarrass my sister now, Mrs. Devering?"

Lucinda slowly shook her head. "No, indeed, Captain. Any lady would be proud to claim you."

"Is that so?"

He flashed that pirate's grin, and Lucinda raised her chin. "Quite so, Captain," she said firmly. The last thing the man needed was to know how attractive she found him dressed in English clothing.

"Absolutely! You can go everywhere with us," Meg exclaimed.

"I'm happy to hear it."

A clatter sounded behind him, and Garrett stepped aside as Stephens arrived with the tea tray.

"I'd better get back upstairs before Stobbins swoons," he said. "He doesn't trust me out of his sight for five minutes. I don't know what he thinks I'm going to do to these clothes." He flashed Meg a grin. "Save me some of those tarts, puss. I'll be back down directly."

Meg giggled and settled down on the sofa as Garrett left the room. Stephens began to set out the platter of berry tarts he had brought up from the kitchen, but Lucinda barely noticed. Her gaze lingered on the doorway where Garrett had disappeared.

That had been the Duke of Raynewood's heir.

Chapter 9

London.

Lucinda took a deep breath as the carriage drew closer to Lady Renfrew's ball. This was the true test. Meg was to be put on display for London society, and hopefully Lucinda's tutelage had been sufficient.

"What the devil is taking so long?" Garrett demanded from the seat across from her. He looked absolutely devastating in stark black evening clothes, but his impatience practically shimmered around him.

"There's a parade of carriages ahead of us, my boy," Lady Agatha said. "Lady Renfrew's ball is always the veriest crush, as it is the first fashionable event of the season."

"Seems like a waste of time to me."

"Oh, Garrett," Meg said with a sigh. "Can't you please behave?"

Garrett scowled and looked out the window, but he remained silent.

As if it wasn't enough that Lucinda's future rested on Meg's success tonight, now she had to worry about Garrett. Hopefully he would not mortally offend someone tonight with his blunt American ways!

And though he had yet to mention it, she was very much aware that their bargain had ended when the carriage had arrived at Stanton House earlier that afternoon.

"Knightsbridge is bound to be there," Lady Agatha announced. "The dear boy knows how close Aurelia and I are, so he makes a point to attend her ball every year."

"Knightsbridge?" Garrett inquired.

"My grandson, the Earl of Knightsbridge. Your second cousin, I believe," Lady Agatha explained. "He's only a year or two older than yourself."

"Fine boy," the duke interjected. "Good man to show you about Town, acquaint you with the clubs and whatnot."

"I look forward to meeting him," Garrett said to Lady Agatha, ignoring the duke's comment.

"We're here," Lucinda said, as the coach halted in front of the Renfrews' townhouse.

"Here we go," Meg breathed, as a footman opened the door. "My first ball!"

Garrett reached out and touched Meg's hand. "You'll do fine, puss."

Meg gave him a radiant smile and stepped from the coach. Garrett looked at Lucinda, and her heart lurched. His eyes still held some of the softness he usually reserved for Meg, and for that one instant, she felt as if she could see all the way to his soul.

She broke the contact, uncomfortable with the feelings his nearness brought out in her. She could not afford to play Garrett's flirtatious games, and she needed to keep her head clear and her wits sharp.

Lucinda smiled and nodded as they moved along the receiving line to greet their host and hostess. That done, she gathered every ounce of control she possessed as they entered the ballroom. This was it. She needed to concentrate on Meg now, not the brooding American who loomed behind her.

"Oh, my," Meg whispered reverently, looking around at the elaborate decorations. Lady Renfrew had elected to follow a Grecian theme for the evening.

"It's all very grand," Lucinda agreed.

"Well, it looks to me as if everyone in society has come out for this bit of foolishness," the duke said. "I see old Pemberly over there. If you ladies will excuse me, I will go speak with him."

"Of course, Your Grace," Lucinda replied.

The duke smiled at Meg and touched her hand. "Have no fear, my dear. You look lovely, and you will take society by storm. Just listen to what Mrs. Devering tells you."

"Yes, Grandpapa," Meg answered.

The duke looked at Garrett. "And you, young man. I trust you will take advantage of Mrs. Devering's advice as well."

"I have no intention of embarrassing my sister tonight, if that is what worries you."

"See that you don't," the duke warned. Then he took himself off to visit with his crony.

"You rascal," Lady Agatha said, thwapping Garrett on the arm with her folded fan. "Don't tease your grandfather like that. It bedevils him so."

"I rather think that was the point," Lucinda retorted.

"Are you insinuating that I would deliberately upset my grandfather, Mrs. Devering?" Garrett's face was the picture of innocence. "That would hardly be the act of a gentleman."

Lucinda cast him a cynical look. "Just so, Captain."

"Appearances, please," Lady Agatha chided.

"I'll behave if Mrs. Devering will," Garrett said with a roguish grin.

Lucinda gave him her coolest stare. "At least I know how to act in polite company, Captain. Kindly make an attempt not to completely ruin the experience for your sister."

Without realizing it, the two of them had stepped toward each other until they were practically nose to nose, a fact that was brought home to her when Meg pushed between them.

"Will you two *please* stop? It's like listening to two children squabble."

"Exactly so," Lady Agatha agreed. "Mind your manners now, as Knightsbridge is on his way over."

Algernon Strathwaite, the Earl of Knightsbridge, was a tall, slender man with light brown hair and green eyes. He, too, had the bold Stanton nose and slashing dark brows that seemed at odds with the air of geniality that surrounded him. His full lips parted in a sincere smile as he bent over Lady Agatha's hand.

"Good evening, Grandmother! I see Great-uncle Erasmus hasn't driven the smile from your eyes."

"What nonsense!" Lady Agatha replied. "Meg, dear, this is my grandson, Algernon Strathwaite, the Earl of Knightsbridge. Algie, this is your second cousin, Miss Stanton-Lynch."

Knightsbridge turned a charming smile on Meg and lifted her hand to his lips. "Enchanted, cousin. I see I shall have to be diligent in my duties to such a lovely relation, and beat away the rascally suitors who would seek to win your heart."

Meg giggled, and Lady Agatha thwapped Knightsbridge on the arm with her fan. "Cease your prattle, foolish boy, and say hello to Mrs. Devering before she believes you a complete clod."

"Ah, yes, Mrs. Devering," Knightsbridge said with a bow. He lifted her hand to his lips. "Always a pleasure."

"And this is Lady Margaret's brother, Lord Kelton. Erasmus and I were hoping you would introduce the boy around, as he is newly from America."

"Kelton, pleasure to meet you," Knightsbridge said, shaking Garrett's hand firmly.

"Garrett, please," Garrett corrected.

"Nonsense!" Knightsbridge said cheerfully. "In London, one is called by one's title. Therefore, you are Kelton and I am Knightsbridge. Do you play cards?"

Garrett bared his teeth in a scarcely tolerant smile. "Some."

"Excellent! What say we visit the card rooms after we've done our duty by the ladies?"

This time Garrett's smile was genuine. "Sounds good to me."

"Good, good. Now, cousin," Knightsbridge

said, crooking his arm at Meg, "may I have this dance?"

Meg smiled and nodded, then went off on his arm. Lady Agatha gave a sigh of pleasure. "Meg is safely in the hands of Knightsbridge, so now the two of you can dance, as well."

Lucinda started. "Ah . . . that's not necessary, my lady."

"Nonsense! Kelton, my boy, surely you have no objection to leading Mrs. Devering out in the country dance, do you?"

Garrett's blue eyes gleamed. "None at all."

"I shall remain here and wait for Meg," Lucinda insisted, her pulse skipping wildly. "There is no need for His Lordship to worry about me."

"But I insist," Garrett said, taking Lucinda's reluctant hand and placing it on his arm. "After all, you're supposed to be teaching me whatever I need to know while I'm here in London. How can you judge if my dancing needs improvement if you don't dance with me?"

"Just so," Lady Agatha agreed. "Off with you now, Mrs. Devering. I shall go pay my respects to Lady Bowen across the room and see if I can obtain an invitation to her daughter's come-out ball this week."

Trapped, Lucinda had no choice.

Thank heavens it was not a waltz, she thought as they took their places. In a country dance they would not even touch, except for their hands. She could get through this.

The music started, and she moved and turned by rote, her childhood dancing lessons coming back to her in an instant, even though she hadn't performed the steps in quite a while. She finally relaxed.

The she made the mistake of looking into Garrett's eyes. He watched her as if he wanted to devour her, as if at any moment he would take hold of her and carry her off to someplace private. Thrilled that such a look was directed at her, she nonetheless schooled her features into a frown of disapproval.

He kept looking at her anyway.

Her next mistake was not realizing how just the pressure of his hand around hers would affect her as he led her through the movements of the dance. Somehow that fleeting contact was more arousing, more tempting, than if he had swept her into his arms and carried her away.

Perhaps it was the lure of the forbidden. As the grandson of a duke and a marquess to boot, Garrett was far above her touch. But still, she wished she dared give in to her feelings.

The dance came to an end, and as the music faded away, Garrett bowed before her and lifted her hand to his lips. "All bets are off," he murmured. When Lucinda snatched her hand back, he grinned.

Lucinda turned and left the dance floor, but she could feel Garrett right at her heels. Knightsbridge approached with Meg on his arm. The young girl's cheeks were flushed pink from dancing.

"Mrs. Devering," Knightsbridge declared, "I daresay my young cousin will momentarily be besieged with suitors, as she dances like an angel and has a face to match."

As if he had been heard, several young men began to make their way through the crowd, their eyes on Meg. Lucinda gave a small smile of satisfaction. Meg was well on her way to becoming a grand success.

Between the two of them, Knightsbridge and Lucinda managed introductions between Meg and her many suitors, and Garrett helped keep the young men in line simply by looking the dark and forbidding brother. Meg accepted a dance with the son of a marquess, and Lucinda smiled indulgently as she watched the young girl happily take her place for the next set.

"Botheration," Knightsbridge said, gazing across the room. "Grandmother has nodded off again. I'll see about waking her, and then you and I shall go off to the card room, eh, Kelton?"

"I'll wait here for you," Garrett replied. "I'd like a word with Mrs. Devering."

"Excellent." With a genial grin, Knightsbridge set off toward his dozing grandmother.

"There is no need for you to remain with me, my lord," Lucinda said, not looking at Garrett. "I am quite capable of taking care of myself."

"Perhaps I wished to dance with you again."

"That is simply not done. Have a care not to dance more than once with *any* lady, Captain, lest you find yourself engaged by morning."

"You must be joking."

She turned to face him. "I am not. If you dance once with a lady, it is noted. If you dance twice with the same lady, there is speculation. If you dance three times with the same lady, her papa will expect your addresses within the week."

He bowed. "Thank you for educating me, Mrs. Devering. Knowing that, I will take care to remain in the card room with Knightsbridge until you are ready to leave."

"Oh, you are impossible!" she said, turning her back on him.

He leaned close until his breath brushed her ear. "I'm going now, Lucinda, but just remember . . . we're in London now."

"I'm aware of where we are," she hissed. "Probably more so than you!"

He chuckled. "Tonight we go home to the same house. And I know exactly where your bedroom is."

"Please leave," she gritted out.

"As you wish," he said, his tone ripe with amusement. He turned to go, only to have a young lady barrel right into him, bumping him back into Lucinda.

"I'm so sorry!" the girl cried. She squinted up at him. "Please forgive me, sir. I did not see you standing there."

"Charlotte, is that you?" Lucinda asked.

The girl now squinted at Lucinda. "Oh, good evening, Mrs. Devering. So nice to see you in Town."

"Wherever are you going in such a hurry?" Subtly, Lucinda tapped Garrett's forearm, and he dropped his hands from where he still steadied the girl by her elbows.

"Mother bade me fetch her some punch," Charlotte answered, casting her gaze shyly away from Garrett. She was attractive in an ordinary sort of way, though her mother insisted on doing her brown hair in fat curls that only emphasized her round face. She was wearing a white gown as befitted a young girl, though the style unfortunately emphasized the plumpness of her figure.

"I shall have to say hello to her," Lucinda said with a smile. "In the meantime, may I introduce you to His Lordship? Miss Charlotte Benton, this is Lord Kelton."

All color drained out of Charlotte's face, and she sank into a trembling curtsy. "I'm so sorry for my clumsiness, my lord," she stammered. "I just . . . Mama won't let me wear my spectacles to these affairs, and . . . oh, I suppose I should not have said such a thing!"

"Nonsense, Miss Benton," Garrett said before Lucinda could reply. "It was I who was clumsy by stepping into your path. I do hope you will forgive me and allow me this dance?"

Charlotte was not the only one who stared at Garrett with her mouth hanging open. Lucinda recovered herself quickly, unlike poor Charlotte, who blushed and stammered as she accompanied Garrett out to the dance floor.

Lucinda watched them go, her heart melting in her chest. She could see that Garrett made an effort to charm Charlotte, whose mother would no doubt be in raptures once word got out that her daughter had danced with the Duke of Raynewood's grandson. Garrett kindly overlooked it when Charlotte made a misstep, and he smiled at her as if she were the most beautiful woman in the world.

His kindness to the shy young girl slipped past Lucinda's defenses. Her heart seemed to squeeze in upon itself as she watched Garrett laugh at something Charlotte had said. Good heavens, what was she going to do? He made it more and more impossible to resist him.

"Good evening, Lucinda," came a voice from behind her.

She stiffened. She knew that voice as well as she knew her own, and the sound of it brought dread to the pit of her stomach. Slowly she turned to face the smiling blond man behind her. "Good evening, Malcolm."

Malcolm Devering, Viscount Arndale, kept his expression pleasant, no doubt so that anyone looking their way would note simply that the viscount regarded his sister-in-law with polite affection. Only Lucinda was close enough to see the greedy light in his pale blue eyes as he ran his gaze over her body.

"You are looking well, dear sister-in-law," Malcolm purred. "Good enough to eat, in fact."

"What do you want, Malcolm?" she demanded, ignoring his sexual by-play.

He looked wounded and placed a hand over his heart. Dressed in stark black evening attire that emphasized his blond good looks, with an ancient title and considerable fortune behind him, he was every young girl's dream of the perfect husband.

But all Lucinda saw was the man who had tormented her for eleven long years.

"Why, merely to pay my respects, my dear," Malcolm said. "After all, I haven't seen you in weeks."

"And it has been peaceful," she retorted. "I know you too well to believe that you have approached me simply out of duty. What do you really want, Malcolm?"

"You know what I want," he murmured, low

enough for only her to hear. "I want what I have wanted for the past eleven years. You, dear Lucinda, in my bed."

Revulsion filled her, but years of experience allowed her to keep that from showing on her face. "My answer is the same as it always is. No."

"Come, Lucinda, you know that is not what I want to hear." He took her hand in an unyielding grip and placed it on his arm. To anyone else, the gesture no doubt looked brotherly. Only Lucinda felt the caress of his fingers along her bare arm as he began to lead her along the edge of the dance floor.

She walked because she had no choice, but she kept her eyes on Meg. "I cannot go far. I am here with the Duke of Raynewood, and I promised Lady Agatha that I would watch out for his granddaughter."

Malcolm smiled at an acquaintance and murmured, "So you think you have found shelter with the duke? You cannot stay there forever, my dear. At some point, you will have to deal with me."

"I will get the money to pay off Harry's debts," Lucinda whispered icily. "I shall *never* share your bed, Malcolm. Accept that now, and leave me alone."

"I cannot," he replied, nodding at yet another acquaintance. "I have dreamed of having you ever since we were interrupted all those years ago, Lucinda. I saw the fire in you, and I mean to have it for myself."

She couldn't suppress a shudder at his words. *Never*.

"You know you have no choice," Malcolm whispered. "It is only a matter of time before someone discovers your financial difficulties. They are already discussing your lack of children."

"You started that rumor," she returned with barely controlled anger. "You know very well why Harry and I did not have any children."

"Indeed," he said with a chuckle. "A man has to visit his wife's bed in order to conceive a child—which Harry did not do. However, all society sees is a woman who was married for ten years and produced no offspring."

Color burned her cheeks. Harry had not visited her bed after their first year of marriage due to mutual agreement. Why, oh, why had Harry confided such an intimate secret to his brother?

"Just leave me alone, Malcolm," Lucinda hissed. "I won't let you win."

He chuckled at that. "I will have you, Lucinda, one way or the other. Who's going to stop me?"

She opened her mouth to reply, but another voice entered the conversation.

"Pardon me, Mrs. Devering, but Meg is looking for you."

Lucinda and Malcolm turned to see Garrett

standing behind them, big and forbidding in his black evening clothes. Something burned in his blue eyes, a possessive light that made Lucinda's mouth go dry.

"Who are you?" Malcolm asked with hauteur. Lucinda almost laughed as she realized that Malcolm had to look up at Garrett, even as he condescended to him.

"I'm Kelton," Garrett replied shortly. "And Mrs. Devering is needed elsewhere."

"Kelton?" Malcolm repeated, startled.

"Kelton," Garrett confirmed. He held out an arm to Lucinda. "If you please, Mrs. Devering."

Lucinda gladly took his arm. "Thank you, my lord. Malcolm, do have a good evening."

For the briefest instant, Malcolm's face twisted with frustration. Then the darling of the *ton* was back, a pleasant smile on his lips—but his eyes promised retribution.

As Garrett led her away, Lucinda resisted the urge to laugh with joy at finally thwarting Malcolm, even in such a small way.

Chapter 10

Garrett reined in his anger with difficulty. Lucinda had clearly started her hunt for a husband, and the knowledge infuriated him. Why did she seek out every man but him?

He led Lucinda away from the impeccably dressed, blond Englishman who watched her with hungry eyes and led her to the terrace doors that stood open to allow the evening breeze to cool the overheated ballroom. He knew the moment when she realized his intention. She dug in her heels in an attempt to stop his progress, but he gave a good yank of her arm that forced her to catch up with him.

"I'm not going out there with you," she hissed.

He halted and glared down at her. "I have things to say to you, and you would probably prefer that I say them in private. I have no problem stating my opinion in front of everyone, though."

Her eyes widened at his rough tone, and then she glanced around at the pampered busybodies who surrounded them. Giving a slight nod, she allowed him to lead her out to the terrace.

Once they were away from the crowd, she broke his hold and stepped away from him. "What is it you want to say to me?" she asked coldly, rubbing her arm where he had held her. "Meg is going to be looking for me."

"Who was that?" he demanded.

"Who was who?"

He ground his teeth at her innocent tone. "The man you were just talking to."

"Oh, him." Her careless dismissal didn't fool him for an instant, especially since she couldn't meet his eyes. "That was Lord Arndale."

"And who is he to you?" Garret moved toward her, forcing her to back up until she touched the stone railing. "Tell me the truth, Lucinda."

She stared at him. "You're being ridiculous."

He knew that he shouldn't go off on a tirade simply because Lucinda had been talking to another man. He knew that he really had no rights where she was concerned.

But something inside him had snapped when he saw her walking on the arm of the perfectly blond Englishman. He didn't like the greedy look in the other man's eyes one bit. Something primal inside him had made him separate her from the herd of glittering pretenders inside the ballroom to remind her that he wanted her, and intended to have her. And no pasty-faced Englishman was going to get in his way.

He moved in on her until their chests practically touched. She watched him with those big dark eyes, her expression scandalized. Her breasts rose and fell rapidly above the low neckline of her rose-colored gown, making the pearls she wore ripple in a most interesting manner.

"Captain, kindly keep your distance," she said, raising a hand to push against his chest.

He didn't move. "You haven't answered my question, Lucinda. What is this Lord Arndale to you?"

"He's my late husband's brother," she said impatiently. "Now are you satisfied?"

"Not for an instant." He refused to move, though she pushed against his chest. "I haven't begun to be satisfied with you yet."

She gave a sigh of exasperation. "Are we back to that, Captain? Didn't I make myself clear the first time that I am *not* interested in sharing your bed?"

"And I thought I made it clear that it was just a matter of time," he replied. "Unless, of course, you are planning on taking your precious viscount to your bed, in which case I would have to stake a prior claim."

She gasped. "You are a barbarian, sir!"

"I'm just a man," he said, stroking his thumb along her jaw. "A man who wants you very badly, Lucinda. And I've been very patient these last few days."

She tried to jerk away from his touch, but with her back pressed against the stone railing, she was unable to escape him. "Captain, please," she whispered. "I need to get back to your sister."

"In a moment. First, there is something I need to do."

Before she could protest, he kissed her, taking her mouth with a thoroughness designed to wipe all memory of the Englishman from her mind. Brother-in-law or not, this Lord Arndale had more than a brotherly interest in Lucinda.

Garrett intended to be the only man in Lucinda's life, at least until he left for America.

Lucinda moaned softly as Garrett kissed her, and fought against the overwhelming urge to press herself against his strong body and forget about everything else. How could this man so easily breach her defenses, even when she was furious with him?

His palm found her breast through the thin silk of her gown, and she whimpered as her body flushed with heat. Meg and Malcolm and all her problems faded away as the power of Garrett's touch took over her mind and soul.

When she was weak-kneed and clinging, he

broke the kiss but remained where he was, keeping her against the terrace railing. His breath came in sharp pants, and she could distinctly feel his arousal through the layers of clothing that separated them.

What kind of woman did it make her that she thrilled at the knowledge that his reaction was for *her*, who had not been enough of a woman to keep her own husband in her bed? How could she have forgotten years of breeding to turn into a wanton who melted at a man's slightest touch?

The *wrong* man's touch.

After all, if she hadn't been good enough for the son of an earl, she certainly wouldn't be good enough for the grandson of a duke.

But, oh, how she was tempted to take Garrett to her bed and experience full-blown passion for the first time.

He continued to hold her, his breath brushing her temples, and she wanted to close her eyes and shut out the world. For this one moment, she had everything she ever wanted.

A woman's giggle jolted her back to her surroundings. Realizing how it would look should anyone see her in Garrett's arms, she pushed at his chest with both hands and this time succeeded in moving him back a step. "We cannot be found this way, my lord. And I must return to Meg."

"Don't call me that," Garrett chided gently, brushing his fingers along her cheek. "You know I hate it. Call me Garrett."

She pulled away and ducked beneath his arm. "You called yourself Kelton when you spoke to Malcolm. I thought you had accepted your title."

His voice tightened. "I only used my title because I knew it would intimidate that weasel . . . Malcolm, is it?"

The moment of closeness was gone, both of them retreating to their corners like a couple of pugilists. "Yes," she replied.

"Funny how you can call him by his first name, but you can't call me by mine."

She wasn't fooled by his silky tone. "Believe me, Captain," she retorted, "you don't want to know the names I call that man."

His sudden stillness told her that she had startled him. Good. Garrett Lynch needed to learn that he did not know as much as he thought!

"I take it you are not overly fond of your brother-in-law?"

"I detest him," she said vehemently. "I want nothing to do with him, but he was Harry's brother, and I cannot alienate him without doing damage to my own reputation."

"What did he do?" Garrett demanded. "Has he ever harmed you?"

For a moment, Lucinda was tempted to tell

Garrett everything—about how Malcolm had been pursuing her for years, about his refusal to do the honorable thing and pay his brother's debts, about the vicious rumors he had started about her being barren to make sure she would never be able to secure another husband and be free of him. But from his aggressive stance and the light of battle in his eye, she wasn't certain what he would do. Drag Malcolm from the ballroom and beat him to a bloody pulp, perhaps.

She would give her mother's pearls to witness such a spectacle, but it would certainly do Meg's reputation little good.

"He has never physically harmed me, Captain," she assured him. "Malcolm is a man who wields his power in other ways. I have been handling him for years."

"If he bothers you again, come and get me," Garrett commanded, his tone deadly serious.

Fisticuffs at Lady Renfrew's ball would be in very bad taste, indeed. "Rest assured, Captain, there is no need for you to interfere."

"Promise me," he insisted.

She sighed. "Very well, I promise."

A long moment of silence passed between them, and tension grew slowly, aided by the quiet chirp of insects and the music drifting out from the ballroom. Garrett watched her with eyes that hid nothing, and she couldn't suppress a shiver at the naked desire on his face.

How she wished things were different, and she could step into his arms without fear. She had the sudden urge to get him alone and show him all the passion she had been hoarding for the past ten years.

He would never look at another woman ever again once she was finished with him, she thought, licking her dry lips.

He must have seen something in her face, because he let out a low growl of need and took a step toward her. Just then, Knightsbridge appeared in the doorway with Meg on his arm.

"There you are, Kelton," he said with his affable grin. "And you, as well, Mrs. Devering. Kelton and I are for the card room, if you would take charge of my charming cousin."

"Have you two been fighting again?" Meg asked, looking from Garrett to Lucinda suspiciously.

"What else?" Lucinda replied with a dismissive shrug. Somehow she forced her weak legs to move away from Garrett and toward Meg. "Have you been dancing, Meg? Perhaps you would care for some punch?"

"I've already had three glasses of punch," Meg replied. "If one more gentleman brings me a glass of punch, I cannot predict my reaction!"

Lucinda couldn't help but laugh at the exasperation in the girl's tone as they stepped back into the ballroom. "You can always refuse, you know."

"I can?" Meg turned around and sent Knightsbridge an accusing glare. "You said I would have to accept all the glasses of punch or else I would offend someone, and then Garrett would have to fight a duel!"

Lucinda's mouth dropped open. "My lord, you didn't!"

Knightsbridge burst out laughing. "Just a little joke," he explained.

"Meg, do not listen to a word your cousin tells you!"

The girl narrowed her eyes at Knightsbridge. "Don't worry, I won't."

He clapped a hand over his heart. "Cousin, I beg your forgiveness."

"In a pig's eye," Meg retorted indelicately. "I know better than to believe that charming grin of yours, *Algie*."

The young lord burst out laughing. Shaking her head, Lucinda met Garrett's amused gaze. The mirth faded from his expression to be replaced by something hotter and infinitely more dangerous.

Desire.

The heat of the ballroom suddenly felt stifling. Or was it the intent in Garrett's eyes that made it hard to breathe? Her head spun with answering need, and for the first time, Lucinda wondered why she was fighting so hard.

Why shouldn't she grab what happiness she could, and learn what passion was all about before she committed herself to another loveless marriage? As long as they were discreet, no one would care. Looking into those endless blue eyes, she couldn't think of a single reason why she should resist any longer.

"There you are, my boy," came the duke's booming voice, shattering the moment. Lucinda jerked her gaze away from Garrett and turned a polite smile on the duke. Then the smile froze on her face. Beside the duke stood a paragon of perfection.

The young lady with him was every inch the English debutante. From the top of her perfectly coifed golden hair to the tips of her delicate slippers, she was an inspiration to every young girl just out of the schoolroom. Every curl was in place. Her eyes were blue, her complexion the ultimate roses and cream. Her sweet features bespoke excellent bloodlines, from her evenly placed eyes and dainty brows to her straight little nose and her cupid's bow mouth. As if that wasn't enough, one tiny dimple creased her cheek as she smiled briefly at Garrett.

She was neither too tall nor too short, and her

excellent figure was enhanced by her pure white gown. Pearls graced her throat, as was only proper for a young, unmarried lady, enhancing the luster of her gorgeous skin and bringing attention to the gentle curves of her bosom.

Garrett stared. Knightsbridge stared. It was like a carriage accident, Lucinda thought sourly. The men could not tear their eyes away.

"Lady Penelope Albright, allow me to introduce my grandson, Lord Kelton."

Perfect Penelope, Lucinda thought with a sigh as Garrett made his bow. Here was the best reason of all for not getting involved with Garrett.

"My name is Garrett Lynch," Garrett corrected, smiling at Perfect Penelope. "Not Lord Kelton."

"Stanton-Lynch," Meg chimed in.

Lady Penelope's flawless brow furrowed with confusion. "I beg your pardon, my lord?"

"My grandson has a strange sense of humor," the duke said, glaring at Garrett. "Lady Penelope, allow me to introduce my granddaughter, Miss Stanton-Lynch."

Meg said with a grin, "It's a pleasure to meet you."

Lady Penelope inclined her head regally, then looked at Lucinda. "Good evening, Mrs. Devering. A pleasure to see you again."

"Lovely to see you, as well, Lady Penelope."

How could she have forgotten the duke's plans for Lady Penelope and Garrett, even for an instant?

The duke continued with the introductions. "And, of course, you know my nephew, Lord Knightsbridge."

"Ah, Perfect Penelope," Knightsbridge said with a hint of a sneer that made Lucinda stare at him in amazement. "You're in fine looks tonight, but I suppose you know that already."

The duke, after a moment of utter shock, looked thunderous. Garrett and Meg stared at Knightsbridge.

Lady Penelope's features settled into a perfect mask of cool politeness. "And you, Lord Knightsbridge, are ever the buffoon."

"Better to be a buffoon than an ice carving."

"That's enough, Knightsbridge," the duke snapped.

Knightsbridge jerked his gaze from Penelope and gave his uncle a baleful look. "I'm going to the card room. Coming, Kelton?"

Before Garrett could answer, the duke jumped in. "My grandson was just about to dance with Lady Penelope."

"I can't imagine why he would care to do such a thing," Knightsbridge said. "But if that is so, then I shall see you later, Kelton."

For one instant, an expression of genuine hurt crossed Lady Penelope's features. At first, Lu-

cinda thought she was the only one who had
seen it. Then she saw the speculative look on
Garrett's face, and realized that he had, as well.

"Of course I want to dance with Lady Penelope," Garrett said smoothly. "It would be my
pleasure."

Penelope smiled at him, then accepted his arm
as he led her out to the dance floor. Knightsbridge glared after them for a moment, then
spun on his heel and stalked away.

"I don't know what's gotten into that boy," the
duke grumbled, watching his grand-nephew's
retreat. "Never saw him cut anyone like that before, much less a lady. At least Garrett is doing
the right thing, though I'm surprised to see it."

"Knightsbridge hurt Lady Penelope's feelings," Meg said. "And as much as Garrett seems
to like thwarting you, Grandpapa, he would
never do so at the expense of a lady."

The duke grunted. "At least the boy has some
sense of honor."

"Of course he does," Meg replied. "He just has
a nasty temper as well. I think he gets it from
you."

The duke gave a bark of laughter at that, then
patted Meg's arm. "You're a treasure, my dear."
He looked back at the dance floor. "They make a
fine couple, don't you think, Mrs. Devering?"

Lucinda nodded, swallowing back an explo-
sion of emotion that threatened to bring her to

tears. She was unable to tear her gaze away from Garrett and Lady Penelope, and she was not the only one. As a couple, they looked spectacular. Tall, dark Garrett, dressed in stark black, was the perfect foil for the petite blond Penelope in her white gown. They looked like opposite sides of the same coin, big and small, dark and light, male and female.

How could she have thought, even for a minute, that she could possibly engage Garrett's affections for more than a fleeting time?

No doubt Garrett pursued her only for the thrill of the chase, not because he truly wanted her. All she could ever have with him was a few nights of passion—if she was even enough for him in that way.

Oh, she was fine when it came to kisses and caresses. But when the moment came to take a man inside her, things changed. Pleasure turned to pain. Hot passion turned to cool distance. She was incapable of enjoying the sexual act.

Unable to watch anymore, she turned away. No man could resist such delicate beauty. It looked like the duke was going to get his wish.

Chapter 11

It had been a splendid evening—or so every-one said.

Garrett sat in a comfortable chair in the library and scowled down into his glass of brandy. He could barely believe it, but he had actually enjoyed some of the evening. Though not nearly as much as Meg had.

He couldn't remember the last time he had seen her laugh so much or have such a good time, and it bothered him that she seemed to love it here in England. What if she never wanted to come home with him?

That thought had made brandy seem like a damned good idea.

He'd taken off his coat and tugged loose his cravat, which now dangled around his neck. He had also unfastened a button or two on his shirt.

No doubt Stobbins would have a heart attack if he saw him like this.

And what would Lucinda do if she saw him like this? Probably accuse him of running around naked again. He took a sip of brandy. Perhaps he'd wander upstairs to her room and ask her.

The notion of breaching her bedchamber made him hard in an instant. The fantasy of what he would do once he gained entrance made him even harder.

That kiss on the terrace had been hot enough to make him forget his surroundings and think about dragging Lucinda into the bushes for a quick, hard coupling. What would she have said to that? Probably something along the lines of, "Captain, how could you!"

He would have shown her how he could. As many times as he could.

But somehow, before they went home, she had cooled toward him. On the carriage ride back she had barely spoken to him. He had done his best to make as many obnoxious comments as possible, but Lucinda had remained stubbornly silent. All he had succeeded in doing was starting a fight with his grandfather, who had seemed unusually interested in what Garrett thought of Lady Penelope. But *he* was only interested in when he could get Lucinda alone.

She had eluded him by going upstairs with Meg when they'd arrived at the duke's townhouse. But she couldn't avoid him forever. He would seek her out once he finished his brandy.

Twenty minutes later, just as he drained the last drop, Lucinda entered the library.

Lucinda had crept downstairs with the idea of fetching a book from the library to help her sleep. A medicinal draught of sherry had proved to be a bad idea last time; better to find some boring tome. She had to do something, lest she toss and turn all night, thinking of Garrett.

She wanted him, but she couldn't have him. She had to focus on her practical goal and ignore these disturbing emotions that kept her awake at night. Garrett Lynch would either marry Lady Penelope or return to America. In either case he would be out of her life, and she needed to concentrate on what would happen to her after he was gone.

Still, she couldn't help but admit that she was very tempted to take Garrett Lynch for a lover, if only for one night.

As she entered the library it took her a moment to realize that she was not alone, and by that time it was too late to retreat. She pulled her wrapper more tightly around her nightdress and raised her chin as if she were fully dressed for battle.

"Good evening, Lucinda," Garrett said, caressing the empty brandy snifter in his hand. She wondered how much he had imbibed.

"Captain," she acknowledged with a stiff nod. "If you'll excuse me, I will be out of your way once I have fetched a book."

He rose from his chair, looking lean and predatory in his disheveled evening clothes. "Do let me assist you."

"That's not necessary," she said, edging toward the nearest bookcase. "I was just looking for something boring to put me to sleep."

"Trouble sleeping, Lucinda?" He stopped just beyond touching distance, then reached above her and pulled a book from the shelves. "Let's see. How about the classics? This is Virgil." He opened the book and flipped some pages, then began to read.

> *"Thus every Creature, and of every kind*
> *the secret Joys of sweet Coition find—"*

"Give me that!" she exclaimed, yanking the book from his hands. Her cheeks flamed red. Coition indeed!

"Not partial to the classics? Let's see what else we can find," Garrett said, perusing the shelves.

While he wasn't looking, Lucinda surreptitiously glanced at the rest of the erotic poem, then slammed the book shut, heat flushing through her body.

"Perhaps the Bard?" He pulled out a thick volume that contained the works of William Shakespeare and leafed through the pages. "Here we go.

"Her breasts like ivory globes circled with blue,
A pair of maiden worlds unconquered,
Save of their lord—"

"I think not, Captain." She pulled that volume from his hands as well and shoved it back on the shelf. "I can choose my own reading material, thank you."

"You find my taste objectionable, Mrs. Devering?"

"I find you objectionable in every way, Captain!"

"Really?" He pulled another book from the shelf. "I doubt you can call this one objectionable." He held it up so she could see.

"The Bible?" She raised her brows. "I'm amazed you know of its existence."

He actually looked wounded. "Of course I know of its existence. Here," he said, flipping through the pages. "This part is one of my particular favorites." He held out the book to her.

She gave him a skeptical glance, but really, what sort of mischief could come from reading the holy Bible? Turning her attention to the page, she began to read.

"Thou hast ravished my heart, my sister, my spouse; thou hast ravished my heart with one of thine eyes, with one chain of thy neck."

Gasping with surprise, she gave him an accusing look. "Leave it to you to desecrate a holy book!"

He laughed. "I didn't desecrate anything. This is from the Song of Solomon." He reached out and traced her cheek with one finger. "The ancients did not deny their desire, Lucinda. They rejoiced in it."

She pulled back from his touch, but the emotions it brought forth echoed throughout her body. "It's scandalous."

"It's human nature," he corrected. He removed the book from her hands and reshelved it, then cupped her face in both of his palms. " 'Thou hast ravished my heart,' " he quoted softly.

"Nonsense," she whispered.

"Truth," he countered. "I cannot get you out of my mind."

"That is just because I have refused you."

"No, Lucinda." His voice was serious, his blue eyes intent. "It is you I want, though I do not know why you do not believe me."

"Come, Captain," she scoffed, but her voice was shaky. "I am a sensible woman. Men do not lust after the likes of me. I am convenient, that is all."

He frowned at her. "Who told you such nonsense? What idiot man did this to you?"

"No one has done anything to me."

"Certainly in not the right way," he muttered with a scowl. "Lucinda, you are a beautiful woman. Any man would be privileged to make love to you."

Oh, how she wanted to believe him! But she had learned the truth years ago. "Thank you for your kind words. Now I will simply get my book and leave you in peace."

"*No.*" He grabbed hold of her shoulders when she would have stepped away, and he pulled her against him. "Kind words be damned, woman. Can't you see that I want you?"

Surprise gave way to excitement as he wrapped his arms around her and kissed her with open-mouthed passion. The heat of his hands on her back seemed to burn through the thin material of her nightclothes. For one panicked moment, she wondered if she would be able to stop him. What if he ravished her?

A thrill ran through her. She *wanted* him to ravish her. No, she desired it. No, *craved* it. And she wanted to ravish him right back.

"God, I want you," he muttered, nuzzling her neck. The nip of his teeth at her throat made her shudder. Her eyes slid closed, and she tightened her grip on his shoulders as her emotions got tossed about like a ship on stormy seas.

Did she dare steal this bit of pleasure for herself?

"Tell me you want me." He pulled back to look into her eyes. "Say it, Lucinda. Say it, or I'll stop now."

She stared at him, her lips parted. How easy it would be to simply let him seduce her, let him sweep her away with passion. Easier for whom, though? Easier for him? Or easier for her, so she could absolve herself of blame in the morning?

The thought of saying the words, of surrendering herself into his keeping, terrified her. But even more frightening was the thought that this moment might never come again.

"Please," she whispered.

He cupped her face in his hands. "Say you want this, too, Lucinda. I will not have you accusing me of taking advantage of you come the morning."

She hesitated, then lay her palm against his where he cupped her cheek. "I do want you, Garrett," she whispered.

He made a low, growling sound and pulled her face to his to kiss her.

As soon as his lips touched hers she melted against him, the amazing rightness of his touch making her hunger. She put her arms around his neck and kissed him back with everything inside her.

One night—she would allow herself one night to explore this thing between them.

His arms banded tightly around her body as if he would imprint her on his own. One large hand slid down, cupping her bottom and surprising a squeak from her. But as his large hand began to massage her sensitive flesh, she gave a low moan of surrender.

"What is it about you?" he murmured, mouth gliding from her ear down her throat and back again. "No matter how many times you refuse me, Lucinda, I always end up back here, begging for your touch."

"Oh, my." She let her head fall back as his teeth found her throat. "You want my touch?"

"Desperately." He cupped his big hand around the back of her head and stared deeply into her eyes. "Touch me, Lucinda. Please." The last word came out as a groan as he resumed nibbling her neck.

"Where?" she whispered.

"Anywhere," he murmured.

Anywhere? A thrill shot through her at the

idea of touching this magnificent male . . . anywhere. It was totally scandalous. Deliciously
scandalous.

Tentatively she stroked his shoulders, grazing
the muscles with her nails. He gave a muffled
groan and took her mouth in a hot kiss that had
her knees melting.

"More," he whispered.

She kissed his throat and thrilled as he closed
his eyes with a hard sigh of need. She nuzzled
her nose into the chest hair visible above his
open buttons and boldly licked his firm flesh. His
hands tightened around her waist. Encouraged,
she smoothed her palms over his chest, delight-
ing in the hard muscles beneath the thin shirt. He
made a sort of purring sound and stretched beneath her touch like a cat being stroked.

She ran her nails down his chest, grazing the
flat masculine nipple beneath the material, and
his eyes sprang open. He looked at her with such
heat, she was amazed she didn't incinerate on
the spot. Slowly, his eyes never leaving hers, he
flicked open the laces of his shirt, then took her
hand and placed it on his naked chest, over his
heart. She stroked him, tangling her fingers in
the curling dark hair that sprinkled his flesh. He
made a low hum of approval, then reached over
and tugged open the ribbons of her wrapper,
slipping it from her shoulders and leaving her
clad only in her thin nightdress.

She swallowed her instinctive protest, then dug her fingers into his chest as his fingers brushed the tip of her breast. She had always been sensitive there, and his touch made her pulse skip wildly as her nipple hardened in response.

He kissed her again and she closed her eyes, giving herself into his hands, trusting him in a way she had never quite trusted any other man. He seemed to know exactly how to touch her, first kneading her flesh, then gliding the edge of his thumb over the aching nipple.

It had never been this good for her. Perhaps she would finally experience the pleasure she had heard so much about.

He stopped touching her, and she opened her eyes on a whimper of protest. He only smiled at her and took her hand from his chest to kiss her palm. Then, holding her hand, he led her to the nearby sofa.

He sat down, legs sprawled in front of him, and guided her between his spread thighs. Her limbs trembling, she could only stand before him like some offering to a deity as he reached out and loosened the ribbon at her neck, then slid off her nightdress.

She closed her eyes, unable to look at him as she stood naked before him.

"Lord in heaven, you are beautiful," he murmured, tracing a hand down the side of her breast, along her waist, and coming to rest on her hip. "Look at me, Lucinda."

She opened her eyes, and saw that he watched her with a gentle smile, this incredibly attractive, aroused man. How had she come to this? And did she dare continue?

He must have seen the fear in her eyes, for he took her hand and brought it to his mouth, pressing a kiss to the palm. Then he placed her hand flat against his chest. "Come sit on my lap, Lucinda."

She flushed all the way to her toes, she was sure of it. "I can't. I'm too big to do such a thing."

He chuckled, then tugged and shifted until she straddled him. "You hardly weigh anything."

She just knew her face was beet red. How had this happened? How had she come to be naked in Garrett Lynch's lap, her legs spread wide across his thighs, her bare breasts in his palms? What madness possessed her?

He bent his head and took her nipple into his mouth, and suddenly she knew what madness possessed her. The same madness that sent desire streaking straight to her woman's parts, the same madness that made her tip her head back, arch her spine, and let out a groan of deep hunger.

She tangled her fingers in his long hair, holding his head to her as he suckled strongly at her breast. Her thoughts swirled, fading away as arousal took hold. Her breath hissed through her teeth as his strong hands closed over her thighs and kneaded the muscles there, and a whimper escaped her as he trailed his fingers along the insides of her thighs.

Oh, there. Oh, yes, there! He touched her gently between her legs, carefully stroking the delicate folds. She quivered in his arms, clinging to his head as he switched his suckling to her other breast, then let out a cry of surprise as his fingers brushed an incredibly sensitive spot.

He made a low, humming sound of approval and slowly released her nipple from between his lips. Looking into her eyes, he continued to stroke her woman's parts, making her shiver as he leisurely drew circles over her damp, sensitive flesh with his fingers. She shifted her grip to his shoulders and clung, her nails digging into the firm muscles.

"Let go, Lucinda," he whispered. "Let go."

She shivered, then closed her eyes and moaned as he gently slipped one finger inside her. It felt so strange and yet so familiar to be touched this way, and her body seemed to know how to move, undulating against his hand in a basic rhythm. He stroked his thumb over that especially sensitive spot again, and she stared at him, open-mouthed, as pleasure streaked through her.

Good heavens, was *this* what all the fuss was about?

Another jolt shook her, and as he continued to caress her, she felt something building, a deep wave of pleasure that started where his skillful fingers played and spread through her whole body, stronger and stronger, making her tremble and shake. He bent his head forward and took her nipple in his teeth—and she cried out with the shuddering ecstasy of her very first climax.

One moment she was shuddering in his arms, and the next moment they lay tangled together on the sofa, his hands stroking her back as he murmured soothing words in her ear.

She was still shaking, and Lord help her, she couldn't look at his face. She was panting, and she was sweating, and her limbs felt so heavy she didn't want to move. She nuzzled her face into his throat, tears inexplicably stinging her eyes.

What had the man done to her?

"Are you all right?" he asked, stroking back a tendril of hair that had escaped from the braid she habitually wore to bed.

She couldn't speak, only nodded.

"Good." He shifted beneath her, working at the fastenings of his breeches. "Because I'm not done with you yet."

She lifted her head at that, eyes wide in amazement. He chuckled, then gently reached out to flick an errant tear from the corner of her eye.

"It's all right," he said softly. "We can stop if you like."

Wordlessly, she shook her head, then slowly shifted until she sat astride him. He lifted his hands to her breasts, watching her with inquisitive eyes as she reached into his unfastened garments and gently touched his erect shaft.

He jumped, his eyes closing halfway as she tentatively explored his male flesh. His reaction pleased her, and she giddily realized that she had the power to reduce him to mind-numbing rapture just as he had done to her.

The knowledge gave her courage.

She tugged his breeches and small clothes down over his hips far enough that his erection sprang free. Taking him in both hands, she explored the hard length of him, marveled at the silky smoothness of his skin, and wondered at the tiny drop of clear liquid that appeared at the tip.

"You're killing me," he groaned. He clenched his hands on her thighs, and his breath hissed from between his teeth as he let her explore.

"Do you like this?" she asked, amazed at her own brazenness.

"Can't you tell?" His hips lifted off the sofa as she tentatively circled the tip of him with her finger.

"I think you do," she murmured. "What else do you like?"

His hot blue gaze locked on hers. "I want to be inside you."

The breath whooshed from her lungs, and her body surged with renewed desire. "Yes—please."

He tugged her forward until the entrance to her body was directly over his straining flesh. "Take me inside you, Lucinda," he whispered. "Take me as your lover."

His bold words echoed through her, and with a deep breath, she slowly lowered herself, allowing him to guide her. The blunt tip of him rubbed against her damp folds, then suddenly he was inside her, stretching her inner walls with the unaccustomed size of him. Her eyes slid closed, and she let out a low cry as their bodies fused completely.

Her body protested, unused to such activity. He held her in place with his hands on her hips, and slowly she could feel herself adjusting. Never had she felt like this with a man inside her!

Though it wasn't exactly comfortable, the pain she'd felt before was absent. Still, the longer she remained in her current position, the better it seemed to get. She could feel the little pulsations of adjustment deep inside her, and she shifted a little, to try and get a better fit. He groaned, and she realized that such a movement gave him pleasure.

Well, well, well.

She shifted again, squeezing inner muscles that she never knew she had, and was rewarded by a strangled sound of surprise and the clamping of his fingers on her hips.

His eyes were closed, and sweat beaded his forehead. His jaw clenched. She realized that he was trying to hold back his natural movements until she was ready for him, and a wave of tenderness swept over her.

"Garrett," she whispered. He opened his eyes, revealing a smoldering heat that thrilled her. She reached out to cup his face. "Help me. I don't know what to do."

His nostrils flared at her words, and his eyes narrowed to slits, but then he took the hand that cupped his cheek and pressed a gentle kiss into the palm. He placed her hand flat against his chest. Then, holding her hips, he showed her how to move.

It started out as a gentle rhythm, and she braced her hands on his torso, lost in the amazing feel of making love to this man. She caressed his chest, tangling her fingers in the curling dark hair, brushing his flat male nipples. He surged upward at that, filling her to the limit, and she gave a cry of surprise followed by a sweep of desire. She began to experiment, running her hands over his body, discovering the places that made the breath hiss from between his teeth and made him thrust harder inside her. Every forceful plunge excited her more and more. When she leaned forward and playfully licked one of his nipples, he lost all control.

With a fierce growl, he pulled her to him for a passionate, open-mouthed kiss. His other hand clasped her backside, her squeal of surprise swallowed up by his mouth. Harder and harder he thrust inside her, his tongue following the movement, tangling with hers. A keening noise rose in the back of her throat as her head spun and her climax rose up, slamming through her with a force that made her moan, low and loud and deep.

He followed a moment later, thrusting upward into her shuddering body, his hoarse groan lost in their kiss.

Minutes later, or maybe hours, he raised his head from where he'd buried it in her neck. Kissing her softly, he whispered, "Stay with me tonight."

Just one night, she thought. "All right."

Then she let him lead her once more down the road of sensual delights.

Chapter 12

What an excellent start to an affair.

Garrett smiled as he thought back to the night before. After he and Lucinda had realized that the library door was unlocked, they had sneaked up to his room to continue in more private surroundings. When he had awakened early that morning she was gone, which he had expected. Had she been discovered in his bed, her reputation would have been ruined. But still, he had missed the feel of her in his arms.

Given their late night the evening before, the ladies had slept past noon, then dressed and gone out on their rounds of social calls. Garrett had bided his time, but now it was teatime, and he would at last see Lucinda. He wanted to look into her eyes and share a secret smile about their night together.

He wondered what shade of pink she would turn.

Chuckling, he went downstairs to the drawing room. Despite her initial reluctance, Lucinda had taken to carnal pleasures with a natural sensuality that had surprised her more than it had him. Her responses were so innocent that he suspected she'd never enjoyed lovemaking before. Obviously her husband hadn't had the skill to bring out that side of her.

Unlike him, he thought with a smug smile.

He arrived in the drawing room, and there she was, looking good enough to eat in a pale green dress, her hair arranged in becoming curls. Meg was with her, happily regaling the duke with tales of their social calls. The old man smiled indulgently and sipped his tea.

"There you are, Kelton," Lady Agatha called out. "We've started without you, and if there are no more of Cook's berry tarts, you have only yourself to blame."

"You would be right, Aunt Agatha, but I do hope you saved me some." He smiled at Lucinda, but she wouldn't look at him. Was she shy now, in the light of day?

"Oh, Garrett, there are plenty left," Meg said with a giggle. "Come have tea, and I shall tell you everything we did today. Lucinda and I have secured invitations to Alexandra Bowen's come-out ball. It is the most sought-after invitation of the Season!"

"I'm happy for you, puss." He sat down and smiled at Meg, then turned his attention to Lucinda. "And I'm certain Mrs. Devering is pleased with herself today, as well."

Lucinda finally looked at him, but there was no answering spark in her dark eyes. "Indeed, Captain, I am most satisfied with the day's accomplishments."

"And what about last night?" Garrett asked, pushing for some glimmer of acknowledgment. "Were you not satisfied with the night's entertainment?"

"Lady Renfrew's ball was most enjoyable," Lucinda replied coolly. "Meg was quite a success."

"A stunning success," Erasmus chimed in.

Garrett frowned at Lucinda. What was wrong with her? There was no shared smile of understanding, no knowing glint in her eye. There should have been *something*, but she acted as if she had not spent the night in his arms.

What the hell was going on?

Garrett sat through the rest of the interminable tea staring broodingly at Lucinda. He noticed how she refused to look at him. Did she regret last night?

Hell, was she going to stop the affair?

He wouldn't allow that to happen. Never had he spent a more satisfying night in a woman's arms. He had been enchanted by her hesitant touch, undone by her innocent blushes as she learned how to please him. They had made love three times altogether, and each time she had let herself go more and more until she had actually cried during her last climax, before collapsing into a deep sleep in his arms.

He had never had a woman so driven to passion that she'd cried in his arms. If Lucinda was just discovering this side of herself, he wanted to be there as she uncovered each new facet. He was certain it would be a fascinating journey.

He glanced at her closed expression and waited until tea was over. The duke excused himself, and the ladies followed him. Garrett pulled up the rear and laid a hand on Lucinda's arm just before she followed Lady Agatha and Meg from the room. "A word with you, Mrs. Devering."

She whirled to face him, taking a step back so they no longer touched. "Your sister—"

"My sister can do without you for a few moments."

"Lucinda, are you coming?" Meg asked, poking her head back into the room.

"I want to ask Mrs. Devering some questions about tonight's ball," Garrett said to Meg. "I wouldn't want to embarrass you, puss."

"All right, I'll see you upstairs, Lucinda."

Lucinda nodded, and with a flash of dimples, Meg left them alone.

"What is it you want, Captain?" Lucinda asked, her expression coolly polite.

He gently touched her cheek, and she pulled away. He frowned. "Did I hurt you last night?" he asked. "Is that why you won't look at me to-day?"

"Not at all, Captain." She glanced away.

He took her by the shoulders, holding on when she tried to shrug him off. "Talk to me, Lucinda. Last night was one of the best experiences of my life, and I would like to continue that way."

"Then I am sorry to disappoint you, Captain. Last night is over, and it will not be repeated."

Garrett stared at her. Where was the passionate woman he had taken to his bed last night? He had thought that she had warmed to him. Hell, she had practically burned up in his arms!

"What do you mean, it will not be repeated?" he demanded. "I thought we were lovers."

"Will you keep your voice down?" Flushing, she glanced toward the open door. "We *were* lovers, for one night only. Now we must both go on with our lives."

"What the hell are you talking about?" He pulled her to him and pressed a kiss to her lips before she pushed him away. "Damn it, Lucinda!"

Lucinda took a step back, hiding her shaking

hands by folding her arms across her chest. Why was he making this so difficult? Didn't he know how hard it was for her to look at him and resist touching him and kissing him?

"Garrett, don't make this harder than it is," she begged softly.

"Don't make what harder? We started an affair, and now you are saying it is finished. Why?"

"It wasn't an affair," she said. "It was just one night, a gift to myself, because I wanted you so much. But we can't continue this way. There is no future for us."

"Of course there's a future. What about all the nights ahead of us before I leave?"

"No, Garrett. I can't look for a husband if I'm spending my nights in your bed."

"Why are you so stuck on the matter of a husband? Can't we just enjoy each other now, and you can find a husband after I leave?"

"An affair could ruin my chance at marriage! Oh, why can't you be reasonable about this?"

"Why can't you?" he shot back. "Damn it, woman, I can't recall a more erotic night in my entire life, and I have no intention of giving that up!"

"Get used to disappointment," she snapped, finally losing her temper. "You and I are from different worlds, Captain. My life is here, in a country you hate. The only honorable option for a gently bred lady is marriage. You have already said that you are not interested in a wife." She folded her arms and tilted her head, narrowing her eyes at him. "Of course, if you have changed your mind, then we might have something to discuss after all."

"No, I haven't changed my mind," he retorted. "I have no desire for a wife holding me down."

"And I have no desire for a casual lover," she shot back. "I want security and companionship, and that means marriage."

"Financial security, you mean."

She jerked her head in a nod. "Exactly."

"I didn't think you were as mercenary as other women, Lucinda," he said with a faint sneer. "I should have known better."

"I have no choice, Garrett. It's either marry, or I starve."

"What about working?" he demanded. "Hasn't anyone in this blasted country ever heard of doing a day's work for a day's wages?"

She tilted her chin proudly. "No Northcott has ever gone into trade, Captain. I don't expect you to understand about duty to the family name, as you cannot bring yourself to accept your own responsibilities to your title. But I will do everything within my power to not damage my family's reputation."

"So rather than earning a living like any de-

cent human being, you would marry some un-
suspecting fellow and leech onto his money."

She paled. "That is a crude and simplistic way
of putting it. I would point out that he gains
someone to run his household and give him an
heir."

"And what about passion, Lucinda?" His fingers tightened on her shoulders. "Where does
passion fit into your nice, tidy little picture?"

"Maybe it doesn't," she said, jerking away
from him. "But passion often fades, whereas
good, solid companionship can last forever. I am
not looking for a love match, Captain."

"Maybe you should be."

She laughed bitterly. "I learned my lesson
about that years ago, Captain. I am not some
green girl to fall for pretty words and a handsome face. A woman in my position has to be
practical."

"Some things just aren't practical, Lucinda."
He pulled her back to him for a long, hard kiss.
When he released her, her body roared its
protest. "This isn't over by a long shot," he
warned. "I haven't had my fill of you yet, Lucinda Devering."

As he stormed from the room, she raised a
trembling hand to her lips, acknowledging a
truth she had not wanted to face.

She hadn't had enough of him yet, either.

*   *   *

Lady Westlake's dinner dance was the entertainment for the evening, though Garrett found precious little reason to be entertained. Aside from his sister's obvious delight in her many dance partners, he spent the evening pondering the difficult puzzle that was Lucinda.

He should just forget about her and move on. In a city like London, there was bound to be any number of hungry widows or seductive actresses to entertain him. Women who accepted sex for what it was and did not insist on putting the price tag of his freedom on it.

But none of them would be Lucinda.

Damn it all! What was it about the prickly Mrs. Devering that attracted him so?

Maybe before he had sampled her charms, he might've been able to walk away. He usually could even after seducing a woman into bed. But something about Lucinda made him linger. In his arms, she had turned from a proper English lady into a seductive woman with a voracious appetite for bed sport. The transformation fascinated him, especially since she was back to being the oh-so-correct Mrs. Devering today.

If he got her alone, how long would it take to turn her back into that lusty creature?

Looking at her, he pondered the idea.

*   *   *

Lucinda could feel Garrett's eyes on her and tried to pay attention to what Lady Agatha was saying. Still, she found herself getting more and more distracted. She finally cast him a sidelong look of annoyance, but he simply gave her a slow, heated smile that brought forth an answering surge of need from her body.

She turned her back on him.

He placed his hand on her arm. "Mrs. Devering, may I have this dance?"

"No, Captain, you may not," she replied without turning around.

"Now, Mrs. Devering," Lady Agatha said. "Go ahead and dance with the boy. I shall watch out for Meg."

"Good evening, all!" Knightsbridge caroled as he joined the group. "Grandmama, you are looking lovely this evening."

"You young scalawag," Lady Agatha said with an affectionate smile. "I'm surprised you're not in the card rooms."

"Headed there," Knightsbridge declared. "Once I fetch Kelton, here."

"Yes, my lord, why don't you go to the card rooms," Lucinda said with a sweet smile at Garrett.

"After our dance," Garrett replied with easy determination.

Before Lucinda could refuse him, their group

was joined by a gray-haired mammoth of a woman with a dark yellow turban and an equally yellow evening dress. Lady Penelope accompanied the formidable dowager.

"Agatha, my dear!" trilled the older woman. "How wonderful to see you!"

"Sophia, you look wonderful," Lady Agatha replied, returning a fond embrace. "Allow me to introduce you to my great-nephew, Lord Kelton. And of course you know my grandson Knightsbridge. My dears, this is the Countess of Farvendale, Lady Penelope's grandmother."

Knightsbridge immediately bowed over the countess's hand. "Enchanted, my lady," he drawled smoothly. He cast Penelope a less amiable glance. "Lady Penelope, lovely as always."

"My lord," she said with a cool nod.

"Sophia, let's go off and have a coze," Lady Agatha said. "The young people can dance while we talk."

"Excellent notion, Agatha," the countess approved. "Well, lads? Which one of you will lead out my Penelope?"

Lady Penelope looked at Garrett.

Garrett smiled at her. "I'm afraid I've already asked Mrs. Devering for this dance, Lady Penelope. Perhaps I may have the next one?"

Penelope nodded and gave Garrett a shy smile. Lucinda opened her mouth to protest, but

Lady Agatha turned to Knightsbridge. "Well, boy, what are you waiting for?"

Knightsbridge looked as if he had swallowed something particularly distasteful. "Ah . . . Lady Penelope, may I have this dance?"

Lady Penelope didn't look particularly excited about the prospect, but she graciously gave her hand over to Knightsbridge so he could lead her out onto the floor.

Lady Agatha made a shooing motion at Garrett and Lucinda. "Go on with you now, Mrs. Devering. You know how you love to waltz."

"But Meg—"

"Don't you worry about her," Lady Agatha reassured her. "I'll be sitting right here with Sophia, and we'll watch out for her. You go enjoy yourself, my dear."

Garrett bowed to the ladies. "You are most kind, Aunt."

Lucinda could do nothing else but allow Garrett to lead her out in a waltz.

They took their places on the dance floor, his hand lightly on her waist, hers on his shoulder. He clasped her other hand, and as his fingers curled around hers, Lucinda was reminded of the night before, when he had been deep inside her, and he had pinned her hands to the bed on either side of her head and twined their fingers in exactly the same way as he brought her to shuddering climax. She darted her gaze to his, and she could see that he remembered, too.

The music started, and they began to move. As before, they followed the steps as one, sweeping along the floor in gentle rhythm that seemed all too familiar.

The hard muscles of his shoulder flexed beneath her palm as he guided her around the floor, and his scent surrounded her, taking her back to the night before with aching clarity. She instinctively smoothed her hand across his shoulder, then curled her fingers into the material of his coat to stop herself.

But, oh, the memories were irresistible. Had it been only last night that he had held her so tenderly? Had it been only last night that she had learned a woman's power, and how heady it was to caress a man and know you were pleasing him? Was it only last night that she had made this man shudder beneath her touch?

It seemed like eons ago. It seemed like moments ago.

Where their fingers twined, their palms seemed to burn. He locked his gaze with hers and gently caressed her thumb with his. Unable to escape, she could only tremble in response. He pulled her slightly closer, so their thighs brushed. His hand flexed at her waist.

Familiar heat flared and spread. As he spun

her in a turn, she clung to him. Her lips were dry, and she licked them. His eyes darkened.

Good Lord in heaven, she still wanted him.

Waltzing with him was pure torment and pure pleasure. Her body seemed to come alive at his touch, and she remembered how it felt to be alone with him in the darkness, entangled in the cool sheets of his bed. She let out a shaky breath. Her nipples had hardened, and moisture gathered between her thighs. Now she knew why the waltz had been considered scandalous; such close contact with a man awoke sleeping secrets within a woman's body.

Secrets that Garrett already knew, intimately.

They danced near the far edge of the floor, and before Lucinda knew what he was about, Garrett whirled her right through a small door nearly hidden by a potted palm.

Inside the small sitting room, Garrett closed the door behind them and leaned back against it.

"What are you doing?" Lucinda hissed urgently. "Are you mad?"

"Maybe."

His blue eyes burned as he locked his gaze with hers. Passion lit his features, and an answering echo chimed through her body.

They couldn't do this.

They shouldn't do this.

"I want you," he said softly.

"No," she whispered back.

"Oh, yes." He smiled, his eyes narrowing with serious intent. "Come here, Lucinda."

"Garrett, open the door." She took a step forward.

"No." He still watched her with that lazy smile, and a thrill shot through her, followed by a stab of pure sensual hunger. God help her, she wanted to touch him again.

"Kiss me, Lucinda," he commanded in a tone that shivered down her spine. "One kiss, and I will open the door."

"What will people think?" she asked, but she took another step toward him.

"Nobody knows we're here," he replied. "One kiss, and you can go back to the ball feeling much better than you do now."

Heat flooded her face. "You don't know how I feel."

"Don't I?"

He did. She knew he did.

"One kiss, Lucinda," he urged softly. "It will ease the hunger."

She was tempted. She looked at that tasty masculine mouth of his, and she longed to kiss him. But she didn't want to stop with his mouth.

Last night he had lain back and allowed her to taste every inch of his flesh. The memory burned through her, igniting her barely controlled passions, bringing her body to life with a flare of need.

"God help me," she murmured, then stepped forward into his arms.

He met her halfway. Their mouths joined, and she coiled her arms around his neck. He leaned heavily back against the door, kissing her deeply with teeth and tongue, his hands cupping her rear end and scooping her closer to him.

She could feel the hard length of him through her gown, and her body burst into flames.

She tangled her hands in his hair and threw herself into the kiss with everything she had. He groaned and crushed her against him, her breasts flattened against his chest, his hands kneading her bottom.

She tugged at the buttons of his coat, hungry for the feel of his flesh. With a low growl, he turned around, pinning her hard against the door, continuing their kiss with a lusty hunger that she matched tenfold. She clung to his neck and he shoved up her gown, urging her legs up and over his hips. His fingers brushed her bare thighs as he held her in place and rubbed against her.

Too many clothes, she thought desperately. She wanted him naked and inside her, and she wanted it *now*. If she had to wait one more second for him—

The doorknob rattled.

They both froze, and suddenly the enormity

of what she was doing struck Lucinda like a lightning bolt.

Where was her common sense? Where was her pride? Her dignity?

Had she really been about to make love to a man in the middle of a ball, backed up against a door like the veriest tart?

Apparently so.

The doorknob rattled again, and voices came from the other side of the door. Then she heard footsteps, as if the people trying to get in had walked away.

"Damn it," Garrett whispered.

She squirmed. "Let me down!"

Slowly, he let her legs slide down until she stood on her feet, and she brushed furiously at her gown, making sure there were no wrinkles.

"We're not done yet," he warned her.

She patted her curls, amazed that her hair was still in place. "Oh, yes, we are." Satisfied with her appearance, she turned and grabbed the door-knob. "Fix your hair."

He raked his fingers through his hair, trying to straighten where her fingers had tousled it.

"This is over, Captain." She stared straight into his eyes. "This can *never* happen again."

She opened the door and swept back into the ballroom.

Chapter 13

By some miracle, Garrett had the presence of mind to wait a few minutes before exiting the room after her. For a moment, Lucinda stood spellbound and watched his tall figure weave through the throng toward Lady Penelope and Knightsbridge.

What was *wrong* with her? Hadn't she learned her lesson when Malcolm almost ruined her? She needed to keep her reputation spotless if she were to find a decent husband. Garrett Lynch and his intoxicating kisses would either be off to America or wed to Lady Penelope soon enough, and she would be left languishing alone if she did not accomplish what she had set out to do.

At the moment, however, her most urgent need was to get back to her duties. She couldn't take the chance of annoying the duke on top of everything else!

She found Lady Agatha sitting on a settee in the corner. Her head bobbed forward, and she snored softly. The Countess of Farvendale was nowhere to be seen.

Neither was Meg.

Lucinda whirled around to look at the dance floor, desperately searching the faces of the dancers. She saw Garrett and the lovely Penelope, but the brief stab of pain at seeing them looking so perfect together was squashed by panic. She did not see Meg. Where was the girl?

"Would you care to take a turn?" Knightsbridge asked, approaching her.

Grateful for potential assistance, Lucinda laid a hand on his arm. "I need to find Meg," she said urgently. "Perhaps you can aid your grandmother."

She gave a nod in the direction of the settee. Knightsbridge sighed as he spied Lady Agatha. "Not again! Ah, well, never fear, Mrs. Devering. I shall revive Grandmama at once."

"Thank you," she said. "I'm going to look for Meg."

She hurried off, searching the odd corners and hidden sitting rooms leading off from the ballroom. While she appeared to be calmly making her way along to anyone who watched her, she still kept her pace brisk as she methodically searched every place a smitten young man might nip off to with a lovely girl like Meg.

With every moment that passed, her panic escalated. Was Meg ill? Or had she been swept away by some eager suitor?

That seemed the most likely scenario, and if so, then scandal was imminent. The duke would be furious if Meg's reputation were ruined.

So sorry, Your Grace, she thought as she made her way toward the terrace doors. *I was busy lifting my skirts for your grandson, instead of protecting your granddaughter from scandal.*

God help her if she did not find the girl!

As she stepped out into the cool night air, she heard a familiar giggle. Relief rushed through her as she turned toward the sound. Meg was there, on the terrace.

With Malcolm.

Relief turned to alarm as Malcolm met her eyes over Meg's head and smiled smugly. What was the man about? What evil did he perpetrate now?

"Meg," she said quietly.

Meg whirled around, her eyes laughing and her dimples flashing. "Hello, Lucinda! Do you know Lord Arndale?"

She had no idea how much danger she was in, Lucinda realized. The girl's face was alight with innocent joy, no doubt due to Malcolm's practiced flirtations.

"Of course Lucinda knows me," Malcolm

said, never taking his eyes from Lucinda's. "She was married to my dear brother, God rest his soul."

Meg's mouth dropped open. "I had no idea! What an interesting coincidence."

"Very interesting," Lucinda replied dryly. "Meg, you know you're not supposed to go off alone with a gentleman."

The girl flushed. "I'm sorry, Lucinda, but it was so very hot in there. Lord Arndale very kindly offered to accompany me outside so I could catch my breath."

"Still, you know the rules," Lucinda said, keeping her voice calm with effort. "How would your grandfather feel if he got wind of this situation? And Malcolm, you know better."

Malcolm gave her a nod. "My thanks for your correction, sister-in-law. But I'm afraid I was swept away by Miss Stanton-Lynch's beauty and lost my head for a moment." He lifted Meg's hand to his lips and brushed a kiss across her knuckles.

Meg giggled, and Lucinda ground her teeth. Over Meg's head, Malcolm flashed Lucinda a smile of fiendish satisfaction.

"Please go inside, Meg," Lucinda said. "I will be along in a moment. I wish to have a word with Lord Arndale."

"Oh, all right." Meg curtsied to Malcolm. "It was very nice to meet you, my lord."

"And a pleasure to meet you, Miss Stanton-Lynch," Malcolm replied with a brief bow. "I expect we will meet again."

"I'm sure we will." Head held high, Meg made an effort to walk with dignity from the terrace, but the dimpled grin on her face spoiled the image. She disappeared inside the ballroom, and Lucinda faced Malcolm.

"What are you up to, Malcolm?" she demanded.

He raised his brows. "Whatever do you mean, Lucinda?"

"Stay away from Meg," Lucinda warned. "She's not for the likes of you."

"The likes of me?" He looked down his nose at her. "You have nerve, my dear, to imply that I am not good enough for the duke's granddaughter? My title and fortune are more than adequate. *I* am not the one who was deemed not good enough for the peerage."

She ignored the barb. "I know exactly what you are, Malcolm, and I will not allow you to despoil an innocent like Meg!"

"Despoil? Really, Lucinda." He clucked his tongue. "However do you propose to stop me? I find the young lady to be charming. She would make an excellent viscountess."

"You have no intention of marrying her," she scoffed. "You're just toying with her."

"Dear Lucinda, you are so sure of everything." Malcolm brushed an imaginary bit of lint from the sleeve of his Spanish blue coat and gave her a smile that chilled her bones. "I do have to set up my nursery eventually, you know. Young Margaret would make a lovely bride."

He chuckled. "Do you really think the duke would refuse my offer? Especially since my dear father is plagued by illness and will no doubt stick his spoon in the wall at any moment now? That would make me the Earl of Witting, more than a match for the granddaughter of the Duke of Raynewood."

Dread crept over Lucinda as she realized that he was serious. He was actually considering a formal courtship.

She would have to warn the girl. There was no way she could stand by and watch Meg marry a viper like Malcolm; he would make the girl's life miserable! He would break her heart and steal the innocent joy from her eyes. And that was only the beginning of how he would hurt her.

"I won't let it happen," she warned. "I will go to the duke."

He leaned back against the railing and folded his arms across his chest, the moonlight creating a nimbus around his blond head. "The Honorable Mrs. Harry Devering telling the Duke of Raynewood what to do. How I would love to be present for that little encounter."

She held her ground and did not allow her doubt to show on her face. Like most predators, Malcolm sniffed out weakness and took advantage of it.

"There are plenty of other potential brides to choose from."

"I fear dear Margaret has stolen my heart," he drawled, a mocking glint in his eyes.

"She's American," Lucinda pointed out, knowing what a high stickler he was.

"That just makes her all the more interesting." He leered. "A wild American! How exciting my marital bed will be!"

Lucinda pressed her lips together and tried again. "Her mother was Irish."

He shrugged. "Lamentable, but the duke's patronage is enough to make me overlook that."

Words hovered unsaid on her lips, but she choked them back. She was too much of a lady to say what she really thought of him, even to Malcolm. She gave him her most disdainful glare instead.

He laughed. "So fierce, Lucinda?" He pushed away from the railing and sauntered toward her, arrogantly confident in his appeal. "Perhaps we can discuss the matter in a more . . . intimate setting."

He stopped close enough to draw his finger along her arm. She flinched away as if an insect had touched her, but she didn't retreat. To do so was to show weakness. "You haven't changed, Malcolm."

"Did you really expect me to?" He gave her a charming smile that had no doubt sent many a society miss into a swoon.

"One always hopes that evil will be redeemed."

"Evil?" He laughed again. "You enchant me with your wit, Lucinda. You always have."

"Is that why you won't let me be?" she challenged. "I should think that after all these years, you would have met some other woman far more amusing than I."

His eyes narrowed as if he sighted down the barrel of a pistol. She could practically hear a weapon cock as he lifted a hand and stroked her cheek. "No one will ever take your place, Lucinda. I *will* have you, no matter how long you keep me waiting."

"Why?" she cried. Fear turned her legs to water, and she stumbled back a step. "Why me? You have refused to pay Harry's debts as you should. You have started false rumors that I am barren so that I will not be able to find another husband. All this to force me into your bed. For ten years, I have refused you, Malcolm. Why can you not accept that?"

"I must have you, Lucinda," he rasped, his

face sharp with hunger. "I will not rest until we finish what we started all those years ago."

He's mad.

How had she never seen it before? He was obsessed with her. He would never give up.

She backed up another step, watching him as if he were a snake about to strike. He had stalked her for years, always there in the shadows like a nightmare she could not escape.

Watching.

Waiting.

Lusting after her with that terrifying gleam in his eyes.

How had she ever thought she loved him?

"You're disgusting," she blurted.

Anger twisted his features. "I will have you in my bed," he vowed. "You have always been a challenge, Lucinda, and I shall not rest until I have taken my pleasure between your soft . . . white . . . thighs."

With every word, he stepped closer, the pale blue irises of his eyes almost disappearing as his pupils dilated. Looking into his eyes, she felt as if she were gazing into the windows of hell.

"Never," she whispered. She backed away. One step. Two. He stayed where he was, a faint smile of cruel amusement on his face. Then she slowly turned her back on him and returned to the ballroom at a dignified walk.

Keeping her head up high cost her the full measure of her control—a control that almost faltered as his soft chuckle followed after her.

Garrett moved through the steps of the minuet by rote, his mind on the woman he had held in his arms only minutes before.

Lady Penelope was chattering on about something, her perfect lips moving. As he looked down into her face, he wished that her mouth was wider, that she was taller, that her hair was darker and curlier.

He wanted brown eyes, not blue. And a tall, slender body, not this petite, curvaceous one. He wanted a woman who would look at him with honest emotion in her eyes, not this expression of polite admiration.

He wanted Lucinda.

He smiled and nodded as Lady Penelope continued her stream of polite small talk, and searched the ballroom for Lucinda.

She would no doubt avoid him for the rest of the night. What they had almost done had shocked her—hell, it had shocked even him. He hadn't expected passion to flare so fast and so hot.

A few more moments, and he would have been inside her.

Still, his only regret was that he hadn't had time to complete the act. He wanted nothing more than to have Lucinda beneath him again, to feel her body pulsing around him in climax as she made those little keening noises in the back of her throat.

He really, really liked those little noises.

He moved through the dance, smiled at Lady Penelope again, then scanned the ballroom. Where *was* she?

He saw her then, coming in from the terrace. The relief he felt turned swiftly to concern as he noted her pale face and wide eyes.

Something had upset her.

Was she still distressed by what had happened between them?

Then someone else stepped in from the terrace: the blond man Lucinda had been speaking with at the ball the other night, her brother-in-law. As he watched, the man gave her a nasty little smile. Lucinda lifted her chin and turned away, her face a pale mask of indifference.

And her brother-in-law watched her rear end as she walked away, his eyes hungry.

What the hell was going on between these two?

Garrett almost stopped in the middle of the dance floor, and his slowing down caused Lady Penelope to step on his toes.

"I'm so sorry, my lord!" she cried, face flushing red with mortification.

"It was my fault," he said, watching as Lucinda made her way to Lady Agatha and Knightsbridge, who stood with Meg.

"No, it was me. I . . . oh, I'm so clumsy!"

The music ended. Lady Penelope gave him a hasty curtsy, then hurried away from him. He frowned after her. Had those been tears in her eyes?

Blasted women. Who could understand them?

He started toward Lucinda, but before he could reach her she darted off, heading for one of the little retiring rooms. He hesitated. He knew what would happen if he followed her into that isolated little room. The same thing that had almost happened a little while ago.

Follow her, his body urged.

He tamped down on his unsated desire and tried to think with his brain. Did Lucinda really need him charging after her when she was clearly upset? But he wanted to comfort her, which surprised him. He had never felt such a thing for anyone but family before. Obviously, Lucinda was starting to matter to him. He wasn't sure what to make of it.

As he stood there debating with himself, he saw Lucinda barrel into an older gentleman in her dash toward the sitting room. She stopped, flushed with embarrassment. He could see her fumbling to utter an apology, and then she looked up, and her expression lightened.

She knew this fellow.

The man said something to her, and suddenly, her face crumpled. She folded in on herself, and her acquaintance quickly moved to herd her behind an ornate sculpture for a moment of privacy. His large body blocked her from the view of the dancers.

Garrett could only stare. He had *never* seen Lucinda break down. Ever. Of all the stiff-lipped British he had met, Lucinda had seemed the most emotionally controlled of all of them.

Now she looked like a woman who had reached the end of her rope.

He started across the ballroom. If that old man had hurt Lucinda, there would be hell to pay.

"There now, my girl," Sir James Whigby said, fishing a handkerchief from the pocket of his plain black evening coat. "Surely it's not as bad as all that."

Mortified, Lucinda could do nothing more than take the snowy piece of linen from his hand and dab at her teary eyes. No doubt she looked a fright with a red nose and red-rimmed eyes. Everyone would know in an instant that Lucinda Northcott Devering had lost her famous composure.

"You look fine," Sir James said with a smile, seeming to read her mind. "No one will know you have been crying, believe me."

"I would like to believe that." She sniffed.

"It's the truth, as sure as I'm standing here. I whisked you out of sight rather quickly, if I do say so myself. It's nice to know I can still move that fast."

Lucinda gave a little laugh at his self-deprecating tone. "Oh, Sir James, you are not that old."

"Over fifty, my girl, and I've seen a lot in my time." He smiled gently. "Would you care to indulge an old friend and tell me what brought this about?"

Lucinda sniffed again and fought the urge to blurt out everything to this man who had been her father's friend. Though more than a decade had separated the two men in age, General George Northcott and Sir James Whigby had been fast friends. Sir James and his wife, Portia, had come to visit the Northcotts many times as Lucinda grew up. Once Sir James's wife had died, he had retired to the country for a long time. This was the first time she had seen him out in society in at least six years.

He was a kind man, and still handsome despite his years. His once jet-black hair had turned gray, and his skin bore the evidence of wind and sun that had been his legacy as a ship's captain in His Majesty's Navy. But his hazel eyes still shone with innate good humor, and his body was still lean, though more with age than with muscle.

Having reached her emotional limit between Garrett and Malcolm, Lucinda had needed nothing more than Sir James's mention of her father to shatter the last thread of her composure.

"I am sorry to have turned into a watering pot," she said, trying to pull the shreds of her dignity about her. "The evening has been rather taxing."

"Are you here with your husband?" Sir James asked.

Lucinda shook her head. "Harry passed on over a year ago. I am . . . assisting the Duke of Raynewood with his granddaughter. The girl is from America and lacked companionship." The lie nearly choked her. It was so difficult to tell a falsehood to such an old family friend, but no one could know of her financial difficulties, or of her bargain with the duke.

"So you have taken the girl under your wing," Sir James said with a nod. "You always were a good-hearted young woman, Lucinda."

No, just a desperate one.

"What brings you to London, Sir James?" she asked, trying to steer the conversation to less dangerous topics.

"Loneliness," he replied with a self-mocking grin. "Life just has not been the same for me without my dear Portia. I thought the gaiety of London might ease my heart."

She laid a sympathetic hand on his arm. "Oh, Sir James."

"It's all right," he said, patting her hand. "I have Roger. He's married, you know, and they have two children. I'm a grandfather now."

"You're too young to be a grandfather," Lucinda said with a smile.

He chuckled. "You're good for me, my dear. It's a pleasure to see a familiar face in this huge city. I vow, I don't know anyone anymore. Would you consider me too familiar if I asked to call on you tomorrow?"

"Of course not!" she exclaimed. "You have been a dear friend of the family ever since I can remember. I would be delighted to receive you, Sir James."

He took her hand delicately in his. "Lucinda, my dear, I am not asking to call on you as a friend of the family. I have decided to marry again. And now that I know you are a widow, I would be honored if you would allow me to call on you for purposes beyond friendship."

Startled, she barely kept her mouth from falling open. "Why . . . of course, Sir James. As I said, you are always more than welcome to call."

He laughed. "I've shocked you, I can tell, though the Northcott dignity would hide it from anyone who hasn't known you for as long as I have. Don't worry, my dear, I shan't rush you. I would simply like the opportunity to court you."

He lifted her hand to his lips, and she blinked

in surprise. "Of course, Sir James. Though I have to admit, you have startled me."

"My dear Lucinda," he said with a grin, "I have startled myself. You may expect me in your sitting room tomorrow."

"Very well," she said. He bowed and walked away, and she stared after him with wide eyes.

Good heavens! She had a suitor.

Chapter 14

The foyer smelled like a damned funeral parlor.

Garrett paused in descending the stairs and gazed at the dozens of floral arrangements that sat upon every flat surface in the foyer. Like a couple of honeybees, Lucinda and Meg moved from arrangement to arrangement, reading the cards and buzzing on about who sent what.

Good Lord, were all these flowers for Meg? He scowled as he realized his sister had become quite popular with the useless London dandies. The sooner he got her back to Boston, the better.

The thought came almost from habit, and suddenly, he wondered what he was waiting for.

Meg had made her court appearance already, and yet he felt no urgent need to bundle her aboard the nearest ship and sail back to America.

It certainly wasn't because he liked England, he thought fiercely. A more useless bunch of people he had yet to meet, not an honest day's work out of any of them. And it was for no great love of his family, though he liked Lady Agatha and enjoyed Knightsbridge's company.

No, the reason he was still in England was right in front of him, wearing a pink dress and looking as sweet and tasty as something in the bake shop window. He and the lovely Lucinda had unfinished business, and he refused to leave until it was concluded to his satisfaction.

"Lucinda!" Meg squealed. The high pitch of her voice echoed through the foyer and made him wince. "Lucinda, look! These are for you!" The skirts of her green-striped gown spun as Meg whirled to face Lucinda with a tasteful arrangement of spring flowers in her hands.

"What?" Lucinda gasped.

What the hell? Garrett echoed silently.

"These are for you! I didn't even know you had an admirer!"

"Neither did I." Hesitantly, Lucinda took the arrangement from Meg and reached for the card. "Goodness, it's from Sir James."

"Lucinda, you sly thing! Why didn't you tell me you had a suitor?" Meg asked with a grin.

"It all happened rather suddenly." Closing her eyes, Lucinda buried her face in the flowers and inhaled their scent. A smile of pleasure crossed her face.

Garrett remembered seeing that same expression on her face when she had run her fingers through his hair two nights ago in his bed.

Damn and blast, didn't she know that he had prior claim on her attentions? Oh, he had overheard her conversation with this Sir James last night. The fellow was fifty if he was a day. What could he offer a passionate young woman like Lucinda?

Aside from the respectable marriage she craved.

"So who is Sir James?" Meg teased. "I haven't seen you dance with anyone but Garrett at the affairs we have attended!"

Lucinda blushed. "He's an old family friend. I saw him last night at the ball."

Meg's face fell. "Oh, then he's not a suitor?"

Lucinda hesitated, then cleared her throat. "Actually, he did ask to call on me, and he made it quite clear that it was for reasons other than friendship."

"Oh, I'm so excited for you!" Meg grabbed Lucinda in a hug that nearly crushed the flowers. "Now we shall both receive gentleman callers today."

"Apparently so," Lucinda replied with a fond smile at the girl. She looked up and saw Garrett on the stairs, and her smile faded.

Meg followed her gaze. "Garrett, there you are! Look at all these flowers! Even Lucinda got some."

Garrett forced a smile to his lips, his eyes locked with Lucinda's as he descended the stairs. "I doubt there's a posy left in all of London, puss."

"I'm going to tell Lady Agatha to come see!" Meg rushed up the stairs past Garrett.

Lucinda continued to watch as Garrett slowly approached her. She hadn't said a word to him after their encounter last night, and she'd hoped he would've gone out before the afternoon callers arrived.

Before Sir James arrived.

He stopped in front of her. "Lovely flowers," he said.

"I . . . yes, they are."

"From an admirer?"

She lifted her chin. "Yes."

"From that man I saw you with last night, the older one with the gray hair?"

"Yes, Captain." She raised her brows in mock inquiry. "Is there anything else you would like to know?"

"May I read the card?"

"No, you may not! It is none of your affair, sir."

His eyes narrowed. "*My* affair is not going at

all as I planned. The woman I am having the affair with is receiving flowers from another man!"

"Will you hush?" she hissed. "Sir James is a perfectly nice man, and an old family friend."

"And he wants you," Garrett added. "I was there last night, Lucinda. I heard what he said."

Her mouth dropped open. "You were *spying* on me?"

"I saw you were upset." He waved his hand, as if searching for words. "I wanted to help."

She gave a harsh laugh. "You had done enough at that point, Captain."

"Garrett," he corrected.

"Captain," she insisted.

They stared at each other, neither willing to give way.

"Two more minutes, and I would have been inside you," he murmured. "Two more minutes, and you would not have seen any other man but me."

"Two more minutes, and I would have disgraced myself," she corrected in a low voice.

"You wanted me," he insisted.

"Yes, but to do *that* where we were, to neglect my responsibilities and abandon my dignity, would have destroyed me."

A footman walked by, and both of them held their tongues until he was out of earshot. Then

Garrett leaned closer to her. "You are making too much of this, Lucinda. It's just sex."

She stiffened. "Exactly, Captain. Not love, and not worth sacrificing everything I have for a few moments of pleasure."

"That's not what I meant." He clenched his hands into fists. "This Sir James. He's old, Lucinda. You're a passionate young woman. He won't be able to satisfy you."

"Oh, but he can," she replied. "His intentions are honorable, Captain. Unlike yours, which are the basest of motives."

He took the flowers from her hands and plunked them down on a nearby table. "If you can't tell the difference between casual lust and sincere admiration, then you have much to learn, my dear."

"And I assume you see yourself as my teacher?" she asked coolly.

Taking her arm, he lowered his voice. "Do we finish this in private, Lucinda, or do we continue this here, where the servants can listen to every word?"

He would do it, too, she realized. He had nothing to lose, and the servants were used to his barbaric ways. But there were things she wanted to say to him, as well.

"Very well," she said. "Let's go into the sitting room."

He bowed, sweeping his arm in a gesture that

indicated she should precede him. With a sniff, she walked ahead of him into the sitting room.

He followed her in, then closed the door behind him.

"Open that door," she demanded.

"No." He leaned back against it. "We are going to have this out, Lucinda."

"There is nothing to have out, Garrett," she replied. "You and I have been at cross purposes from the beginning."

"I rather thought we were in agreement two nights ago," he murmured.

At the look on his face, Lucinda almost groaned. Even now, she wanted him. "I have never made any secret of the fact that I need a husband, Captain, just as you have never made any secret of the fact that you are leaving England. That puts us at cross purposes."

"It doesn't have to be that way."

"It does," she insisted. "What would you think of a man who wanted nothing from Meg but an affair?"

His face darkened. "I would kill the bastard. My sister is worth more than that."

"And I am not?"

He opened his mouth to answer, then closed it again.

"It's not the same," he said finally.

"But it is." She smiled sadly. "I am worth more than a few nights of passion, Garrett. You have taught me much about that side of myself, and I thank you. But my place in society requires that I marry, not indulge in love affairs.

"I respect your decision, Garrett, as you must respect mine. Do I come to you, begging you to wed me? No. As you said, we are two adults, and we have had a discreet liaison. But my goals are different from yours. You cannot give me what I want, so I must look elsewhere."

"I don't have what I want yet," he said in a low growl, looking as if he would devour her right there.

She took a deep breath. "I'm sorry, but I have given you everything I can afford to."

He stepped toward her. "Don't try and tell me that you don't want me, Lucinda. I would hate to call you a liar."

"I do want you." She laughed at his surprised expression. "I am honest with myself, if nothing else, Garrett. I may not *want* to want you, but my body does not always do my bidding."

"What harm can there be in continuing our affair?" he cajoled. "We can be as discreet as you want."

She lifted her chin. "I have reasons, Garrett. You don't know everything there is to know about me. Please just accept that I must do this."

"If Sir James asks you to marry him, you'll say yes, won't you?"

She nodded. "Probably. I am fond of Sir James,

and I have known him all my life. I could do much worse."

"Did you love your first husband?"

She stiffened. "I prefer not to discuss my marriage to Harry."

He raised his brows. "I take that to mean you didn't love him."

She walked over to a table and toyed with the flowers in a Chinese vase. "Our marriage was arranged by our families. Such things are done all the time."

"And Lord Arndale?" he asked softly. "Where does he fit in?"

She whirled on him and glared. "Malcolm is Harry's brother. That's all he is and all he ever will be to me."

"So vehement," he noted. "Are you in love with him?"

"What is this obsession you have with whom I love?" she cried. "You certainly do not love me, Garrett. I believe you are incapable of it."

He scowled. "Certainly I am capable of it."

"Of course." She gave a dismissive wave of her hand. "That is why you have spent your life running away from your emotional responsibilities."

"What the hell are you talking about?"

"I am talking about you." She put her hands on her hips and stared him right in the eye. "Being an outsider in this family, I observe much that probably escapes you. You, sir, are afraid of emotional entanglements."

"The hell I am!"

She didn't even flinch at his use of language. "I know that you love your sister."

"Of course I do. I would do anything for her."

Lucinda nodded. "Anything but be there for her."

His face grew thunderous. "I have always taken care of her and of my mother. *Always*."

"Financially, yes. But you've spent the better part of Meg's life away at sea. You didn't have to do that, Garrett. You own the company. You could have run it from Boston, but instead you chose to separate yourself from your family. You loved them, you sent them money. But they wanted you there with them, and you couldn't do that."

"Perhaps I should have," he snapped. "But I'm here now, right? I came all the way to god-damned England and *stayed* here because of Meg."

"A step in the right direction," Lucinda agreed. "But while here, you have done your best to maintain your antagonism toward your grandfather."

"You know what he did," Garrett snarled. "He destroyed my family."

"He was trying to protect your family," Lucinda corrected. "In doing so, he made a huge mistake, one that cost him as much as it cost you. Didn't it ever occur to you that he was just as hurt as you were when your father died? Your father was his *son*. How do you think that made him feel, to know his actions had precipitated the death of his child?"

"I don't think the old bastard has a heart."

She laughed. "The same could be said for you. You're both afraid of love, both afraid to be hurt again."

"Trying to make me fall in love with you, Lucinda?" he challenged.

"I have practical reasons for what I do, reasons that have nothing to do with how I feel about you, Garrett. *Your* reasons stem from fear."

"I'm not afraid of anything," he scoffed.

"You're afraid to forgive your grandfather."

"I should have grown up here," he answered fiercely. "I should have known the life my father knew." He walked to the window, looked out onto the streets of London. "He used to talk about it. How green England was, how much he loved riding across the land his ancestors had owned. But my grandfather denied me the life I might have had."

"He's offering it to you now."

"But I like America, too," he said, turning to face her again. "People are different there. Everyone is equal. I miss it."

"It's your home. Of course you miss it. And

this is my home. I love England as much as you love America."

"I suppose you must," he said slowly.

"And I love my family as much as you do," she continued. "Though they are all dead, there is a certain tradition that must be carried on. I am the last Northcott living. I must do my duty by my family name and make a respectable marriage so that I can continue to move about in society. *Not* engage in a scandalous affair that might damage my reputation and shame my family name."

"No one has to know," he said, but she could hear the uncertainty in his voice.

"I would know," she said.

"Damn it, Lucinda," he said, but there was no heat in his words. "I can't get you out of my mind. I want you in my arms, and the thought of you with this Sir James fellow makes me crazy."

"I'm sorry about that," she said. "But I have reasons for what I'm doing."

"Tell me," he demanded.

She shook her head. "I do not answer to you, Garrett."

"Then how do you expect me to understand?" he asked fiercely. "Are you in some kind of trouble, Lucinda? Do you *have* to get married?"

She sighed and headed for the door with determined strides. "I am done discussing this, Garrett."

"What about children, Lucinda?"

She stopped, her hand frozen in mid-air where she reached for the doorknob. "What?"

"What about children?" he repeated. "Don't you want children some day? Sir James seems a little too old to be a father."

She whirled to face him, hands clenched at her sides. "Haven't you heard, Captain? Rumor has it that I cannot have children, so you need not concern yourself with such things." To her horror, her voice broke on the last words.

"Back to 'captain' again, are we?" he muttered. Then he looked closely at her, and she pressed her lips together, refusing to meet his eyes. "So you cannot have children?"

She shrugged. "That is what they say."

"That's not what I asked you." He stepped closer, but she sidled away from him. "Lucinda, tell me what's wrong. *Are* you in some sort of trouble?"

"Don't concern yourself with me, Garrett." She looked at him then and gave him a brittle smile. "You just worry about your ships and your sister. I can take care of myself."

"Can you?" he challenged softly.

Turning her back on him, she jerked open the door. "I have no choice."

She exited the room, but did not manage to close the door before he responded.

"There is always a choice, Lucinda."

Chapter 15

There is always a choice, Lucinda.

The words haunted her all day.

Garrett didn't know what he was talking about, she thought fiercely as the maid buttoned her favorite brown dress for a drive in the park with Sir James. Garrett knew nothing about her problems, nothing about how hard it was to hang on to something intangible, like her family's reputation, in the face of something as unforgiving as English society.

He knew nothing about Malcolm's obsessive pursuit, nothing about the financial problems that haunted her every day, nothing about her fragile arrangement with the duke that was all that might save her.

Garrett Lynch was a man in control of his own life. He owned his own business and did what he chose. Unlike a woman, he did not have to sell himself into marriage merely to survive.

Her own bitterness surprised her.

She had been raised an English lady and knew her duty. So why was she now angry about what she must do to survive? Why was she even thinking about how wonderful it would be to marry for love and not survival?

Sir James was a good man. He was older than she was, yes. A good twenty-five years older, in fact. But he was a kind man, and she trusted him. He didn't seem bothered by the rumors Malcolm had started, and she knew he was well off financially. By some miracle he had returned to London in search of a wife just as she had been seeking someone exactly like him for a husband. A month ago she would have thanked God for such divine intervention.

A month ago, she had not been yearning for Garrett.

She sighed, then left the room to go receive Sir James.

Garrett stepped into the drawing room and immediately wished he hadn't.

"Garrett, dear boy!" Lady Agatha greeted him. "Do come and meet Sir James."

The last thing Garrett had expected when he had come looking for Meg was to be confronted with Lucinda's suitor. The older man sat in an armchair across from the settee where Lady Agatha and Meg rested. He was dressed simply yet elegantly in plain, well-made clothing that Garrett himself might have selected. Sir James rose as Lady Agatha made the introductions.

"Garrett, may I present Sir James Whigby? Sir James, this is my grand-nephew, Garrett, Lord Kelton. Sir James has come to take Mrs. Devering for a ride around the park," Lady Agatha added with a beaming smile.

"Pleasure," Sir James said with a respectful nod.

"Sir James." Garrett nodded back, struggling to remember why it would be a bad idea to challenge the fellow. He had to respect Lucinda's choices, had to allow her to live her life without his interference. It was what he would expect of anyone else, and so he was trying his best to accord her this courtesy.

Unfortunately, his instincts urged him to warn the other man away from the woman he had claimed for himself, no matter how primal that seemed.

Lucinda chose that moment to enter the room. She stopped just inside the doorway as she saw Garrett standing there, and their gazes met and held for a long, charged moment.

She looked beautiful in a walking dress of a soft brown, shades darker than her hair. The color made her complexion look creamy and flawless, and her doe-like eyes look fathomless. Her mouth appeared soft and pink and lush, an invitation to any man breathing.

Don't go, he thought.

Her expression softened, and her dark eyes filled with a tenderness that made his heart ache. She cared for him. It was there in every inch of her posture, in the yearning in her eyes, in the curve of her smile.

How could he not have known she had feelings for him? Why hadn't he realized that?

He had been a fool. Lucinda was not a woman who gave herself lightly, and he felt ashamed of himself for trying to treat her that way. She deserved as much respect from him as Meg or any other woman of his acquaintance. Somehow his lust for her had eradicated his good manners, and there was no excuse for it.

So when Sir James rose from his chair and approached her, Garrett stepped aside. When the older man took her hand and brushed a kiss to the back of it, Garrett reined in his primitive instincts and did *not* jerk Lucinda away from Sir James as he longed to.

She looked back at him once, as Sir James opened the door to the drawing room and ushered her out. He saw gratitude in her eyes, and a longing that seemed to echo back from within himself.

Good Lord, he realized with shock. He had

feelings for Lucinda! Feelings that had nothing to do with lust. Feelings that felt uncomfortable and awkward, and yet somehow so right.

Yet he could only stand there, shaken, as she swept out of the room on the arm of another man.

Lucinda tried not to think about the brief flare of emotion that she had seen in Garrett's eyes as Sir James handed her into the curricle. Sir James was the man she should be thinking about, and she gave him a brilliant smile as he climbed into the seat beside her.

To her surprise, he didn't smile back.

"Are you certain this is what you want, Lucinda?" he asked quietly.

"Whatever do you mean?" she asked, startled.

Sir James looked back at the house, his expression somber. "I did not miss the look between you and the duke's grandson, Lucinda. What is he to you?"

"He is . . . I mean . . ."

"He's watching you from the window."

Lucinda whipped her head around and saw that Garrett was indeed watching her from the window of the drawing room. Their gazes met for an instant; then he disappeared from the window.

She let out a little sound of distress. Sir James touched her hand, and she turned to look at him.

He touched her cheek gently. "Forgive me, Lucinda. I didn't mean to sound harsh. I would just like to know if I should consider Lord Kelton as a competitor for your hand."

She twisted her lips bitterly. "Not at all, Sir James."

"Like that, is it?" Sir James took up the reins and set his matched pair of grays trotting toward Hyde Park. "Would you care to talk about it?"

She hesitated.

"Lucinda, I have known you since you were a child," he reminded her. "Much has happened to you since your father's death, and I would like to think that you can confide in me. I assure you, I shall not think less of you for it."

The sincere compassion in his voice brought tears to her eyes, and she fought to control herself. How she longed to have someone to confide in! But she did not dare talk to him about Garrett, especially since Sir James was a suitor.

But, oh, how she wanted to.

At her continued silence, Sir James let out a sigh. "All right, if you feel you can't tell me outright, let me tell you what I have surmised. I can see that there is something between you and Lord Kelton. Obviously marriage is not involved here, because you said he does not pursue your hand. And it seems to me that you want to marry again."

"Yes, I do," she replied, facing him at last. He

continued to keep his eyes on the road, but she could tell she had his full attention.

She took a steadying breath before continuing. She had to tell him the truth, for what if Garrett succeeded in taking his sister back to Boston before Meg could contract an advantageous marriage? Lucinda's bargain with the duke had not taken Garrett's stubbornness into account. "I must be honest with you, Sir James, because our families have been friends for so long. My late husband left behind some substantial debts."

"Ah," Sir James said, comprehension spreading across his features. "And I take it your current finances will not cover the amount?"

"That is correct."

"So you wish to marry again for financial security."

"That is part of it."

He glanced at her. "And I take it young Lord Kelton has no desire for marriage, though he does seem to have some desire for you."

She blushed. "Something like that."

"As I suspected." He paused. "I am not going to ask for details. You are from a good family, Lucinda, and whatever is between you and the marquess is your business. However, should we marry, I would not tolerate infidelity. Perhaps that is old-fashioned, but it is how I feel."

Mortified, Lucinda looked down at her hands.

"I am not like that, Sir James. Should we marry, I would be a faithful wife."

"I'm glad to hear it." He turned the horses into Hyde Park. "Do you love him, Lucinda?"

"No!" she said, appalled by the thought.

After a moment of silence, he said, "Do you think you could come to love me?"

"I could try," she said softly.

"That is all a man can ask." He nodded at a society matron in a passing carriage. "We will not speak of this again."

Garrett went back to the window, but the curricle had already left, carrying Lucinda away with it.

He clenched his hands into fists as he stared blindly at the street below. Confusion churned in his gut, stirring up unfamiliar emotions. How could he have let her leave with Sir James?

How could he have stopped her?

He flexed his hands helplessly, desperate to grab onto something of his own, something real. He had lost everything now. His parents were gone, and with every day that passed, Meg grew more and more attached to England. She might want to stay permanently, and he loved her too much to deny her anything, as much as he wanted her to come back home with him.

And he had lost Lucinda.

That was the most crushing of all, because it

was his own fault. He had held her in his arms, had claimed her so briefly, yet he had lost her because of his own pigheadedness. Once she realized that he could not offer her what she needed, she had looked to another man.

And why shouldn't she? Scowling, he turned from the window. All she wanted was marriage. Yes, she was secretive about her reasons, but he had to respect her for sticking to her goals and not settling for less than she deserved. Lucinda was a proud woman from a good family, and she was not made to be a man's plaything.

So why didn't he just marry her?

The jolt of apprehension that he expected never came. The idea of Lucinda as his wife seemed comforting rather than alarming, and having her in his bed every night promised hot encounters even on the coldest winter nights. The notion that she would be at his side to talk to and to hold for the rest of his life made him realize what he had been missing all these years. He had been a damned fool to wait so long.

What had he been afraid of? Losing her? Hell, he'd never had her! By not treating her honorably, he had all but shoved her into Sir James's arms.

Was there any chance that she might come back to him if he wooed her as a suitor should? They could marry here in England, and then he would take her back to Boston . . .

The thought stopped him cold. Lucinda had no desire to leave England. Everything she had done, she had done so that she could continue to live in high society. How could he possibly convince her to leave England? What if she refused to marry him?

"Damn it!" he muttered, scowling at a painting of a bowl of fruit that hung on the wall.

"Garrett, why are you talking to that painting?" Meg asked.

He had forgotten that he was not alone in the room. He turned to face Meg and Lady Agatha, who watched him with puzzled expressions, but he was saved from answering when the duke came in.

"We have visitors," Erasmus said, just as the butler announced the names of those visitors.

"The Countess of Farvendale and Lady Penelope Albright!"

"Sophia!" Lady Agatha cried with delight as the countess, clad in brilliant green from top to toe, swept into the drawing room. Lady Penelope, clad in a soft shade of blushing pink, followed at a more sedate pace. As the older women embraced, she sent Garrett a shy smile.

Meg joined the fray, and as Garrett watched all the women greet one another, he wondered how he could discreetly escape.

Somehow, his plan of greeting the ladies and slipping from the room got waylaid, and he found himself seated beside Lady Penelope on the settee, with Meg on the other side, and across from the countess and his great-aunt. And if that wasn't enough of a trap, the duke had also settled down in an armchair to socialize.

"Tell me about America," Lady Penelope said to Garrett, her blue eyes wide. "Is it as wild as I have heard?"

"We're from Boston," Meg answered with visible patience. Obviously, it was not the first time she'd been asked such a thing. "It's quite a large city and very civilized."

"There are no savages there?"

"Of course not," Garrett replied. Really, was the girl such a twit that she had never heard of the great city of Boston? "It's a lot like London, actually."

"Really." Lady Penelope sounded as if she did not believe them, but manners forbade her from saying so.

"Garrett has sailed all over the world," Meg said, clearly changing the subject. Garrett glared at her, and she smiled sweetly at him, the little instigator. "He's seen so many great cities and exciting places. He owns his own business, you know."

"You're in *trade*?" Lady Penelope gasped, drawing the attention of the duke and the two older ladies. She stared at Garrett as if he were some creature she had never seen before.

"That was before he inherited," Erasmus assured her, casting Garrett a warning glance.

"I'm still in trade," Garrett declared, earning a black look from the duke. "When the *Trinity* arrives back in England, I will be going back to Boston where I belong."

"But I thought . . . whyever would you want to return to America when you can have so much here?" Lady Penelope asked, a wrinkle appearing between her delicate brows.

"Because I live there," Garrett replied.

"Oh, Garrett, I thought you were staying for the whole season," Meg complained with a pout.

"This is all very unexpected," Lady Farvendale said, casting a telling look at the duke.

"The boy's a bit headstrong." The duke glared at Garrett.

"I don't belong here, puss," Garrett said to Meg, ignoring the rest of them. "Surely you can see that."

Meg sighed. "I had hoped you would stay for a while, though."

"Are you serious?" Lady Penelope gasped. "You are really *not* staying here in England to claim your title?"

"I don't understand any of this," the countess snapped, her eyes narrowing. "Are you saying that you have no intention of claiming your title *or* staying in England?"

"That's correct."

"*I see*," the countess bit out. She rose to her feet. "Come, Penelope, we have other calls."

"But Grandmother—"

"My dear Lady Farvendale, if I might have a word with you?" the duke asked.

"Your Grace, I believe everything is perfectly clear," the countess said with a haughty sniff.

The duke stiffened and looked down his nose at her. "Lady Farvendale, I require a word with you at once!"

"I think not, Your Grace. It is quite clear to me that the prospects here for Penelope are not what I was led to believe."

Meg groaned. "Oh, Grandfather, you didn't!"

"What prospects?" Garrett demanded.

Lady Agatha let out a soft snore, her head bobbing forward.

The duke waved a dismissive hand at Meg. "Don't concern yourself with this, Margaret."

"Don't concern myself?" Meg leaped to her feet and planted her hands on her hips. "You're trying to sell off my brother into marriage, and you expect me to stay out of it? I'm not a child, Grandfather!"

"He did *what*?" Garrett roared.

Lady Agatha jerked awake. "What was that? What?"

"Good heavens," Lady Penelope exclaimed,

placing a hand on her bosom. She stared at Garrett as if he had grown horns and a tail. "My lord, must you act the savage?"

"Yes, I must," he bit out, glaring at the duke. "Whatever made you think you could arrange my life for me, old man? Didn't you learn anything from what happened to my father?"

"I only want what's best for you," Erasmus replied, lifting his chin and staring his grandson down.

"You just want what's best for your precious title!"

"Lady Penelope is an excellent match," the duke defended.

"Indeed she is," Lady Farvendale agreed with a firm nod of her head.

"Impeccable breeding," Lady Agatha agreed. Then she sent a puzzled look at Meg. "A match for whom?"

"For Garrett," Meg said with a snort.

"Garrett? And Penelope? Good heavens, no!" Lady Agatha exclaimed, laughing. "Why, they would never suit."

"Agatha!" Lady Farvendale gasped in shock, slapping a palm to her ample bosom.

"Oh, don't get on your high horse, Sophia," Lady Agatha said. "Your granddaughter is a fine girl, the cream of the crop. But she and Garrett would never make a match of it."

"I'm glad *someone* in this house can see reason," Garrett growled.

The butler entered the room. "The Earl of Knightsbridge," he announced.

"Hello, all!" Knightsbridge sang out as he entered the room. Upon seeing Lady Penelope, he stopped cold. "Oh, *you're* here."

"The rudeness of your family knows no bounds, Agatha," Lady Farvendale sniffed.

"I think it's rather rude to arrange someone's life without asking him first," Meg retorted, glaring at the duke. "Grandfather, you had best not plan on arranging any matches for *me*, or I will return to America so fast, you'll think my presence here was just a dream."

The duke paled. "Margaret, please!"

"Who's getting married?" Knightsbridge asked, helping himself to a biscuit off the tea tray.

"No one, my lord," Lady Penelope said, rising from the settee. "Grandmama, I believe it *is* time we were leaving."

"Grandfather is trying to play matchmaker between Lady Penelope and Garrett," Meg said to Knightsbridge.

He choked on a biscuit. "What!"

"Utter nonsense," Lady Agatha said with a wave of her hand. "They would never suit. You, on the other hand, would be a perfect match for dear Penelope, grandson."

"What!" Knightsbridge and Penelope exclaimed at the same time.

"Indeed," Lady Farvendale said slowly, looking from one young person to the other. "I see what you mean, Agatha."

"I make my own decisions about my life," Garrett said, pointing a finger at his grandfather. "*I* will decide whether I stay or go, and whether I marry or not."

"Don't you use that tone with me," the duke warned.

Meg threw up her hands. "Oh, you two are so much alike!"

"We are not!" the duke and Garrett shouted at the same time, then glared at each other.

"I need to sit down," Knightsbridge said, sinking into an armchair.

"Utterly perfect," Lady Farvendale said to Lady Agatha.

Lady Agatha nodded. "They're already half in love with each other," she said.

"We are not!" Penelope exclaimed.

"I should say not!" Knightsbridge chimed in.

The two older ladies merely smiled as the butler entered the room again.

"Ah . . . Mr. Tim O'Brien," Stephens announced.

"He's back," Meg whispered dismally, as the seaman entered the room.

Garrett came forward to greet his first mate. "Tim, how goes it?"

"Well, Captain, there's a problem with the harbormaster in London harbor, and I think you need to come and see to it yourself," Tim said. He nodded at Meg. "Good day, Miss Meg."

"Hello, Tim." She sank back down on the settee, her expression glum.

"What kind of problem?" Garrett demanded.

"He's charging us way too much for dropping anchor in the harbor," Tim said. "And one of the boys overheard him bragging about how he was going to stick it to us Americans by cleaning out our pockets."

"Did he, now?" Garrett said softly. Then he gave the man a predatory grin. "Let's go have a chat with the harbormaster, Mr. O'Brien."

"You will do no such thing!" the duke interjected. "We have guests, Garrett."

Garrett cast his grandfather a glance that made the old man's haughty look falter. "No, sir, *you* have guests. I have business to attend to."

He left the room, Tim O'Brien right behind him.

Chapter 16

Lucinda returned from her carriage ride in a cautiously hopeful mood. Aside from their initial uncomfortable conversation, everything had gone splendidly. She had every hope that Sir James would eventually declare himself.

Upon entering the duke's home, she handed her hat and pelisse to the butler. "Where is Miss Stanton-Lynch, Stephens?"

"In the Blue Salon, Mrs. Devering."

She set off down the hall. When she opened the door to the blue salon, she took one step into the room and stopped dead.

"Good afternoon, sister-in-law," Malcolm said with a charming grin.

He leaned against the fireplace mantel, the epitome of the dashing London bachelor in his perfectly tailored bottle-green coat and meticulously tied cravat.

"Lucinda, I'm so glad you're back," Meg said, rising from the settee. She gave Lucinda a telling look, then jerked her head in the direction of Lady Agatha, who sat beside her.

A soft snore echoed throughout the room.

Cold fear knotted Lucinda's stomach. Good heavens, Meg had been alone with Malcolm for who knew how long without benefit of a chaperone! She met Malcolm's eyes and saw unrepentant glee in his gaze. He knew what he was doing, the snake!

"My lord," she said in her frostiest voice, "would you care to explain what is going on here?"

"I am simply paying a call on Miss Stanton-Lynch," Malcolm said, all innocence. "We were well chaperoned until a few minutes ago."

"It's not Lord Arndale's fault," Meg said, clearly concerned that she had done something wrong. "It just . . . happened."

Lucinda remembered well how things tended to "happen" around Malcolm. She would not let Meg fall into the same trap she had been prey to all those years ago!

"Be glad the duke did not find you here with his granddaughter," she said to Malcolm as she came forward and sat down in an armchair near the settee.

"But you are here now, dear Lucinda," Malcolm replied. "And propriety is once more restored."

"Yes." She gave him a warning look. "And I will be here every time Meg receives you."

"As it should be," he agreed, but she could see the laughter in his eyes.

Meg let out a relieved breath and sank back on to the settee, obviously glad there would be no repercussions from the incident. "Lucinda, the viscount was just telling me about his estates. They sound beautiful," she sighed.

"You shall have to see them sometime," Malcolm said. "Perhaps I shall have a house party in the summer."

"That would be lovely," Meg said.

"I doubt that we could attend," Lucinda said at the same time.

Meg frowned. "You don't know that, Lucinda."

"Don't fret, Miss Stanton-Lynch," Malcolm said, amusement in every word. "The lady is only looking out for your welfare."

"Why does everyone think I'm some sort of ninny?" Meg huffed. "The last thing I want to do is hurt Grandfather by causing some sort of scandal, especially after he has been so kind to me."

"We don't think you a ninny," Lucinda answered, reaching out to touch the girl's hand. "Let's change the subject."

"Unfortunately, I fear I must be going," Malcolm said, "as much as I hate to leave such delightful company."

Lucinda quickly rose to her feet. "I'll see you out, my lord."

He raised his brows at her obvious desire to be rid of him, but took his time in bowing over Meg's hand. "Enchanting as always, Miss Stanton-Lynch."

Meg blushed. "Thank you for stopping by, Lord Arndale." She giggled, and the sound woke Lady Agatha.

"What was that?" the old lady bellowed.

"Lord Arndale was just leaving, Aunt," Meg said.

"Arndale?" Lady Agatha squinted at Malcolm. "Oh, yes. It's been delightful, my lord. Do call again."

"Come, my lord," Lucinda said, leading the way to the door.

Malcolm followed her silently until they left the Blue Salon and reached the hallway. "So eager to be alone with me, my dear?" he purred.

"I warned you to stay away from her," Lucinda hissed.

"My dear Lucinda, I doubt there is much you can do about it." They reached the foyer, where Stephens handed him his hat and walking stick. Malcolm donned the fashionable beaver hat and gave her that charming smile that always made her blood turn to ice. "I will continue to court her," he murmured. "Unless, of course, you wish to make a bargain."

Lucinda clenched her hands into fists. "I don't like your bargains."

"Then we have nothing to discuss. Good day, dear sister-in-law."

He left her standing there and never looked back.

Garrett sat in the chair at his desk on board the *Trinity* and listened to the sound of the waves gently lapping at the side of the ship, the creak of the boards, the snap of an untrimmed sail in the wind. He closed his eyes and let it soothe him like a lullaby.

He had lived most of his life on a ship. It was the only true home he had ever known. Familiar smells surrounded him: wood, salt, and tar. The gentle sway of the ship as she bobbed at anchor in London harbor all but rocked him to sleep.

Yet something was wrong. It wasn't quite the same.

He opened his eyes and stared at the wood plank ceiling of the cabin. He felt unsettled somehow. He had never felt that way aboard ship; being at sea had always eased his restlessness.

He blamed it all on Lucinda.

She had done something to him. Somehow she had looked deep into his soul and saw the loneliness he had always kept hidden. Was she right? Did he fear loving people? Had he been running away from his emotions all these years?

It certainly hadn't stopped him from developing feelings for *her*.

A quick double knock came on the door of his cabin, the prearranged signal he had discussed with Tim. Sitting up in his chair, he picked up one of his sea charts and scanned it. "Come!" he called sharply.

Tim creaked open the door. "Begging your pardon, captain, but Mr. Cuthbert, the harbormaster, is here to see you."

Garrett scowled. "Show him in."

The portly Mr. Cuthbert swaggered into the room, a superior grin on his face. He looked around the cabin as if assessing its value.

"Mr. Cuthbert?" Garrett said, drawing the man's attention. He took enormous pleasure in the way the harbormaster's eyes widened at the sight of his fine London clothing. "I understand there is some confusion with the rates to drop anchor in London Harbor."

"No confusion," Cuthbert said, recovering from his initial surprise. He puffed out his chest. "The rates are just like I quoted to your man here."

"I see." Garrett consulted his pocket watch. "Mr. Cuthbert, I am due at Almacks this evening, so I do not have much time to argue about this.

Perhaps I should just have you removed from your post and be done with it."

"What!" The man's eyes bulged. "You can't do that!"

"I'm certain that I can." He gave the man a smile that showed all his teeth. "I'm sorry, I've neglected to introduce myself. I am Garrett Lynch, captain of this vessel."

"I know who you are," the man sneered.

"I am also the Marquess of Kelton," Garrett continued, watching the sneer disappear from the harbormaster's face. "And while I am rather new to London—just inherited, you know—I'm certain my grandfather, the Duke of Raynewood, knows whom I can speak to in order to get you discharged."

"N-n-no need of that, my lord," Cuthbert stammered. "There must have been some sort of error with one of my clerks. I'm certain that's what happened here."

Garrett raised his brows. "A clerical error? I am quite relieved to hear it. So what *are* the rates for dropping anchor here?"

Cuthbert quoted a figure that was a third of what he had told Tim.

Garrett nodded in approval. "Much better, Mr. Cuthbert. If you go with my mate, Mr. O'Brien, he will see that you are paid the correct amount."

"Thank you, my lord. Thank you very much."

The man bowed and then humbly followed Tim from the room.

Tim gave Garrett a knowing wink before he closed the door behind himself.

Garrett leaned back in his chair and waited for the feeling of satisfaction that normally would have filled him at beating the harbormaster at his own game.

It never came.

He surged from the chair and began to pace the length of his cabin. What was *wrong* with him? Why didn't he feel at home on the *Trinity*? And why had he relied on his title to resolve the matter? In the past, he would have used sheer will and American stubbornness to wear the man down.

He didn't feel like himself anymore. And he didn't like it a bit.

Lucinda had done this to him. She, with her pride and her passion. She had changed him somehow, with her talk of duty and family loyalty, and now he wasn't content with his life anymore.

His ship, which had once been his escape, now seemed an empty shell of a once-consuming dream. Lonely and vacant, lacking in warmth, void of companionship. Just a vessel of travel, not the lifelong friend he had once thought it was.

He dropped his head into his hands and

rubbed his palms across his face. Lucinda had made him care about things he had never cared about before. He had thought he needed to be aboard ship, to start planning his voyage home, to ease the restlessness that plagued him.

Wrong.

He needed *her*.

But he had the feeling it might already be too late.

Meg was clearly starry-eyed over the handsome viscount, and since Malcolm's pedigree made him a completely eligible suitor for the girl, Lucinda knew there was only one thing she could do to make sure this match never happened.

She went to the duke.

Just before changing for dinner that evening, she found him alone in his study. She knocked firmly, but her hand shook as she twisted the knob in response to his barked, "Enter!"

The duke sat behind his desk. "Yes, Mrs. Devering, what is it?"

"Forgive the intrusion, Your Grace, but I want to speak to you about Meg."

"Oh?" The duke waved a hand at a chair, then sat back and steepled his fingers. "You've done well there, Mrs. Devering. She's become the most sought-after young miss on the marriage mart— not that I had any doubts that she would."

"Thank you, Your Grace. That is what—"

"I wish I were as pleased with my grandson's behavior. The boy embarrassed me beyond the pale this afternoon when he told me in no uncertain terms that he would not wed Lady Penelope! And he did so in front of Lady Penelope herself, as well as her grandmother, Lady Farvendale."

"Oh, no," Lucinda whispered. But a small part of her heart rejoiced at the news.

"Indeed! Agatha has some misbegotten idea that Lady Penelope and Knightsbridge would suit, but I cannot envision such a thing."

Lucinda could very well envision it, but said nothing.

"At any rate," the duke continued, "I have been very pleased with the stream of eligible young bucks paying their calls on Margaret this past week."

"Which brings us to the subject I wanted to discuss," Lucinda jumped in. "I do not think it would be wise to allow Lord Arndale to call on Meg any more."

"Oh?" The duke raised his brows. "And would you care to enlighten me as to your reasons, Mrs. Devering?"

"I've known the viscount for a long time," she said, despite his clear displeasure. "I feel they would not suit."

"Why not?" the duke asked. "He's from an old and respected family, and when his father passes on, he will bear an old and respected title. Not to mention that he's rich as Midas, and he's handsome to boot. What else could a young girl want?"

"Not everything is as it seems, Your Grace," she said. "Just because he is handsome physically does not mean he is the same inside."

"Nonsense!" The duke dismissed the idea with an aristocratic wave of his hand. "Unless you can provide me with some specific reason why the viscount would not suit, I am afraid I cannot accommodate your request."

Lucinda opened her mouth, then closed it again. If she told the duke of her own close brush with scandal at the man's hands, he might consider her an inappropriate person to associate with Meg. The reason he had originally chosen her was because of her spotless reputation. If he were to find out the truth, it would destroy any chance she had of having a future.

But if she didn't tell him something, then he might allow a match between Malcolm and Meg, which would destroy Meg in the end.

"I am waiting, Mrs. Devering."

Torn, she said, "Your Grace, please trust me when I tell you that Malcolm has not always dealt honorably with young ladies."

"Details, Mrs. Devering." The duke pinned her with his dark-eyed gaze. "I have promised my granddaughter that she may wed whom she wishes, as long as that man has either a title or fortune—preferably both—that is worthy of her."

And Malcolm had both.

She took a breath to fortify herself and began. "I've known the viscount for a long time," she said. "Since before I married his brother."

"Yes, yes." The duke grimaced, then took a deep, shaky breath.

Lucinda frowned at his odd behavior, but continued, "Your Grace, Lord Arndale has made improper advances toward me over the past several years."

The duke's face reddened, but when she stopped, he indicated with an impatient wave of his hand that she should continue.

"I have always refused him, but still he persists. I do not think such a man would make Meg a good husband, so—"

The duke gasped, turned completely pale, then clutched his chest with one hand and grasped at the drawer of his desk with the other.

"Your Grace!" Lucinda jumped to her feet and rushed over to the elderly man. He continued to gasp for air as he clawed at the drawer to his desk. She yanked open the drawer. "What is it? What do you need?"

He shoved her away and reached for a small bottle. She attempted to help him with the stopper, but again, he pushed her hand away and managed to uncork the thing himself. Then he sipped at the vial, breathing heavily the whole time.

Gradually, over a span of minutes that felt like hours, he began to breathe easier. His complexion slowly returned to normal, though ruddy color remained high in his cheeks. With hands that trembled, he put the stopper back in the bottle and returned it to the desk drawer. Then he looked up and shot her a sharp look of warning.

"You will not speak of this," he commanded. "Do you understand?"

She stared. "But, Your Grace, you are ill! That was laudanum, wasn't it?"

"I said you will not speak of this!" he thundered, then spoiled the image by falling into a coughing fit.

Lucinda waited until he recovered, then said, "Perhaps we can discuss the matter."

"There is nothing to discuss." The duke glared up at her. "Must you hover over me?"

Lucinda took a step back. "Very well, I will say nothing of this."

The duke grunted in satisfied agreement.

"*If*," she continued, "you do not allow Meg to marry Lord Arndale."

"Blackmail!" he spat, outrage flashing in his dark eyes. "Mrs. Devering, you astonish me."

"And you astonish me," she retorted. "Why haven't you told anyone how ill you are?"

"It's no one's business but my own."

"You are the most stubborn man alive," she said. "Now I see where your grandson gets it!"

"Enough, madam!" he roared. "For your information, that young whelp gets his contrariness from his father."

"Then it must run in the family," she snapped.

The duke pulled forth a handkerchief and dabbed at his upper lip. "Mrs. Devering, considering you wish me to grant your request, you seem amazingly unconcerned that you are very close to angering me."

"Wrong, Your Grace. I am *very* concerned, especially about Meg." She took a deep breath to calm herself and folded her hands in front of her. "I am ready to discuss the matter."

"There is no discussion," the duke replied. "I shall decide which of her suitors are appropriate matches for my granddaughter, not you. And you shall speak to no one about my condition, else you shall find yourself alone in society without the Raynewood influence to sustain you."

Or the Raynewood money.

The words remained unsaid, but the knowledge echoed between them for a long, silent moment. She gave him a stare of disapproval that made even the duke shift uncomfortably in his chair.

"The matter may not even arise," he said finally. "Do not concern yourself, Mrs. Devering. I will guard my granddaughter well."

He turned his attention to some papers on his desk, and heart heavy, Lucinda quietly left the study.

She stood in the hall for a moment, staring blindly at the pattern of the wallpaper. She was not satisfied that the duke understood the urgency of the matter, and she was reluctant to push the issue when he was clearly so unwell. Nonetheless, she could not stand idly by while Malcolm continued to court Meg. She cared too much for the girl.

Somehow, she would have to stop Malcolm.

Chapter 17

The duke proved he had not given up when Lady Penelope and her grandmother arrived for dinner that evening. However, Lady Agatha had also invited Knightsbridge.

Knightsbridge and Lady Penelope glared at each other from across the drawing room and never exchanged one word, and the duke spent the entire time watching the doorway for Garrett, who did not appear. By the time dinner was announced, the duke had grown furious. Lucinda watched him carefully in case he had another attack.

"Where is the boy?" he muttered, offering his arm to escort Lady Farvendale into dinner.

"He's on his ship, Grandfather," Meg answered, bitterness underscoring her tone. "We may not see him for days."

Lucinda placed a hand on Meg's shoulder to comfort her, but the girl shrugged it away.

Lucinda sighed. After her confrontation with the duke earlier that evening, she had attempted to warn Meg away from Malcolm, but Meg had not taken the advice very well. Apparently she was becoming enamored of the viscount, for she had even accused Lucinda of wanting the man for herself. Lucinda had not bothered to explain further. She would simply have to find another way to make sure a match between Meg and Malcolm did not happen.

Knightsbridge and Lady Penelope continued to glare daggers at each other over dinner, and Lady Agatha fell asleep over her beef. Lady Farvendale was mortally offended that Garrett had not come to dinner and was haranguing the duke, who had apparently assured her that Garrett had come to his senses about Lady Penelope. The duke smoldered like an active volcano and cast black glares at Garrett's empty chair.

By the last course, Lucinda had a throbbing headache.

She managed to slip away while the ladies were waiting for the gentlemen to join them. She knew she would be missed shortly, so she merely ducked into the library for a few moments of peace.

As soon as she entered the room, she regretted it. Why hadn't she gone up to her room or into the parlor? Instead she had wandered instinctively into the room where she and Garrett had first made love. Everywhere she glanced brought forth some memory from that night. Their time together had been magical, and she longed even now to feel his touch once more.

But it wasn't to be. Garrett Lynch would turn his back on his heritage and return to America, and she would probably marry Sir James and live a life of quiet gentility. Such a life was what she had worked for, and she should be glad it was going to come to pass.

She just wished, with all the longing of the passionate woman she had discovered herself to be, that she could have more.

She heard the door open behind her and whirled, heart pounding as hope soared in her breast. A tall figure entered the room, but her expectation crashed into disappointment when she saw it was Knightsbridge.

"Mrs. Devering," he said with surprise. "So sorry. I didn't realize anyone was in here."

She smiled weakly. "I am developing a headache and thought a few moments of quiet would help."

"I can't say I blame you. Lady Farvendale is the worst sort of harpy." A look of shared understanding passed between them. "I don't mean to disturb you."

"You're not," she assured him. "As a matter of

fact, there is something I wanted to ask you, and since circumstances have brought us together, hopefully you will not find me too bold."

"I'm certain that will not be the case," he said with a careless wave of his hand. "Ask what you will."

"Why do you dislike Lady Penelope so?"

He stared at her in surprise. "That *is* bold."

She blushed. "I will understand if you do not wish to answer, my lord."

"Actually," he said, sitting down rather heavily in a chair, "I find that I do wish to talk about it."

Eyebrows raised in surprise, Lucinda sank down on the sofa across from him.

"I am listening, my lord," she said.

"Lady Penelope is the most beautiful woman I have ever seen," Knightsbridge blurted. "She is perfect in every way."

"I would think this would be a good thing," Lucinda said, puzzled.

"She's *too* perfect!" Knightsbridge exclaimed. "She always looks perfect and acts perfect and dances perfectly. Her conversation is perfect, and her manners are perfect. Even her name is perfect! Albright—she is the brightest thing in my universe."

"Oh dear," Lucinda whispered, as she realized what he meant.

He nodded. "Yes, I am hopelessly in love with

her. But how can someone so perfect want *me*? I am notoriously late, and my valet despairs of my fashion sense. It is only due to *his* that I can be seen in public at all! And I am losing my hair!" He bent forward to show her the top of his head, where she could indeed see that the hair had started to thin.

She cleared her throat. "Nonsense, my lord."

He laughed humorlessly. "You are very polite, Mrs. Devering, but I know the truth. How could I possibly ask Perfect Penelope to be the wife of Knightsbridge the Buffoon?"

"I don't think you are a buffoon, my lord," she replied. "And I think you are doing Lady Penelope a disservice."

He snorted. "She has no interest in me. She wanted Garrett until he told her to her face that he had no intention of marrying her."

"So I heard. But what makes you think she wanted Garrett at all? It seems to me that her grandmother and the duke are pushing for the match, not Lady Penelope."

"But she went along with it."

Lucinda sighed. "My lord, what else could she do? Every time you see her, you are the picture of rudeness."

He had the grace to look ashamed. "I know it. But I see her standing there, looking so perfect and untouchable, and I want to ruffle her feathers a bit. Make her seem human."

"Maybe you should try exercising some of your famous charm on her," Lucinda suggested. "Perhaps you will surprise yourself."

He shook his head. "No, she hates me now. I've seen to that."

For some reason, his defeatist attitude made her angry. "So you would rather say nothing and watch as she marries some other peer? You know that is bound to happen, my lord."

"I know, I know." He swiped a hand over his face. "It's just that I would be completely mortified if she rejected me. I don't want to take the chance."

"So you're not even going to try?"

"I don't know," he whispered.

"What is the matter with you?" she demanded, rising to her feet. "The woman you love is within your grasp, and yet you are doing nothing to win her! Don't you realize how lucky you are?"

He stared at her in shock. "I guess I don't."

She threw her hands up. "Good Lord, Algie, most people have to marry out of duty, or they fall in love with someone outside their class and spend the rest of their lives forever mourning their lost love. The woman you love *is* in your class. You have the chance to marry for love and satisfy duty as well, yet you sit here and mope because things are *too perfect* for you! You should thank God on your knees that you have been given such an opportunity!"

"I never thought of it like that," he said, standing. "Good heavens, Mrs. Devering, but you are quite the general's daughter when you choose to be, aren't you?"

Lucinda flushed. "I apologize for my impertinence, my lord, but not for what I said. I mean every word of it."

"It needed to be said, and I was acting like a cork-brained idiot. Why else would I let love slip through my fingers?"

"Yes, why else?" she repeated, thinking of Garrett.

"I'm going to go back there and charm Lady Penelope," Knightsbridge said with determination. "Thank you, Mrs. Devering, for opening my eyes."

"You're quite welcome, my lord."

"Algie," he corrected with a grin. "You had no problem using my name before."

She blushed.

He started to leave, then looked back. "Are you coming?"

She shook her head. "I don't think so. Meg is a bit put out with me at the moment, and I still have a headache. I think I'll go up to bed."

"Very well; I'll let them know. Thank you again, Mrs. Devering."

He left the room, and Lucinda wearily rubbed her temples. Her attempts to save Meg from Malcolm's clutches had worn down her very soul. There was no one else she could turn to for help, no one else who would believe her.

Except Garrett.

She hadn't wanted to go to him, hadn't wanted to hear him talk of how he would be leaving soon, but she had no choice now. She would have to face him.

She looked back at the sofa, remembering how gentle he had been with her that wonderful night. He had also been discreet. Did she dare tell him the truth about her past with Malcolm?

Anyone else would be shocked at her near brush with scandal so many years ago. And someone else might not believe her current allegations against Malcolm. The duke certainly hadn't batted an eye. But Garrett was an American, not an Englishman, and he loved his sister. He would see to it that Malcolm did not succeed in marrying Meg, even if that meant taking Meg back to America.

She looked around the library, haunted by memories of the most beautiful experience of her life, and wondered if Garrett would still respect her once she confessed her past sins to him.

She squared her shoulders in resolution. Whether he respected her was not the issue. Meg's future happiness was at stake. Lucinda would do anything necessary to ensure that, and Garrett would, too. There was no other choice.

Lucinda left the library and swiftly mounted the stairs. She would write a note to Garrett and have it delivered to his ship. She was certain he would drop everything and come if it involved Meg.

On the way to her bedchamber she nearly collided with Stobbins, who was lugging Garrett's battered sea chest through the hallway.

"Stobbins, where are you going with that?" she asked. "You should get a footman to help you."

"His Lordship has asked me to send his chest around to his ship," Stobbins panted, taking a moment to rest by sitting on the chest. "I believe he may be leaving England soon."

Lucinda froze. "Did he say when?"

Stobbins shrugged. "Soon. The coach is waiting for this, so if you'll excuse me, Mrs. Devering . . ."

The valet rose and continued to lug the chest down the hall as Lucinda stared after him in shock. Was Garrett just going to leave without saying good-bye?

Good riddance to him, then! Smoldering with anger, she stormed down the hall. No doubt her life would be much easier without the handsome lout chasing her all over London, attempting to seduce her. She wouldn't miss him at all!

Of course she would.

Lucinda paused with her hand on the door to her room as sadness seeped into her bones, bringing a slump to her shoulders.

She had at least hoped he would say good-bye.

What if she accompanied the sea chest to Garrett's ship and talked to him in person? Everyone thought she had gone to bed, so she would not be missed. And she would probably have a better chance pleading her case with him face to face than through a note.

It was a daring plan, and if she got caught, her reputation would suffer. No lady ever visited a man at his residence, especially if that residence was at the London docks. It was too risky, too bold for a proper English lady.

She went to fetch her cloak.

Garrett sat back in his desk chair in the cabin of his ship, the remnants of his dinner on a tray before him. The stew and biscuits had brought back memories of home, and he had thoroughly enjoyed every bite. Now that he sat alone with his bottle and a goblet of brandy, however, restlessness once more nipped at him.

He had spent the day handling business, attempting to recapture the contentment he had once felt aboard ship.

Instead, he simply felt lonely.

In the past, he had just gone out to the nearest

tavern in search of an available woman to warm his bed, and had been content. But now Lucinda was the only one who could soothe his soul. Never before had he met a woman who had made him question the way he lived his life or his beliefs or his dreams of the future. No casual romp with a tavern maid would ease this ache in his heart. He needed Lucinda and her starchy ways and her good sense and her courage. But soon Sir James would propose, and she would say yes, and then she would be lost to him forever.

Proposing first wouldn't even solve the problem. She had already told him even if he did so, she would say no. She was bound and determined to live a society life in England, so it seemed as if there was no compromise to be made. She wanted an Englishman, and he was an American. Despite his title, he could never give her what she needed.

His best bet was to set sail for Boston as soon as possible and forget he had ever met her.

A knock sounded on his door, breaking him from his musings.

"Come," he called.

Tim O'Brien stuck his head in. "Begging your pardon, Captain, but there's a lady here to see you."

Puzzled, Garrett asked, "What lady, Tim?"

The door opened further to reveal a cloaked figure standing beside the mate. The woman took a step into the cabin and drew back her hood.

Lucinda.

Stunned, Garrett rose to his feet. "What are you doing here?"

"I need to speak to you."

He could only stare at her. Never had he expected Lucinda Devering to step into his world, yet here she stood, looking like a dream in a pale blue dress with a midnight-blue cloak over it. She wore the delicate pearl earrings and necklace that he had seen her wear many times before, and her curly hair had been temporarily tamed into a sedate coil at the base of her neck.

She looked just as beautiful as if she had stepped out of a London drawing room, but to see her here, surrounded by the wood planking of his ship, with the creaks and groans of the vessel around them, seemed beyond the realm of fantasy.

"Ah . . . do you want me to take the lady's cloak?" Tim asked from the doorway.

Garrett tore his gaze from Lucinda with difficulty. "No, Tim, that's all right. Please close the door on your way out and see that we're not disturbed."

"Aye, Captain."

The door shut behind the mate with a soft click, leaving them alone together.

Lucinda seemed to be waiting for something. Finally she said, "Would you mind if I removed my cloak?"

He shook his head to clear it, realizing he had been staring at her like a green boy who had never seen a woman before. "Of course. Forgive my rudeness, I'm just so surprised to see you here."

"I am rather surprised to find myself here, but I have a matter of some urgency to discuss." She slipped the cloak from her shoulders and handed it to him. He took it and went to hang it on a hook, marveling at the way her scent mingled with the familiar smells of wood and sea and tar.

"May I offer you some refreshment?" He returned to his desk to show her the bottle of brandy. "This just came in from France."

"No, thank you, Captain," she said with a shake of her head that sent the candlelight dancing through her hair. "I don't indulge in spirits."

He grinned. "I seem to recall you indulging in a bit of sherry late one night."

She blushed adorably. "Yes, well, there were extenuating circumstances."

"Yes, there were," he murmured, and her blush deepened. "May I interest you in something else? I can have Tim bring some tea."

"No, thank you." She folded her hands in front of her and twisted her fingers together. "Do you mind if I sit down?"

He winced at his own foolishness. "Of course not. Please do. I'm sorry." She seated herself in a nearby chair and he sank into his own, taking a big gulp of the brandy as he did so. "What did you want to talk to me about?"

"You weren't at dinner this evening," she said.

He raised his brows in amusement. "Did my grandfather send you here to chastise me?"

"Of course not!" She took a deep breath and toyed with the folds of her skirt. "I was just making an observation. Lady Farvendale was very put out with His Grace that you did not arrive."

"Lady Farvendale? Don't tell me that old fool invited Penelope and her grandmother to dinner after I expressly told him I would not marry the girl."

"I'm afraid he did," she confessed. "But take heart, Captain. It seems that Lady Agatha's grandson is interested in pursuing Lady Penelope."

"Knightsbridge? Really? Well, I wish him luck. She never was my type. I wonder what my grandfather was thinking."

"Probably that he wants you to stay in England."

He snorted. "That will never happen."

"I know," she whispered.

An awkward silence fell. Garrett sipped his brandy and watched her, wondering how they had come to this. How had they gone from passionate lovers to polite conversation? The enormity of what he had lost gnawed at him.

"So," he said, realizing too late how harsh his tone sounded. "If you did not come here to chastise me for missing dinner, why are you here? What is this matter of great urgency?"

She bit her lip. "It concerns Meg."

He put down his goblet and focused his complete attention on her. "What's the matter with Meg?"

"Oh, she's in fine health," Lucinda assured him. "It's another matter entirely, and—please forgive me, Captain—but this is rather difficult for me to explain."

He picked up his goblet again. "Difficult how? Difficult as in the story is complicated? Or difficult in that you are embarrassed to tell me?"

"Both," she admitted.

He watched her nibble on her lower lip and tamped back the urge to drag her into his arms. He could hardly believe that she was here, on his ship, unchaperoned, and it was all he could do to remember he was a gentleman.

"We've never had a problem talking to each other, Lucinda," he said quietly.

"I know. But this is a delicate matter, and . . ." She sighed and met his gaze, her dark eyes serious. "No one else will listen to me, and I am worried about Meg."

He set down his goblet, then reached across to lay his hand over hers where it rested in her lap. "I will listen, Lucinda."

She stared down at their hands for a moment. "Garrett," she said, "you may not want me to have any contact with your sister once I have told you my story."

"I doubt that," he scoffed. "You are her dearest friend, and you are the one person I trust with her safety." He slipped his hand beneath hers and twined their fingers. "Now tell me what's bothering you."

Her fingers tightened around his. "Lord Arndale has been courting your sister."

"Your husband's brother?" At her nod, he said, "I've seen him about. I've never laid eyes on a bigger popinjay. Don't worry, Meg won't have anything to do with him."

"I'm afraid you're wrong there," she said. "I tried to tell Meg what kind of man Malcolm is, but she accused me of wanting him for myself." Her lips twisted in disgust. "As if I have eluded his advances for the past eleven years only to become his wife! Ugh!"

Garrett froze, his fingers tightening around

hers. "What do you mean, 'eluded his advances'?" he asked quietly.

She shook her head, not meeting his gaze. "I'm sorry, I should have started at the beginning."

"Lucinda." Garrett waited until she looked at him. He hated the despair he saw in her lovely brown eyes. "Did he ever hurt you?"

"Not in the way you mean. He's been trying to get me into his bed since before I married his brother, but he's never forced the matter. At least, not physically."

Garrett clenched his jaw at the casual way she described years of unwanted attentions. "Lucinda, why don't you start from the beginning."

She sighed. "When I was eighteen years old, I thought I was in love with Malcolm. My father found us in an embrace and demanded that Malcolm marry me.

"Malcolm's father said my background wasn't impressive enough to wed his heir, but since my father was a man of some political power, the earl offered his younger son in order to hush up the scandal."

"What a bastard!"

Lucinda gave him a secret little smile that tugged at his heart. "I often thought the same thing," she confessed. "But ladies don't say such things."

Then her expression grew serious. "Malcolm

never gave up trying to seduce me, even after I was married to his brother," she said. "Knowing what I know of him now, I believe he would have ruined me completely had my father not walked into the conservatory just then."

"I don't doubt it," Garrett agreed roughly. "And this is the rotter who's courting my sister? The bounder won't get her anywhere near the altar!"

"Thank you, Garrett," she said, squeezing his hand.

"Lucinda," he said softly, "this was not easy for you to tell me. I know how much your reputation means to you."

She nodded.

He took both her hands in his. "I'm honored that you chose to confide in me."

A single tear slipped down her cheek. "I had no one else to turn to," she whispered.

He stood, tugging her to her feet, and pulled her into his arms. She nuzzled her face into his shoulder. "It's all right. You can tell me anything, and I'll always love you."

Her head jerked up, her eyes wide with shock. "What did you say?"

"Hell," he muttered as he realized what he had admitted. "I said I'll always love you, though I didn't mean to tell you like that."

"You *love* me?"

"Yes." He cupped her face in his palms, forcing her to look into his eyes and see the truth. "I love you, Lucinda Devering, spotty past and all."

"Heavens," she whispered. Then she kissed him, and he lost himself in the joy of her touch.

Maybe they had a chance, after all.

Chapter 18

Garrett was in love with her!

The world suddenly seemed a bright and beautiful place.

"God, I've missed you," he murmured, taking control of the kiss and making her head swim. "I've been sitting here dreaming about holding you in my arms again."

"I'm here," she murmured. "I was afraid you would hate me."

He pulled back and stared at her. "Why? Because a young girl fell in love with the wrong man? Do you know how many times Meg thought she was in love with some scalawag or another? Why, when she was fourteen, she declared herself in love with Tim, and he left for the Indies until she came to her senses."

"An Englishman would think me disgraced," she said, caressing his shoulder.

"Then it's a good thing I'm no Englishman." His smile turned wicked, and the hungry gleam in his eyes made her knees weak. "I want you, Lucinda," he whispered. "Come to bed with me."

Her heart pounded and her blood bubbled like hot molasses in her veins. She hesitated, unsure of their future. But then he raised her palm to his mouth and gently bit the pad of her thumb, and common sense dissolved into absolute passion.

He loved her. Somehow they could make it work.

"You are so beautiful," he murmured, cupping her face in his hands once more. His kiss was feather soft, and he nibbled gently at her lips, melting her insides like hot candle wax. "Come to bed, Lucinda."

She gave a breathy moan of assent.

He unfastened the many buttons of her dress as she tugged open his shirt and nuzzled her nose into the dark hair sprinkling his chest. He attempted to slip the gown down her arms, but she had managed to completely open his shirt, and when she pressed her mouth to one of his nipples, he hissed in response, his head falling back and his hands clenching on her gown.

She continued to tease his nipple with her lips

and tongue until he pulled her mouth to his, kissing her deeply and slipping his tongue into her mouth.

She moaned and arched against him, twining her arms around his neck until the kiss gentled, and he cupped her face tenderly in his palm.

His gentleness undid her. She could do nothing but cling to him as her dress pooled around her feet, and he caressed her bottom through the thin material of her chemise, nibbling at her lips until she longed for him to take her.

"Garrett," she whispered against his mouth.

He slid a hand beneath her thigh, tugging her leg up over his hip as he worried her lower lip gently between his teeth. She could feel him, hard and ready, through his breeches, but he took his time as if she were a fine liquor to be savored.

"What are you doing to me?" she murmured, lost in sensation.

"Loving you," he whispered, tugging down the strap of her chemise and placing a kiss on her shoulder. "I want to spend all night loving you."

Somehow, they made it to his bed.

Garrett fell backward, taking her with him so she sprawled atop him, and her chemise flipped up, baring her bottom to the cool air. She squealed and tried to tug the flimsy undergarment back into place, but he stopped her with a hand on her bare flesh, caressing her until she forgot everything but his touch.

"I need you," he groaned, slipping a hand between her thighs. His mouth found one of her nipples through the thin chemise and sucked strongly, his fingers stroking her slick folds.

She whimpered and let her head fall forward. She'd already lost some hairpins, so she tugged the rest of them out, letting the toffee-colored, curling mass fall down around them.

He made a sound of approval and tangled his other hand in her hair, bringing her face to his for a hot, open-mouthed kiss. His clever fingers continued playing between her thighs until she thought she would go mad. Hungry, she pressed the flat of her hand to the front of his breeches.

He groaned, breaking the kiss and letting his head fall back against the mattress as she explored him through the fabric of his clothing.

How she had missed this, the beauty of his body and the sheer pleasure of his hungry response. How could she have thought even for a moment that she could forget about what they had together, turn her back on such rare passion in favor of a tepid marriage to Sir James?

Garrett was the only man she wanted, the only man she would ever want.

She straddled him, dodging his questing fingers when he sought the dampness between her thighs again. She grabbed his wrists and pinned his hands to the bed on either side of his head, holding him there, though she knew he could easily break her grip if he wanted to.

They stayed that way for a long moment, breathing hard, eyes locked in silent combat as her hair fell in a silken curtain around them.

"Let me love you," she whispered, leaning down to kiss him softly.

The strap of her chemise drooped over her shoulder, and he grabbed it between his teeth and tugged. "Take this off," he said, letting the material slip from between his lips. "And then take me—if you dare."

His soft command sent ripples of need through her.

"I dare," she breathed, releasing him to trail both hands down his chest. When he shuddered, she smiled with feminine victory.

He reached for her, pulling off the chemise and tossing it to the floor. He hooked a finger around her pearl necklace. "And don't you look the proper lady with your pretty pearls?"

He released the necklace to trail his hand down her body, brushing his fingers against her breast and along the curve of her hip. Her breath caught in her throat.

"Everyone knows a lady is never without her pearls," she gasped.

"And you're very much a lady, aren't you?" he cupped both her breasts in his hands, looking at her body as boldly as you please. She arched into his touch, moaning as he fondled her soft flesh until her nipples hardened.

"Do you want me?" he asked.

She nodded, caught up in sensation.

"What do you want?" he coaxed.

"I want . . . you inside me," she breathed, meeting his eyes with no hesitation.

He gave her that pirate's grin. "And I want to be inside you, my love. Very much. Now why don't you be a proper lady and ask me nicely?"

She raised a brow at him. "Why don't *you* ask *me* nicely?"

Before she could blink, she found herself flat on her back beneath him. He slid his thigh between her legs and nudged them apart, pressing against that part of her that ached for him. "Ask nicely," he commanded.

"Garrett . . ." she pleaded.

"Ask nicely," he repeated, bending his head to tease one peaked nipple. She whimpered and arched her back, offering herself to his mouth, but he pulled back, the devil. Obviously, he would not continue until he had what he wanted.

"I want you," she whispered finally, cupping his cheek.

Her head spun as he bent his head to her breasts, and she clung to him with limbs that had grown heavy with arousal. Somehow he removed the rest of his clothing without taking his mouth from her. At some point she felt him, hard and hot against her thigh. Finally he slipped inside her, that first, hungry thrust that never failed to steal the breath from her lungs.

She clung to him, wrapping her arms and legs around him as he surged heavily inside her. This was what it should be like, a sharing of souls as well as bodies. An expression of emotion that could not be demonstrated any other way.

He met her gaze, blue eyes intent, completely and utterly focused on *her*. It was all she needed to lose herself. She let go, her body singing with release, as he murmured soft words of encouragement in her ear.

"I love you," he whispered, and the world spun away.

Afterward Lucinda lay content in Garrett's arms, the beat of his heart a reassurance against her skin. A glow of happiness suffused her, an emotion she had not felt in a long while.

A miracle had happened—Garrett loved her. The future held more possibilities now. He knew she would settle for nothing less than marriage, so he must be planning on doing so. Perhaps that meant that he was finally ready to forget the past and mend things with his grandfather. He would take on his title, and they would be married.

But what if the duke objected? What if he felt she wasn't good enough for Garrett? Worried, she cuddled closer to Garrett and stroked her hand over his bare chest. He covered her hand with his and twined their fingers together over his heart.

She relaxed. Garrett would not let the duke come between them.

A knock sounded on the door.

Garrett sat up in bed. "I told them we weren't to be disturbed. Blast it." He threw back the covers and grabbed his breeches. Lucinda couldn't take her eyes off his lean, muscular form as he yanked on the garment and stalked to the door, fastening his breeches as he went.

"What is it?" he barked, jerking the door open partway.

"Sorry to disturb you, Captain," Tim O'Brien said apologetically. "It's just that we're having a bit of trouble with the ale merchant."

"Trouble that couldn't wait until the morning?" Garrett growled, stepping outside the door and closing it most of the way.

Lucinda grinned at Garrett's cranky tone and snuggled deeper beneath the blankets. He was obviously put out at the interruption, and the knowledge thrilled her. As she relaxed in the bed that still held the scent of their lovemaking, she could just hear their conversation beyond the partially closed door.

"This can't wait if you plan to leave in two

days like you've said you want to," Tim was saying. "The merchant is being difficult."

Still smiling, Lucinda waited to hear Garrett tell his mate that the plans had changed.

"I still intend to set sail in two days," Garrett replied instead. "Damned English merchants! I'll be glad to see the last of this blasted country."

The smile melted from Lucinda's face.

"What's the fellow's problem?" Garrett continued. "I'll bet he wants more money."

"That would be it," Tim confirmed. "Says he can sell it to someone else for more profit, so if we want it, we have to pay the same price, and we have to take delivery tonight."

Slowly, Lucinda sat up in bed.

"Bloody thief," Garrett snarled. "I'll see to it directly."

"Sorry, Captain," Tim said. "I know you have company."

Lucinda slipped from the bed and picked up her chemise from the floor. She pulled it on, listening for Garrett's answer.

"It's all right, Tim," Garrett said finally. "There's nothing you can do. These people are a greedy lot."

Lucinda sucked in a sharp breath and slipped her pale blue dress over her head. He had never intended to marry her, never intended to stay in England. He hated the English and always would. The shining future she had been imagining shattered.

Thank God she had not told him that she loved him.

"I'll be on deck in a moment, Tim. See to it someone is available to see the lady home."

"Aye, sir."

By the time Garrett stepped back into the cabin, Lucinda had managed to do up almost all the buttons on her dress. It was difficult with no lady's maid to help her, but at least she was decent.

"Hey there," Garrett said with a fond smile. "You got dressed awfully fast."

"I'm going back to the duke's townhouse," she said tonelessly. It was all she could do not to burst into tears.

"I was hoping we'd have a few more minutes together." He laid his hands on her shoulders. The warmth that spread across her skin was more than she could bear, and she shrugged him away.

"I must go," she snapped, unable to keep the bite from her voice any longer. "Where are my slippers?"

"Lucinda, what's wrong?"

She searched out her slippers, thrown to opposite sides of the room. "Nothing's wrong, Captain. We are exactly what we were before, no more and no less."

She sat down in a chair and took extraordinary care in putting on her slippers so that she would not have to look at him.

He came and knelt before her, grasping the arms of the chair and trapping her there. "What's the matter? Are you crying?"

"No." A tear slid down her cheek and made a liar of her. Defiantly, she swiped it away and looked him in the eye. Oh, those beautiful blue eyes. He looked at her with such love, such tenderness.

A lie. An impossibility.

Nothing had changed, and she was a fool to think it would.

"What's the matter? I warn you, Lucinda, you shall not leave until you have told me."

"Don't threaten me." She grabbed one of his arms with both hands and shoved, then rose from the chair. "I am not some young girl like your sister, Garrett. I am a grown woman, and you will treat me like one."

"I thought I just did."

His attempt at flirtation fell flat. She only stared at him, ice forming around the heart that urged her to go to him.

He rose, concern flickering in his eyes. "Lucinda, talk to me."

"Perhaps you had better talk to me, Garrett," she said quietly. "Perhaps you had better tell me exactly what went on here tonight."

"You know what went on." He reached out, stroked her cheek. "We made love."

"Did we?" She jerked away from him.

He scowled. "Don't play these games with me, Lucinda. You never have before."

"I've never been in this position before. I've never made love to a man," she continued, her voice rising, "only to find out moments afterward that he intends to leave me!"

"I don't intend to leave you."

"You are setting sail for Boston in two days—that sounds like leaving to me!"

"Come with me." He took her hand.

She stared at him. "To America?"

"Yes, to America! You don't have to make it sound as if I asked you to accompany me on a trip to hell."

"My home is in England," she whispered.

"You can make a new home in America. With me."

"But I belong here."

"Damn it, Lucinda, you are so stubborn! Why do you want to stay in a country that has treated you so badly?" he demanded. "If you come away with me you can start a new life."

Part of her urged her to go with him, to follow wherever he led. Another part of her, the part that had kept her going for so long, reminded her that her goals were within her reach. She could have everything she ever wanted, if only she said yes to Sir James.

But not everything. She would not have Garrett.

The pain of it made her lash out. "You're calling *me* stubborn? What about you? You still have not settled things with your grandfather," she accused. "Instead, you are running away again. Why do you hide from your emotions?"

He scowled. "How can you say I hide from my emotions when I have just spent the past hour showing you how much I love you?"

"You say the words," she said, "and you are an incredible lover. But nothing has really changed with you, Garrett. You still intend to return to America without taking on the responsibilities of your title. You still have left things unsettled with your grandfather. And you still intend to take Meg with you, despite the fact that she's very happy in England!"

"Didn't you warn me that Meg isn't safe here?" he demanded. "Yet now you say I should leave her here."

"I say you should let her choose."

"Why? I let you choose, and you didn't choose me." He stared at her, eyes bleak. "I don't know what you want from me, Lucinda. You have turned my world upside down. I want you to be my wife, but I can't stay here in England. I have a business to run in Boston, and I have already been away too long."

"You want to marry me?" she whispered, hope swelling in her breast.

"Of course I want to marry you!" he thundered. "Did you think I wanted you to come home with me to make you my mistress?"

"I didn't know," she retorted. "You never asked me to marry you."

"Will you?"

She stared at him, emotions warring within her. If she married Sir James, she knew what her life would be like—exactly what she had always wanted. But there would be no passion. Affection, fondness, yes. But no love.

If she married Garrett, she would have the passion and the love, but she would have to leave behind everything she had ever known for a life that stretched forward in foggy uncertainty.

What would happen if things did not work out with Garrett? She would be lost and alone in an unfamiliar country. At least in England, she knew where she stood.

She couldn't rush into this.

"I love you," she said quietly, admitting it for the first time. "I want nothing more than to be your wife. But if we wed, you intend for us to live in America."

"Yes." He took her face in his hands. "Boston is very much like London, Lucinda, only there isn't as much social snobbery. In America a man is judged for what he has done with himself, not who his ancestors were."

"I don't know if I can do it," she said, her voice shaking. "I don't know if I can leave behind everything I have ever known. I need to think."

He closed his eyes for a moment, disappointment etched on his face. But then he opened them again and smiled at her, caressing her cheeks with his thumbs. "But you are not saying no, right?"

"I'm not saying no," she agreed. "But *you* need to think as well, Garrett. Your grandfather is an old man. Perhaps you should mend things with him before it is too late."

"You don't know what you're asking."

"If you can ask me to leave my past behind, I can ask you to leave yours behind."

He dropped his hands from her face and stepped back. "Does it mean so much to you then?"

"I have difficulty with the fact that you refuse to accept your responsibilities."

"It's just a fancy title," he scoffed, slicing his hand through the air dismissively.

"No, it's more than that," she told him earnestly. "There are estates attached to that title, and people living on those estates who need and deserve a responsible leader. They cannot exist without one."

"They have my grandfather."

"For how long? Garrett, your grandfather is eighty-five years old. It's a miracle he's doing as well as he is! But he won't be able to continue the responsibilities of the peerage for much longer. You need to claim your birthright."

"Is that what you want in a husband, a fancy English title so you can play lady of the manor?" he snarled.

She jerked as if she had been struck. "How can you say that?"

"I have offered you my name and my life in America to share," he said. "But that is not good enough for you."

"You're twisting my words."

"Maybe you had better marry Sir James," he shot back. "Obviously my love cannot compare with fancy estates and the approval of shallow society."

She stalked to the bed and began to search out her hairpins. "If that's what you think of me, Garrett, then we have no more to discuss."

"Then I guess we have no more to discuss."

She paused, barely able to breathe at the pain that stabbed through her at his words. But she was a survivor. She had survived Malcolm's obsession, a loveless marriage, and the disapproval and death of her father. She would survive Garrett Lynch.

She just didn't know if she would have a heart left afterward.

The silence stretched between them. "I will have a man see you home," Garrett said finally.

"Thank you." She slowly began to wind her hair into a knot at the base of her neck, keeping her back to him. If she looked into those beautiful blue eyes of his, she knew she would burst into tears.

She heard him come up behind her, felt the heat of his body as he stopped only inches away. Then he touched her, caressing her bare shoulder.

"I have told Meg I will stay for her come-out ball tomorrow night," he said quietly, "but after that, I am going home." His fingers tightened on her shoulder. "If you decide to come with me—"

She closed her fingers over his, unable to look at him. Unable to keep the tears at bay any longer. "I know."

He took his hand away, leaving coldness where the warmth of his flesh had been. "I'll have someone see you home."

Chapter 19

The come-out ball for Miss Margaret Stanton-Lynch was the grandest event of the season.

Meg looked like a young goddess in a pure white gown shot with silver, and pearls adorning her neck, ears, and hair. A coolness still existed between her and Lucinda, but Meg was so excited at a ball being thrown in her honor that she more or less forgot her anger as the guests began to arrive.

Before long, the house was packed to the rafters. The duke led Meg out in the first dance, and after that, eligible young bucks swarmed the young American, vying for her attention.

Lucinda watched the whole thing as if from a distance. If she were the same person she had been weeks ago, she would have basked in this

triumph. Because of her tutelage, Meg was a total social success. The duke had even gone so far
as to murmur a compliment to that fact. She
should be ecstatic, as all her plans were coming
to fruition.

Instead, she felt like a stranger in her own
world. She watched the dance of the social players as if she were in the audience at a theater.

Did she really care what these people thought
of her?

She waited for shock to strike at such a rebellious notion, but it never came. Amazed at herself, she cautiously explored these new ideas, the
total opposite of what she had believed for so
many years.

How many lives had been ruined by society's
disapproval? How many innocent girls had
ended up in loveless marriages because of one
misstep amidst the convoluted rules of the so-
called Polite World? How many fortunes had
been lost? How many hearts had been broken?

Too many.

Did she really want to spend her life amid
these fickle people, people who would turn on
her in a moment if they thought it would provide
a juicy piece of gossip for their entertainment?
She had fought long and hard to do that very
thing, yet suddenly it all seemed so foolish. Why
had she clung so long to a way of life that had
done her more harm than good?

For her father, perhaps. She had failed him by nearly causing a scandal, and his death so soon after her marriage had left her feeling as if there were unfinished business between them. She realized now that she would never get her father's approval back. He had died before he could give it, and she had to accept that. Perhaps society had taken the place of her father somewhere in her mind, and so she found herself trying to prove herself worthy to a group of people who didn't care for her or even know her at all.

She should have been trying to prove it to herself.

Yes. A surge of rightness swept through her, and it was as if someone had lifted her burdens off her shoulders. Why did she work so hard to make herself accepted? She didn't answer to anyone but herself and her maker.

As she looked around the opulent ballroom, she realized that England's glittering peers did not provide her with the security she needed in order to be happy. She had to create her own feeling of security within herself, and to do that, she had to be brave enough to trust herself and leave the past behind.

A movement near the ballroom doors caught her eye, and she watched Garrett enter the ballroom.

How different this entrance was from the first

time she had met him! The wild American barbarian was gone, and in his place stood a dashing and elegant marquess who looked every inch
the grandson of the Duke of Raynewood.

Garrett had dressed in the plain black that he
favored, the starkness broken only by the pure
white of his shirt and neck cloth. His dark hair
was combed back and fastened in a queue, emphasizing the noble Stanton nose and the slashing eyebrows. His blue eyes glittered like
gemstones as he surveyed the throng.

He strolled into the room, no doubt searching
for Meg, and Lucinda couldn't help but notice
that he'd walked just as proudly across the deck
of his ship as he did through the duke's ballroom.

They were the same to him, no more, no less.

He turned his head and saw her. For a moment, he hesitated. Then he started across the
room toward her.

Her heart pounded as he approached, excited
by his mere presence. He didn't have to say anything, didn't have to do anything. He had only
to exist in the same room with her for her to react
to him.

This was what she wanted. She wanted to feel
alive. She wanted to feel beautiful and desired.

This man wanted her, simply and completely.
And she wanted him right back.

America suddenly took on a different hue. Instead of appearing to be a land of dark uncertainty, she now saw it as a bright and shining opportunity for discovery.

And marriage to Garrett seemed even more so.

"May I have this dance, Mrs. Devering?" The familiar voice jerked Lucinda's gaze away from Garrett. Sir James smiled down at her, having approached without her noticing. She glanced again at Garrett, but all she saw was his back as he retreated into the crowd.

Her ingrained good manners took over. Even as she took Sir James's hand to accept the dance, she realized that her future might not be as certain as she had once thought it would be.

And the prospect did not alarm her at all.

When Garrett saw Sir James approach Lucinda, he turned and walked away. Once he would have continued on and competed with the other man for Lucinda's attentions—and won. He would have enjoyed challenging the other male, and he would have enjoyed Lucinda's outraged reaction as he walked away triumphantly with her on his arm.

But she had to make her own decisions, and he had to let her. Even though it killed him to stand aside and watch her dance in the arms of another man.

He helped himself to a glass of champagne,

wishing it was brandy, and watched the spectacle of Meg's come-out ball.

Meg was dancing with some red-haired
young pup with big ears, and looked like she
was having a wonderful time. She looked like
she belonged here.

His gut knotted. He didn't want her to belong
here in England. He wanted her to come home
with him.

What if she didn't want to leave?

He sipped the champagne, steering away
from those painful thoughts. He didn't want to
contemplate the idea that he might very well
have lost everything that mattered to him.

"So you're leaving tomorrow, are you?" The
duke had come up beside him while he wasn't
looking. He glanced at the old man, but his
grandfather was watching Meg, a soft smile on
his face.

"That's my plan."

"Are you thinking to drag Margaret along
with you?" Erasmus looked at him then, his dark
eyes sharp and searching. "Whether or not she
wishes to go?"

A cutting remark rose to Garrett's lips and
hovered there, unsaid. "I don't know," he admitted, surprising himself.

He had surprised his grandfather, too. A flash
of emotion crossed the old man's face before he
could hide it, and it shocked Garrett to the bone.

Loneliness. And hope.

The all-powerful Duke of Raynewood was just as painfully lonely as he himself often was, but in the duke's case, it was all his own doing.

Maybe they were more alike than he thought.

The idea made Garrett take another gulp of champagne. He didn't want to think of his grandfather as human. He didn't want to look at him and realize that the monster of his childhood was nothing more than a tired old man who suffered the same demons as he did.

Lucinda's words came back to him. *Didn't it ever occur to you that he was just as hurt as you were when your father died? Your father was his son. How do you think that made him feel, to know his actions had precipitated the death of his child?*

Garrett had no children, but he had Meg, who had at times felt more like his daughter than his sister. How would he feel if he did something that resulted in Meg's death?

The pain and grief would rival all the fires of hell.

"So you have come to your senses?" his grandfather challenged. "You will allow Margaret to stay?"

Once he would have taken umbrage at the old man's querulous tone, but now he saw the duke's aggression for what it was: fear.

"Meg is a grown woman," he said mildly. "She will make her own decisions."

Hope flared in the duke's eyes. "And what of you, boy? Will you stay as well?"

"I can't." His gaze strayed to Lucinda.

"I see."

"I have a business to run," Garrett continued, looking away as Lucinda slipped out onto the terrace on Sir James's arm. He met the duke's gaze. "I don't expect you to understand, but there are people depending on me for their livelihood. I have already been away too long."

The duke snorted. "No one would understand better, boy. I have hundreds of people depending on me for the very same thing." He glanced across the room. "Blast it. Agatha's gone off again. I'd best wake her."

The old man set off across the room, leaving Garrett stunned by the fact that the two of them were not so very different after all.

The moon shone full and bright, illuminating the small garden with a sweeping shaft of cool light. Lucinda went to the railing and stared down at the bushes and flowers and the marble statues that glowed in the eerie moonlit night.

She had a feeling she knew why Sir James had sought this moment of privacy with her, and for the first time, she wasn't sure she wanted to hear what he had to say.

He took her hand, drawing her gaze to his face. "Dearest Lucinda—"

"Sir James—" she began in the same moment.

"No, Lucinda, please let me get this out." He took a deep breath. "It's been many years since I offered for a woman, and I'm a bit out of practice."

Lucinda raised one trembling hand to her bosom. "Sweet Lord," she whispered, uncertain if she was excited or terrified.

"Lucinda, I have always admired you," Sir James continued. "Your father was my dear friend, and I have watched you grow from a sweet child into a beautiful woman. In that time I have come to care for you a great deal, and I would be honored if you would consent to be my wife."

As he smiled down at her, his brown eyes warm and kind, emotion clogged her throat.

"I can see you are uncertain," Sir James said, when she did not respond. She opened her mouth to speak, but he held up a hand, silencing her. "Don't say anything. Think about my proposal, and I shall return on Thursday for your answer."

"Thank you," she said quietly. "I would like time to consider your kind offer."

"May I escort you back inside?" he asked, gallantly proffering his arm.

"Actually, I would like to be alone for a few moments," she said, apology in her voice. "To think."

"Of course." He raised her hand to his lips. "Perhaps you might save me a waltz later."

She gave him a weak smile. "Perhaps."

He did not press her further. He sketched a brief bow and retreated into the ballroom, a smile on his lips.

Lucinda watched him leave, confusion tangling her thoughts. At last she had what she had always wanted . . . but she wasn't sure she wanted it anymore.

She had never expected to have a choice.

The beauty of the garden beckoned her, and she walked down the curving stone steps into the tiny patch of greenery that served as the garden. She sank down on a stone bench, her emotions churning.

She stood at a crossroads. She could walk one path with Sir James at her side and live a life of ease in England as a respected member of the Polite World. Or she could walk the other path with Garrett—become his wife, and go back with him to America. She had no idea what to expect, but with Garrett's love to sustain her, she had no doubt they could weather any storm.

Both men were wealthy enough to pay off Harry's debts, and both men were more than enough to discourage Malcolm's determined pursuit. But which one should she choose?

Sir James would treat her with kindness and

respect. Years of quiet peace stretched before her as Lucinda Whigby. Should she wed Garrett, she had no doubt that the two of them would continue to engage in heated discussions. No doubt she would constantly feel the desire to fling a vase at his head when he was acting stubborn, but when it was over, she would always be secure in his love.

Garrett loved her. Sir James was fond of her. There really was no choice at all.

Garrett was the man she loved, and she would marry him, though it meant possibly leaving England for good. She would miss England, but how bad could America be, if Garrett wanted to return there so badly? And there were things she would *not* miss here, like the snobbery of England's peerage and the constant fear of scandal. All in all, she might even look forward to going to America.

"Well, well, well," came a voice that shattered her thoughts and chilled her blood. "Good evening, dear Lucinda."

Lucinda leaped to her feet as Malcolm stepped out of the shadows of the garden behind her. "What are you doing here?" she demanded, her heart thundering in her chest.

"I was invited to the ball, of course." The moonlight turned his blond hair to silver gilt as he came closer. He wore dark clothing, which was why he had blended into the darkness so well. She refused to retreat a step, though every instinct in her body urged her to do just that.

"The ball is in the house, Malcolm," she said.

"What kind of gentleman would I be if I left a lady all alone in a secluded garden?" he purred. "Unlike your suitor, I would never consider leaving you alone, dear Lucinda."

The words held a casual menace that froze her with its subtle threat. He reached out and stroked his hand down her cheek. A wave of revulsion shook her free of her trance, and she jerked away from him.

"Keep your hands off me!"

Quick as a snake, he grabbed her by the arms and hauled her up against him. "Never, Lucinda dear. I have waited too long to get my hands on you."

She struggled, but he was amazingly strong. "Release me at once, Malcolm!"

"You are not the pigeon I had hoped to snare tonight, but I will accept fortune's choice."

She opened her mouth to scream, but he swiftly clamped an arm around her struggling form and closed his other hand around her throat. She cast him a frightened look, barely able to breathe, much less summon help.

His eyes glittered in the moonlight. "You're mine, Lucinda. At last, you are mine!"

Black spots edged her vision, and his face began to blur. She struggled to breathe, but she couldn't seem to pull in enough breath. Everything began to fade . . .

Meg stood frozen in the shadows of the terrace, her dark cloak hiding her from anyone who might be watching.

Shocked, she watched Malcolm choke Lucinda into unconsciousness and then carry her limp body through the small garden gate and away from the house. She couldn't even shout for help; she couldn't even run for assistance.

The man she loved had turned into a monster.

You are not the pigeon I had hoped to snare tonight.

With fingers gone cold like ice, she crumpled the note he had sent her into a small, tight ball. If not for a trick of fate, she would now be happily riding to Gretna Green in Malcolm's carriage, determined to become his bride.

What a fool she had been!

A tear trickled down her cheek, and she swiped it away. She should never have listened to his promises—his lies. She had gone to him when she was angry at Lucinda, had believed him when he told her that Lucinda had been chasing after him for years. Lies, all lies. And then, afraid that Garrett might drag her back to America against her will, she had been only too receptive to Malcolm's suggestion to run away and get married. She had convinced herself that her grandfather would understand.

Why had she ignored the advice of the people who loved her? Because of her foolishness, Lucinda was now in danger.

While *she* stood about, wallowing in self-pity!

She whirled and raced up the stairs toward the house.

Garrett would know what to do.

Chapter 20

Garrett was doing his best not to watch the terrace doors when Meg appeared. He knew immediately from the look on her face that something was wrong. Heedless of the stares she attracted—what was she doing wearing a cloak?—she hurried over to him, her eyes wide with distress.

"Lucinda's been taken," she gasped, grabbing his arm.

Alarm roughened his voice. "Damn that Sir James—"

"No, not him. It was Malcolm."

Malcolm. The very man from whom Lucinda had sought to protect Meg. Fury smoldered, then burst into flame. "Tell me what happened."

The duke came over and interrupted just as she opened her mouth to speak. "What the devil is going on here?" he demanded in a whisper. "Margaret, why are you dressed this way? Everyone is staring!"

Guilt flooded Meg's face, the same expression she had worn at age three when she had dumped salt into the sugar bowl. Though urgency nipped at his heels, Garrett stepped in and said calmly, "There has been some trouble. Perhaps we should discuss this in private."

A look at Garrett's set face made Erasmus snap, "Very well—let's adjourn to my study. Agatha can handle things here."

Moments later, the three of them were alone in the duke's study. Garrett shut the doors behind them, then cut right to the heart of the matter. "Lord Arndale has abducted Lucinda."

"Good God, are you certain?" the duke exclaimed. He paled and slowly made his way to the chair behind his desk. "That is a very serious accusation."

"I saw it, Grandfather," Meg interjected. "I was in the garden, and I saw him take her."

"Perhaps she went willingly," the duke suggested. "She was angling after a husband, after all."

Meg shook her head, and her voice trembled as she said, "He put his hand over her throat and choked her until she fell unconscious. She might even be . . . dead."

"No." Garrett's tone held more certainty than he felt, but he didn't want to think about the alternative. "She's not dead. He would have just left the body if she were dead."

"He said something about waiting too long to get his hands on her—he sounded like a madman," Meg whispered.

"What were you doing in the garden?" Erasmus asked. "And for God's sake, why are you wearing a cloak in the middle of your come-out ball?"

Meg cast her gaze to the floor. "I was supposed to meet him," she admitted in a small voice. "We were going to Scotland to get married."

"What!" Garrett roared.

"But why?" the duke rasped, sinking heavily into his desk chair. "Why would you do such a thing?"

"I thought I was in love," she replied softly. "And I didn't want to go back to America. I thought I could stay here in England if I married Malcolm."

"Foolish girl," the duke muttered.

"I wouldn't have forced you, puss," Garrett choked, stunned at his sister's narrow escape. "But Lucinda warned me about Malcolm. She said he was evil, and I would never have let you marry him."

"She warned me as well," Erasmus said, regret heavy in his voice. "And because I didn't want to limit Margaret's choice of husband and lose her as I did your father, I didn't listen."

"She tried to warn me, too," Meg said with a sob. "But Malcolm told me Lucinda wanted him for herself, and I believed him. I've been so stupid!"

"The important thing is to get Lucinda back before Malcolm harms her," Garrett said. "Where could they have gone? The trail grows cold as we stand here."

"We were going to Gretna Green." Meg took a deep breath in a clear effort to calm herself. "He said he had made arrangements at an inn along the way."

"There are several decent inns on the road to Scotland," the duke said. "But those grays of his are very distinctive, and if he wanted to move swiftly, using his own prime horseflesh would be his best bet."

"I'm going after her," Garrett decided. "Give me directions."

"That's good of you to offer, my boy."

"To hell with that," Garrett snarled. "I intend to marry Lucinda."

"Oh." The duke blinked, as if assimilating the information.

"Oh, Garrett!" Meg cried, clearly delighted.

"Then you'd best take Knightsbridge with

you," his grandfather continued. "He knows the way, and he'll prevent you from killing Arndale."

"He can try," Garrett growled, heading for the door.

"Beat him senseless if you want," Erasmus called after him, "but don't kill him. I'll not have my heir flee the country for ridding the world of that vermin."

"I've been trying to flee this country since I got here, old man," Garrett replied with a snort. "But I will try to do so of my own will and not the Crown's."

"That's all I can ask," the duke said. "Good luck to you, my boy."

"It's Arndale who needs the luck." Garrett jerked open the door and went to look for Knightsbridge, simmering rage adding fury to his step.

Malcolm had taken Lucinda, but the Englishman had not bargained on Garrett's Irish temper or American audacity. Garrett would take her back.

And Malcolm would pay.

Lucinda slowly recovered her senses. At first she thought she was back in her bedroom at Stanton House, but then she realized that the bed was much harder than what she was used to. It even *smelled* different. She wasn't at home. She wasn't any place she knew. With a jolt, she came fully awake and sat straight up in bed.

And immediately wished she hadn't.

The room swam for an instant, then settled, leaving her with a curious light-headed feeling. She raised one trembling hand to her throat, touching the tender flesh with a wince.

"Never fear, dear Lucinda. I left no bruises."

She jerked her head around at that familiar, dreaded drawl, then instantly regretted the action as the room spun again. When it settled, she found herself looking at Malcolm.

He sat in a nearby armchair, his coat and cravat gone, and his shirt partly unbuttoned. He held a crystal goblet of brandy, and as he swirled it around in the glass, the heavy gold signet ring he wore reflected the light from the nearby fire. His hair glimmered like gold in the flickering of the flames.

The smile on his face was that of a predator who had finally cornered his prey.

"Where am I?" she demanded, her voice much stronger than her body felt.

"At an inn." He sipped the brandy, never taking his eyes from her face. "Don't try to call for help. The innkeeper was very sympathetic to my tale about my reluctant bride."

"I wouldn't marry you if you were the last man on earth," she swore.

His fingers tightened briefly around the goblet, then relaxed. "Not that I would ever have you, my dear. You are certainly good enough for a mistress, but your bloodline just doesn't measure up for the wife of the Earl of Witting."

"Your father has not yet died," she reminded him.

"He lingers still," Malcolm agreed carelessly. "But he is bound to go on to his reward any time now. Then I shall be the earl."

"Don't you care for your father at all?" Lucinda gasped. "How can you be so cold-blooded?"

"I'm not cold-blooded," Malcolm said, making a little *tsk*ing noise. "In fact, I plan to show you how very hot-blooded I can be, dear Lucinda."

"I don't want you, Malcolm," she said coldly.

He laughed. "My dear, I don't care if you do or not." He placed the goblet on a side table and rose, stretching like a tiger in the sun. "I've waited much too long," he said, approaching her.

"Stay where you are," she commanded, holding up a hand.

He paused, then laughed. "How fierce you sound, my dear. I'll have you purring like a kitten in no time."

She rolled her eyes. "Malcolm, you sound like the villain of a poorly written play. Didn't you give this any thought? Don't you think someone is going to come after me?"

"This was just a lucky impulse," he said airily.

"Then what were you doing in the garden?" The answer came to her when he smiled. "Meg. You were going to meet Meg!"

"Yes, dear Miss Margaret is quite in love with me. We were going to Gretna Green."

She was glad that her capture had saved Meg from such a fate, at least. "Won't she miss you?"

"No, I will just tell her that it was too dangerous to go tonight. That word of our plans might have gotten to the wrong ears." He laughed as he came to stand at the side of the bed. "Who do you think convinced her that you were jealous when you warned her away from me? Really, Lucinda, that was not a very nice thing to do."

Lucinda stared up at Malcolm, trying to think through the fuzzy-headedness. Meg was safe. Now she had to come up with a way to escape herself. Once she got away, she would marry Garrett and be off to America, far beyond Malcolm's reach.

In the meantime, he stood much too close to her, close enough for her to smell the brandy on his breath, and he was half naked. Not a good situation at all! She looked around the room, at any place but him, and noticed her reticule still hanging from her wrist. It was a miracle she had not lost the tiny bag when he had carried her off.

An idea struck. Now, if she could only make it work . . .

Out of concern for the duke, she had taken one

of his vials of laudanum and slipped it into her purse in case he had an attack during the ball. If she could somehow get the laudanum out and slip it into Malcolm's brandy, he would fall asleep, and she could escape!

There were obstacles, however, one being Malcolm himself. He stroked a hand over her hair, then let his fingers graze her bare shoulder as she frantically sought an idea that would get her off the bed and away from his touch.

"Do not fight me," he murmured as she shrank from him. "You will only hurt yourself."

She rolled to the other side of the bed and was on her feet before he could blink. They stared at each other across the expanse of the coverlet, Malcolm amused, Lucinda defiant.

"I don't want to hurt you," he said. "I only want what you have been promising me all these years. It's not polite to tease a man, you know."

"I haven't promised you anything," she said hotly. "I may have been seduced by your charm when I was a young girl, but I know the real you, Malcolm. I would rather bed a leper than lie with you!"

He narrowed his eyes. "Have a care what you say, Lucinda. I have better uses for that mouth than spitting at me."

Revulsion churned her stomach. "Don't you understand, Malcolm? I am refusing you."

"Don't *you* understand, Lucinda?" He came

around the end of the bed, stalking her until she backed up against the bureau. "I don't care. I will have you tonight, and it is up to you just how difficult you want to make this on yourself."

Lucinda swallowed hard as he reached out to hold the top of the bureau, trapping her between his arms. Closing his eyes, he leaned forward and nuzzled her hair, inhaling deeply. "You smell delicious," he breathed.

Fear wrung a small sound from her throat. Malcolm pulled back and looked at her, his pale blue eyes almost compassionate except for the lust that lit them. "What ever is the matter, dear Lucinda?"

She had to be clever. She had to get herself out of this. "My nerves are overset. Perhaps some brandy . . ."

"Of course." He stroked his hand over her cheek. "Help yourself, my dear. But do not think of trying to escape—my man is just outside the door."

She nodded, her hands shaking as he stepped back and allowed her to cross the room to the brandy. A soft sound made her whip her head around. Malcolm smiled seductively as he pulled the tails of his shirt from his breeches and unfastened the last of the buttons.

"Hurry, my dear," he purred. "I grow impatient."

She nodded, then reached for her bag.

"What are you doing?" he barked.

She jumped. "Just taking off my reticule, Malcolm." She tugged open the strings on the bag before making a show of slipping it from her wrist and placing it on the table beside the brandy bottle. As she did so, she tipped the tiny bottle of laudanum into her palm.

"All right then," he said. "But be quick about it. I am very eager to claim what's mine."

She made a show of uncorking the brandy bottle and refilling the single goblet, letting the clink of the bottle on the glass disguise the small pop of the stopper on the laudanum bottle. She put down the brandy bottle and tipped the laudanum bottle against the edge of the goblet.

Malcolm grabbed her wrist and jerked her around to face him, the laudanum bottle gripped in her captured hand. "What's this?" he demanded. "Are you trying to poison me?"

He shoved her hard against the wall with one hand on her throat, the other clenched on her wrist. Then he ripped the vial from her hand and threw it into the fire. The glass shattered, and the fire flared as her last chance at escape burned to ashes before her eyes.

"You will regret that," he hissed, shoving his face close to hers as she struggled for breath beneath his punishing fingers. "I didn't want this to be difficult, but you have made the choice."

He tightened his fingers around her still-tender throat, and tears stung her eyes.

He used his free hand to fondle her breasts, his gaze locked on hers. "Now listen to me. You will remove your clothing and lie down on that bed and spread your legs for me as a woman should. And you will take me—and anything I want to do to you—with silence, do you understand?"

He was going to rape her now, and there was nothing she could do about it. She could only hope to get out of this alive.

The door crashed open and slammed hard against the wall. Garrett burst into the room, his eyes fierce. Knightsbridge followed, casually stepping over the body of the unconscious man in the hallway.

"Say, Kelton," Knightsbridge said, "you will have to show me how you do that—" He stopped short just inside the doorway as he caught sight of the occupants of the room. "Good Lord, Arndale, have you lost your senses?"

Malcolm released Lucinda and turned to face the two men. "Gentlemen, you interrupt."

"That's my fiancée you're fondling," Garrett snarled.

"The devil she is!" Malcolm exclaimed. "She's my mistress, you know."

"Liar!" Lucinda rasped, wincing as the effort hurt her throat. She ran over to Garrett, who pulled her close against his side.

"You've kidnapped and abused my future wife," Garrett said to Malcolm, his voice silky with menace. "Give me one good reason why I shouldn't kill you."

"Lies," Malcolm snarled. "The woman came willingly. She's no innocent virgin. She's a lusty widow, as you no doubt know." He smirked. "She all but begged to have me between her legs. Perhaps your future wife is not so virtuous as she would have you believe."

Garrett gave a roar of rage and leaped for Malcolm, slamming his fist into the viscount's nose.

Knightsbridge pulled Lucinda out of the way as Malcolm went down, crashing into the table. "Kelton, do try not to get any blood on your clothing," he called out. "Stobbins would be most put out with you."

Garrett stood over Malcolm, who gingerly picked himself up off the floor, holding his bleeding nose. "Come on, you bastard," he growled. "Let's settle this."

Malcolm drew himself up, stanching the blood with his shirt cuff. "Perhaps in the wilds of America they settle such things like savages, but here in England, gentlemen settle disagreements in an honorable manner."

"No," Lucinda whispered with horror, sensing what he was about to say.

"Name your seconds, sir!" Malcolm demanded.

"What the hell is a second?" Garrett snapped.

Malcolm burst out laughing. "This is price-less," he sneered.

Knightsbridge stepped forward. "I shall serve as your second if you like, Kelton," he said. "Arndale has just challenged you to a duel."

Garret bared his teeth in a predatory grin. "I accept, Arndale. Shall we say Thursday at dawn?"

"Agreed." The viscount gave Knightsbridge a smug smile. "You will need to educate Kelton on the ways of a gentlemen's duel, my lord. He should also choose the weapon."

"Pistols," Garrett said, ignoring the dig.

"You will inform me as to the name of your second, Lord Arndale," Knightsbridge said coldly. "I will expect to call on him tomorrow afternoon to make the final arrangements."

"Of course, Knightsbridge."

"Come, Kelton," Knightsbridge said, giving a tug on Garrett's sleeve. "Let's take your lady home. There's much to do."

"See that you show up Thursday morning, Arndale," Garrett said, "or I'll come find you."

The viscount smiled maliciously. "I wouldn't miss it."

Chapter 21

"**Y**ou can't fight a duel," Lucinda said for the third time in the carriage on the way back from the inn. "Malcolm is a crack shot."

"So am I." Garrett gazed impatiently out the window into the night. Being a man of action, it didn't sit well with him to leave the viscount in one piece back at the inn. But Lucinda's reputation was on the line, and he would follow these blasted English rules if it saved her good name.

Besides, he had the pleasant memory of Arndale's bloody nose to sustain him until the duel.

"And what was all that nonsense about me being your fiancée?" Lucinda ranted. "I do not recall accepting your proposal, sir!"

"It wasn't nonsense at all," Garrett said, turning to face her. "I intend to marry you, Lucinda.

However long it takes to convince you, you will be my bride."

She lifted her chin defiantly. "I will not be bullied into marriage, Captain."

"Captain, is it?" His temper snapped, and he reached across and hauled her into his lap.

"Garrett!" she cried.

"Pardon, Knightsbridge," Garrett said, then kissed Lucinda with all the passion that was eating at him.

"Not at all," Knightsbridge responded politely.

After a moment of initial resistance, Lucinda melted into his embrace, her arms slipping around his neck. She clung to him, and he pulled her closer. He had almost lost her today.

"You're going to be my wife," he murmured, holding her close.

"If you survive," she replied, snuggling into his arms, "then you can ask me—and not before."

"Congratulations to you both," Knightsbridge said with a grin.

Lucinda tried all day on Wednesday to talk Garrett out of fighting the duel, but to no avail. He seemed bound and determined to risk his life for her good name. At one time she would have been pleased, but now she just wanted all of it to be over.

She didn't want to be a widow before she was even a bride. Or a fiancée, for that matter.

Malcolm had named Baron Chumley as his second, a nasty lecher who had been his good friend since they had attended Eton together. Knightsbridge had gone off to meet with Chumley, and he returned with the news that, since Garrett had no intention of apologizing for striking Malcolm and insulting his good name, the duel would go on as agreed at dawn on Thursday morning.

Upon hearing the news over tea, the duke said to Garrett, "I'll tell you again. Wound the fool if you must, but do not kill him. I'll not have you arrested for that idiot's demise."

"I wish you would just call it off," Lucinda said.

Garrett, the duke, and Knightsbridge, all stared at her.

"Matter of honor," Knightsbridge said. "We can't have it said that Kelton is a coward."

"And Arndale must pay for his scurrilous behavior," the duke agreed. "He has insulted my grandson's future bride and behaved like the veriest knave. I, for one, hope Garrett aims true and teaches the cad a lesson."

"I'm not his future bride yet," Lucinda retorted.

"I must do this," Garrett said to her, his voice

low and quiet. "I take care of my own."

"Forget it, Lucinda," Meg spoke up. "Once he's made up his mind, there is no changing it."

"Then let's pray Arndale leaves the country like the coward he is," Agatha said placidly. "Would someone please pass the cake?"

By dinnertime, Lucinda's nerves were drawn to the limit. It didn't help that Meg was also worried and depended on Lucinda to calm her fears. Garrett's mind was on the upcoming duel, and he, Knightsbridge, and the duke periodically locked themselves in the duke's study to discuss the matter, no doubt to avoid alarming the women. But Lucinda would have felt better if she knew what was going on.

Well, maybe feminine wiles would convince the stubborn man.

She waited until the house was quiet. The clock in the foyer had just struck one when she slipped into Garrett's room. He sat up in bed when she entered, the bedclothes falling back to reveal his bare chest and shoulders in the flickering candlelight.

"What are you doing here, love?" he asked softly.

Lucinda locked the door, then turned to face him, her ivory silk nightgown swishing softly in the silence of the room. Her curly hair fell about her shoulders, and she had brushed it one hundred times to make sure she looked her best.

With a seductive smile on her lips, she sauntered toward the bed.

"I came to be with you." Kneeling one knee up on the bed, she leaned over to kiss him, her hair falling forward like a curtain around them.

He responded to her kiss, cupping her cheek in his palm. Then he pulled back and looked into her eyes, his own dark and glimmering in the dim light. "I *am* going to meet Arndale in the morning," he told her.

"I know." Her smile turned sad as her heart grieved at the words. "That's why I'm here."

"You won't change my mind," he warned as she climbed onto the bed to kneel beside him.

"I can try," she whispered. "Or better yet, I can show you what you risk by going through with it."

"I know what I risk," he said, swallowing hard as she tangled her fingers in his hair. "And I know what I risk if I do not do this. Arndale must be taught a lesson."

"Is that lesson worth more than your life?" She held his face in her hands and pressed a soft kiss to his lips. "I have only just found you, my love. I don't want to lose you so soon."

He placed his hands on either side of her waist as she dropped soft, nibbling kisses on his mouth. "You don't have much faith in me, Lucinda."

"I don't trust *him*," she corrected. "He is not

an honorable man, Garrett. If there is a way for him to cheat, he will do so. He believes that his social position will protect him from anything."

She sighed and leaned her forehead against his. "All this time, I have been begging you to accept your heritage. Now, when all I want is the American sea captain, you choose to act the English gentleman."

He chuckled. "Don't count on that too much, my love. I am only doing this for you."

"Why?" she pleaded. "We are going to live in America. Who cares what English society thinks?"

"I do." He took her hands in his. "I have been talking to my grandfather. He has been an invaluable fountain of knowledge about this whole thing."

"I'm so glad that your imminent death has brought you closer," she snapped.

He squeezed her hands reassuringly and continued, "Grandfather and I have come to a sort of understanding. I see now that there is more to being a nobleman than just the title and riches that go with it. As you said, the duke is an old man, and he can no longer keep up with all that is involved with running his many estates. He needs help."

She thought of the duke's illness, but decided

against telling him. The duke would tell Garrett in his own time. "He needs you."

"Exactly. He needs me." He sighed. "Like it or not, I am his only heir. I know that he regrets what happened with my father, and I also know that I cannot hold my grandfather completely to blame. My father played a part in this, too. He didn't have to lose all contact with England, but he was a stubborn man."

"Imagine that," Lucinda murmured, earning a playful slap on the bottom.

"Have some respect for my family line," Garrett admonished, a grin tugging at the corners of his mouth. "We can split our time between America and England. We can come back every year for the Season and spend the rest of the time in America."

"*If* I marry you," she teased. Then she sobered. "Garrett, there is something I have not told you." She took a deep breath. "My late husband accumulated quite a bit of debt before he died. By rights, Malcolm should have paid those debts. It would have been the honorable thing to do."

Garrett snorted. "And we all know how honorable Malcolm is."

"Exactly. He refused to pay Harry's debts unless I became his mistress. He was obsessed with what he called our 'unfinished business' from years ago."

Garrett pulled her into his arms. "I should have killed him when I had the chance," he murmured into her hair.

"I managed to elude him by making a bargain with your grandfather," she continued, snuggling into his embrace. "If I successfully launched Meg into society and got her wed to an eligible suitor, then the duke would pay all of Harry's debts. If I did not succeed, then I was on my own."

"Wait a minute. You have been *working* for my grandfather?"

She gave him a haughty look. "Please. We Northcotts do not 'work.' "

"After all that rubbish about how the English gentry doesn't work for a living, *you* were employed the entire time by my grandfather!" Garrett chuckled.

"It was a bargain we had," she corrected. "The duke paid for my wardrobe and allowed me to accompany Meg to all the social events. There, of course, I hoped to find a husband. It was the only way I could escape Malcolm."

Garrett's shook his head. "And then I came along and played havoc with your plans by trying to seduce you, didn't I?"

"You didn't help matters," she acknowledged.

"But you're marrying me, and I will happily pay off Harry's debts for you."

Lucinda grew serious. "*If* you survive this foolish duel."

"I will survive, my love." He took her face in his hands. "Believe it."

"I do not know what the morning will bring," she whispered. "But tonight I would like to show you how much I love you." She pushed against his shoulders until he leaned back against the pillows, then climbed on top of him. "Just please, come back to me."

"I intend to."

He reached for her, but she pushed his hands away, placing them on the bed on either side of his body. "No. I want you to lie back and let me love you. I need to do this, Garrett. I need to show you so that if the worst happens . . ."

He leaned forward and kissed her, then laid his forehead against hers, blue eyes earnest. "It won't."

She licked her lips, loving the taste of him. "Lie back, my love. Let me remind you what you have to come back to."

He allowed her to push him against the pillows again. She hitched up her nightdress and straddled him, her bare thighs on either side of his beneath the covers. He made to push down the blankets, but she stopped him with her hands on his and shook her head.

He fisted his hands. "I want to feel you."

She smiled at him. "Soon."

"You're punishing me, aren't you?"

"No, I'm loving you." She leaned forward, letting her silk-clad breasts brush his chest, and kissed him, deeply and slowly.

He made a noise of longing and tried to take control of the kiss.

"Stop," she murmured. "For once, let someone else be in control."

"Tyrant," he teased. His breath hissed from between his teeth as she trailed kisses down his neck.

"Tyrant, hmm?" She licked the pulse at the base of his throat and slid her hands down his chest, flicking her thumbs over his flat nipples as she went. He groaned and whispered her name. His fingers clenched on the blankets.

She laughed, low and sultry, feeling like the most beautiful woman in the world. "Do you want me, Captain?"

"You know how much I do." He shifted his hips to emphasize his words, and she clearly saw his arousal outlined beneath the covers.

"Yes, you certainly do," she murmured. She tugged the blankets, to the foot of the bed, leaving him bare before her. Cupping his hard shaft between her hands, she murmured again, "You certainly do."

"Sweet Jesus, Lucinda," he muttered, his head falling back. She continued to caress him, and he grasped the edges of her nightdress in his fists and shoved it up over her thighs.

"You're not playing fair," she chided, bending to flick her tongue across his nipples. "You're supposed to be enjoying this."

"I am enjoying it. Too damned much."

"Poor thing," she crooned. "Maybe this will help . . ." She shifted backward, then leaned down and caressed the tip of his straining shaft with her tongue.

"Good God!" He reached for her, tangling his fingers in her hair. "Where did you learn that?"

She smiled and licked him again, loving the deep groan that rumbled from his chest.

"Don't you dare stop," he moaned. "It feels incredible."

"Tell me if I do something wrong."

"You couldn't," he murmured, caressing her face, her hair. "Just don't stop."

"All right." She continued to stroke him with her tongue, nuzzling him with her lips, finally taking him completely into her mouth. He made a growling sound in his throat, his face a picture of ecstasy, and she increased her motions, loving the way he was undone by so simple a caress. Then suddenly he pulled away from her, rolled them over, and pinned her beneath him.

"That's not fair," she pouted as he loomed over her.

"All's fair in love." Before she could blink, he had stripped her of her nightgown.

"Garrett, what—oh, sweet heaven!" All thoughts of what she had meant to say dissolved from her mind as he dipped his head and sucked strongly at her nipple. She wrapped her arms around him, arching her back and rubbing her pelvis against his as the pleasure mounted like lightning.

"I have to have you," he murmured, switching to the other breast.

"Didn't you like what I was doing?" she teased.

"Any more of that, and things would have been over much too soon." He spread her thighs and nudged himself between them, pressing his erection against her aching flesh.

She arched her hips in supplication.

He thrust inside her and held still for a long moment. "You're mine," he whispered.

She wrapped her legs around his waist, bringing him in deeper. "You're mine, too."

He began to move, and they came together in a passionate kiss, mouths starving for the taste of each other. She clung to him and held him tight, as they sought ecstasy together.

Much later, she snuggled close in his arms, one hand over his heart, the glow of pleasure still surrounding them.

"I can't change your mind, can I?" she whispered.

"No." He kissed her forehead and tightened his arms around her.

"All right." She stroked her hand across his chest. "Just come back to me."

He twined his fingers with hers, over his heart. "Always," he vowed.

Chapter 22

Thursday dawned gray and drizzling. Stobbins would be upset about his rain-spattered boots, Garrett thought, but then again, bloodstains would be worse.

He had left Lucinda alone in his bed, wrapped in his sheets and the scent of their lovemaking. They had come together three times in the night, each time more desperate and hungry than the last. Finally she had slipped into slumber, exhausted.

He would do anything for Lucinda, but he could not allow her good name to be tarnished— and he couldn't allow her abuser to escape unscathed.

Knightsbridge and Chumley were examining the pistols, and across the green stood Arndale, looking smug and confident as he chatted with an acquaintance.

Though dueling was illegal, quite a crowd had gathered. Some placed wagers on the outcome, and some had come merely to watch the spectacle. A couple of young bucks had clearly not been to bed yet and they laughed uproariously at each other's jokes, oblivious to the solemnity of the day.

"Lord Kelton."

Garrett looked up to see Sir James approaching him. He didn't bother to hide his surprise. "Sir James, what are you doing here?"

"I heard what was going on. This is about Lucinda?"

Garrett nodded. "Arndale abducted her and tried to force himself on her, then took offense when I bloodied his nose for it."

"Bastard," Sir James spat. "Bloodied his nose, did you? Is that what happened to his pretty face?"

"Guilty as charged."

"Good for you then. I never liked Arndale." He paused, then looked Garrett in the eye. "Lucinda's father told me what Arndale did to her. I didn't agree with George's solution, but she was not my daughter. I had no say."

Garrett nodded.

"Be aware that Arndale is not honorable. He *will* cheat, if he can."

"I've been warned."

"Good." The older man clapped a hand on his shoulder. "Good luck to you, then. I hear congratulations are in order?"

"If you are referring to the fact that I intend for Lucinda to be my wife, then yes."

"I'm happy for you," Sir James said, "even though I offered for her myself. But she was always in love with you. At least I lost her to the man who loves her. Take care of her, Kelton." The older man turned to leave.

"Sir James, wait," Garrett called.

Sir James turned back, brows arched in inquiry.

"Should things go awry today," Garrett said, "I want you to take care of Lucinda. I need to know she will be safe if I am not here to protect her."

The other man's face softened into a smile. "I have a feeling you will rule the day, Kelton. But if by some mischance that devil's spawn manages to put a bullet in you, you can rest assured that I will indeed wed Lucinda and take care of her for you."

"Thank you," Garrett said, sincerely grateful.

"Kelton!" Knightsbridge called, approaching rapidly. "We are ready to begin."

"Good luck to you," Sir James said again, then he melted into the crowd.

"I'm ready," Garrett said. "Let's get this over with."

* * *

The coach lurched to a halt, nearly throwing Lucinda to the floor. Silently cursing, she slid to the far end of the seat and peered out through the window curtains.

A large crowd of gentlemen had gathered on the green where Garrett and Malcolm were to duel. Both men and their seconds were talking, while a third held open a box that held two dueling pistols. Malcolm made a gesture with his hand, and Garrett selected one of the pistols. Malcolm took the other.

The sight of Malcolm with a weapon in his hand made her shudder, but not nearly as much as the look of malice that the viscount sent at the American's back as Garrett walked away. She twisted her fingers together so hard that her knuckles hurt as the two men took their positions, back to back.

The crowd grew silent as the count began.

"One! Two! Three!"

"Please, God, let him live," she whispered, her gaze riveted on Garrett.

"Four! Five!"

How could she have been so foolish as to refuse to wed him the second he asked her? They could have been halfway to America by now . . .

"Six! Seven! Eight!"

He was doing this for her, she knew. Trying to preserve her good name in a society that meant so little to her now. She loved him for the gesture, but—

"Nine!"

"Look out!" someone shouted.

A gunshot shattered the silence, and Lucinda screamed as her worst nightmare seemed to come true before her very eyes. Garrett went down like a stone, landing face-down on the ground.

"Arndale fired early!" exclaimed a voice from the crowd. "Dishonorable bastard!"

Garrett wasn't moving. He looked so still . . .

The roar of the crowd grew louder, and Malcolm looked smugly pleased with himself. Lucinda's hands shook as she tried to shove open the door, sobs shaking her body and tears streaming down her face. He couldn't be dead. He just couldn't be!

"Wait, he's up!" someone cried.

Lucinda jerked her head up and stared as Garrett slowly picked himself up off the ground. Her hands slid weakly off the door handle as her entire body sagged with relief.

He was safe. By some miracle, he was safe.

Garrett wiped his hands down the front of his mud-stained coat. Stobbins would kill him for certain, he thought. Then he turned to face his opponent.

Malcolm's self-satisfied smirk disappeared as it became obvious that Garrett was unharmed.

The viscount glanced from right to left, but no one would meet his eyes. He stood watching Garrett with growing panic spreading across his face, his empty pistol still clutched in the limp hand hanging at his side.

Garrett had expected Arndale to fire early, but he still nodded in gratitude to Sir James, who had shouted the warning.

"Lord Kelton, you may still take your shot," said the man holding the pistol box. "Lord Arndale, hold your position."

It was worth the mud bath to see the fear on Malcolm's face. Garrett grinned as he sighted down the pistol at his nemesis.

"I will take my shot," he called out. "And I'll put a bullet in your sorry carcass if you ever so much as look at my betrothed again." Then he fired, enjoying Arndale's yelp of fear as the bullet exploded in the ground between the viscount's toes.

The crowd roared with approval, and money began to change hands as wagers were paid. Garrett remained where he was, the excitement draining out of him.

Knightsbridge strolled over. "This little incident certainly has changed the mind of society," he said. "Arndale will never again enjoy the popularity he has in the past."

"Good." Garrett handed the empty pistol to him.

"Going to be deuced dull without you

around," Knightsbridge said. "Maybe I'll come visit you in America."

"We'd be glad to have you."

"In the meantime," Knightsbridge said with a chuckle, "perhaps you had best see to your betrothed, before she comes running out of that coach and completely ruins her good name."

"What?" Garrett whirled and saw Raynewood's coach with its ducal crest at the edge of the green. "What the devil is she doing here?"

"Probably wanted to make sure you didn't get yourself killed," Knightsbridge said, but Garrett had already started toward Lucinda.

Shunned by the other men, Malcolm left the green, surrounded only by his servants. As the viscount's carriage pulled away, Lucinda jumped down from the duke's coach.

"What's the matter with you?" Garrett demanded. "Don't you know you can ruin your reputation by showing up at a duel?"

"Then you'll just have to marry me and save my reputation." She flung herself into his arms and held on tight. "Thank God you're all right."

"I told you I would come back to you." Taking her face in his hands, he pressed a kiss to her lips. "*Now*, will you come with me to America and be my wife?"

She grinned. "I thought you'd never ask."